Also by Tay Marley

YA Novels
The QB Bad Boy and Me
The Summer of '98

New Adult Novels
Meant for Me

The QB, SUMMER, and Me

TAY MARLEY

wattpad books W

wattpad books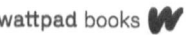

An imprint of Wattpad WEBTOON Book Group

Published in Canada by Wattpad WEBTOON Book Group, a division of WEBTOON Entertainment Inc.

36 Wellington Street E., Suite 200, Toronto, ON M5E 1C7 Canada

Published in the United States by Wattpad WEBTOON Book Group, a division of WEBTOON Entertainment Inc.

5700 Wilshire Boulevard, Suite 220 Los Angeles, CA 90036 USA

www.wattpad.com

First Wattpad Books edition: August 2025

ISBN 978-1-83411-026-4 (Trade Paper original)
ISBN 978-1-83411-027-1 (eBook edition)

Library and Archives Canada Cataloguing in Publication information is available upon request.

155105023

Cover design by Art of Nora

MAY

PROLOGUE

DRAYTON

The school courtyard is a frenzy of activity after the senior class has graduated and thrown their hats in the air. Families are congregating around the beverage tables, sail shades keeping the sun off and upbeat music coming through the PA system.

That's it. High school is over. It's a weird concept to come to terms with. I've spent so much of my life here for as long as I can remember, and today I'll walk out of the campus and never come back.

I peer around at the familiar faces and wonder who I'll keep in contact with and who I won't.

"Drayton."

Coach jogs toward me wearing a suit and tie. I've seen him several times today, but I still crack a grin. I've never seen this man in anything but sweatpants and a hoodie. I am going to miss him. For all his quirks, he's been a damn good coach.

"Yes, sir?"

He shakes my hand. "Congratulations again, kid. You made me proud, and it was a pleasure having you on the team."

"Thanks, Coach."

He locks in eye contact. "I want free tickets to NFL games when you make it to the big time."

I laugh, appreciating the vote of confidence, and then I notice Dallas coming up beside me. "You got it, Coach. It's the least I can do."

"Good man." He claps me on the shoulder before he leaves, off to secure more future season passes from his team, no doubt.

I drop an arm around Dallas. She's holding her graduation cap between her hands, her hair falling down her back. "Your mom is looking for you; she wants a photo with you and your dad."

"Mm-hmm, I'm sure."

My teammate Derek and his mom walk past, and I wave.

"Your dad is tracking down the photographer," Dallas says, moving to stand in front of me. "I haven't seen him, that's just what your mom said."

Dallas has been doing a good job of avoiding my dad for the last few weeks; even though he and I have been working on burying the hatchet, she's still hurt by the things he said to her on prom night, and I don't blame her at all. He blamed her for my interest in UCLA and accused her of ruining my future. I'd never been so close to hitting the man. He plans on apologizing, so Mom says. It'll require Dallas letting him close enough, but I'm not going to push her into hearing him out. He did the damage; he can fix it.

"Nathan and I got some photos done too," Dallas adds.

"Did you get some with Gabs?"

"Yeah."

Dallas and I took pictures together the second we got off the stage, while my mom and dad were busy having a conversation with some of the faculty. Then I slipped away to talk to the boys and confirm our plans for this afternoon. I'd volunteered to host the graduation party, and Mom was thrilled when I told her two days ago. Not.

Speaking of, my mom is blowing up my phone with her exact coordinates and ordering me to hurry the hell up before the photographer moves on. I let Dallas know that I'll be back soon and go find my parents, who are hanging around under a tree, keeping out of the sun. Mom is on her phone, texting me again, no doubt. I can feel it vibrating in my pocket every three seconds. When she sees me, she looks both frustrated and relieved. Dad claps me on the shoulder.

"Congratulations, graduate."

"Thanks," I say before I'm pulled into a crushing hug by Mom.

"I'm so proud of you."

I pat her back. "Thanks, Mom. Now here's a gentle reminder, keep your mouths shut around Dallas."

Mom leans back, jaw dropping. Dad slips his hands into his pockets and gives me a flat glare.

"You know what I mean." I grin, ignoring the disbelieving stares. "UCLA is a surprise. She doesn't know, and I'd like to keep it that way."

As soon as I sent off the letter of intent, I decided that pulling this off as a surprise had the potential to make this summer even more romantic. Time is slipping through our fingers—we have to cling to every moment, bask in the sun like it's the last time we'll ever see it. All of that dramatic flair. Plus, she was pretty adamant I shouldn't choose a college just to be closer to her. I don't think she'll spend the whole summer falling apart over our impending separation, but I do know she'll be happy when she realizes I'm just a half-hour drive away. But keeping secrets? From Dallas? Next to impossible—if anyone breaks, no joke, it'll probably be me.

"Ready, team?" the photographer asks, aiming his camera at us. Mom makes a fuss, straightening my cap, fixing my tie, smoothing the fabric on my shoulders. As soon as she's done, we stand together in front of the tree and smile.

It's hard to ignore the fact that someone is missing. I've lived the last six years without my sister, and it still feels wrong to be graduating without her. I keep waiting for a moment when it doesn't feel so gut-wrenching to be reaching these milestones knowing she's not here to do it with me. Knowing I get to celebrate the life I'm living and she doesn't. Sometimes I think, Well, if she can't live her life, then I should live it for her. And then other times I think, How dare I find happiness? I don't deserve it. It's a little carousel of ever-changing emotion.

The photographer snaps a few shots, scans a QR code for us, and hands the little slip over so we can have them developed. Dad waves to someone passing and lets us know he'll be back as Mom picks her purse up off the ground and looks at me like she knows exactly what I'm thinking.

Her palm comes to my cheek. "You doing okay?"

"Yeah, I'm good."

She tilts her head disbelievingly, but I'm saved when Dallas wanders over, still carrying her cap. Her legs poke out from beneath her graduation gown, tapering into a pair of high heels that give her another few inches of height.

Mom smiles, gives her a hug, and congratulates her before slipping away to talk to some of the other moms.

"I've done my share of mingling," Dallas says, looping her arms around my neck. My hands settle on her waist.

"You're about to do a whole lot more of it." I remind her about the party, and she pouts. "In a bikini."

"We'll see."

I look her up and down. "I hope so."

"Can you believe it?" she asks. "It's so weird. Just like that, we're done. We're never coming back here. Sure, we got up onstage and got a certificate and threw our caps or whatever. But that doesn't feel like enough to express how huge this is. We practically lived at this school for years."

"I hear you, baby."

"And now we have to start the rest of our lives as adults." She sucks in a deep breath. "That's a long time. Adulthood is so long. This went too fast. I feel like it's not balanced enough. We need more time to be kids!"

She's freaking out.

"Well, we have summer. You and me. Every single day is going to be ours. Special." I pull her a bit closer. "Can we promise each other something, right now?"

"Okay?"

"Let's agree not to think about the fall at all," I say and note the little flinch of doubt in her brow. "Let's embrace this summer and not talk at all about what comes after. We don't get sad; we pretend it's not real."

"Except we're literally going to LA to visit CalArts again."

"Apart from that," I say and pull her a bit closer. "What comes after summer is out of sight, out of mind. So we can just enjoy the time we have. Deal?"

"Yeah, deal." She tries to smile, but I can see the little bout of anguish over how short the summer actually is. "Twelve weeks," she murmurs. "That's all we've got."

So she thinks.

JUNE

CHAPTER 1

DALLAS
Eleven weeks to go

The sound of a motorcycle revving the heck out of its engine wakes me up, and I roll over on my pillow, staring at the ceiling through half-lidded eyes. The haze of sleep and confusion begins to clear, and then I sigh.

Drayton did promise me that not one moment of summer would be wasted before we leave for college. So I'm not surprised that he's outside waking me up at the crack of dawn. It's Nathan who is going to have some words about Dray's wake-up call methods. Dray starts his mornings far earlier than we do due to his circuits in the gym. I know his dad has him working with a private coach most of the summer too. It leaves me time to dance, which I spend at least an hour doing each day. I suppose it works that we're both committed to staying on top of our craft.

Flinging my covers back, I stand, then I stumble over to the window in the hopes that I can save the situation from escalating. Too little too late, though.

Nathan's voice is barely audible over the revving engine, but I can hear him shouting even in my bedroom.

Pulling back the curtain, I see Drayton out on the street, leaning casually against his bike with his hand wrapped around the throttle, flicking it back and forth. He tips his head up at me with the biggest shit-eating grin on his face. The neighbors must hate him, that's for sure.

I slowly shake my head at him and then draw a hand across my throat, signaling for him to quit it. He stops suddenly and raises a brow.

"You're going to kill me?" he shouts loud enough that I hear him, as does Nathan.

"Yes!" I hear my brother's muffled voice.

I wave Drayton inside and let the curtain drop. He's an absolute menace. But I can't wait to find out what he has planned for us today. I took some time off work over the next couple of weeks. Wren, one of our newer hires, was more than happy to cover my shifts. She's mentioned the fact that she wants to get out of here after her graduation next May. What she wants to do, however, I don't know. All I know is that she needs the cash, and her willingness to cover my shifts means a little extra time for Drayton and me to spend together. Since the graduation party, he's shown up every morning with a new suggestion.

Yesterday, we made sundaes with about a thousand toppings and sauces. The day before that, we painted portraits of each other and died laughing at how both of our pictures looked they could've been painted by a child. And then we ended up painting each other and kissing and falling a little more in love. That's how it is with him. A never-ending fall. I'm still waiting to hit the ground.

I stand in front of the mirror and run my fingers through my hair as I yawn and attempt to wake up. The door flies open a few moments later, and Drayton saunters straight in, grabs my face, kisses me, and then falls onto my bed.

"Get dressed, Cheer," he says. "We have plans."

"I figured."

He grins.

"How should I dress?"

"The less, the better is my personal preference."

I slide open my closet door and glare at him. "What are we doing?"

"You can't really dress wrong for today, Cheer. Wear whatever you feel comfortable in."

"This." I wave a hand over my little pair of cotton shorts and cami. It's so hot at night at the moment that I would rather wear nothing to bed, but the thought of having to flee the house in a fire or natural disaster won't allow me to sleep in the nude.

Not unless I'm at Drayton's house and we're both in the nude. It's illogical, but there's comfort in not being alone in potentially scrambling around for clothes in the middle of a house fire.

Drayton stands up and walks toward me. I quickly assess his casual black slacks and white T-shirt. His thin chain hangs from his neck. He slips his hand onto my waist and gives me a rough tug into his body, staring down at me with those sensual eyes and his panty-dropping grin.

"I do love these pajamas, Cheer, but you wouldn't be happy with me if I let you go out like this."

"So considerate." I stand on tiptoe and give him a kiss.

Before I can pull back, his hand wraps around the back of my neck, and he deepens the kiss for a brief moment. Then he gives me several quick pecks, steps back, smacks me on the ass, and tells me to get dressed before wandering out of the room. I hear him hollering for Nathan and smile with butterflies in my stomach.

There's a suitcase half packed in the corner of my room for our trip to California next week. I'm not sure why I bothered so early considering I've taken most of the clothes back out to wear. I scrounge through it and find my pale-blue tank top and a pair of wide-leg jeans. I quickly fix my hair and put some mascara on. Before I leave the room, I throw my clean laundry straight at the suitcase.

We're going to California so I can get the lay of the land, scout out my building, and figure out how to get to my dorm and where to park. What's close to the building. Spots I can eat when I'm out. Potential places of work that aren't too far from the campus. Things I'd rather know before I get there. Plus, it'll be a fun little getaway for Drayton and me. We're going to go to Disneyland and Universal Studios and shop on Rodeo Drive.

Well, maybe not shopping because I've never spent more than twenty dollars on a T-shirt. But I'll browse. From outside the store.

I wander down the hall when I'm ready and find Nathan stirring a cup of coffee while Drayton sits at the breakfast bar and scrolls through his phone. I expected conversation, but it's silent instead.

Drayton looks up. "You look beautiful. Your brother isn't talking to me."

"I don't talk to people who wake me up at seven in the morning and also turn the entire neighborhood against me," Nathan says.

"You'll live." Drayton stands up and slides his phone into his pocket. "Come on, baby. We've got things to do."

"Goodbye." Nathan drags out the word as he lifts the cup to his lips and refuses to look at us.

I'm surprised he's this mad; he's a morning person most of the time. Though, it is summer, and he doesn't have to be up for work right now. We have plans to go camping when I get back from California. I'm not much of a camper, but it'll be nice to do something with Nathan that he wants to do. My whole summer's pretty much scheduled, which gives me less time to worry about what's going to happen in the fall. I do my best not to think about the fact that soon, Drayton and I will no longer be within a short drive of each other. Up until graduation, I thought I was totally fine with the situation I'd created, and then we left the campus and reality hit me like a blow to the chest.

Time is counting down, and then everything changes.

~

Drayton pulls the motorcycle into the lookout spot where he brought me when we became official. It's still technically closed to motorcycles, but Drayton rides up the wide gravel walking track with little concern. We hop off, and just as he always does, Drayton fixes my hair when I pull my helmet off. He kisses me, and then I go and stand at the edge, where I look out over the rocks and bask in the clear blue sky and sunshine.

I love coming here. It's where we confessed how we felt about each other. It's where we've hidden from the world once or twice. I turn and look at him over my shoulder, a pang in my chest at the fact I'll have to live without seeing him all the time when we go to college.

Drayton lifts his seat compartment and starts pulling out little snacks and cold drinks. There are churros and croissants and lemon ice tea because I hate coffee. He arranges it all on a plaid blanket.

"Breakfast with the sunrise." He stands at the edge of the blanket and widens his arms. "The sun has already risen because I figured you and Nathan would kill me if I came before five."

"You thought correct."

He nods. "Yeah. Plus, I needed to hit the gym before I came."

I sit down and pop a strawberry into my mouth. "Do you want to come camping with Nathan and me when we get back from California?" I ask, licking the juice off my lips while Dray stares at me like he's hungry for something other than food.

"Uh, I don't know."

I recoil, blinking at him as he stretches out on his side and leans on his elbow. "You don't know?"

"I'm not a big camper, baby. I like hotels and room service and private hot tubs."

"You're such a rich kid," I scoff, tearing off a piece of croissant. "And full of shit. You like being outside. You also said we have to spend every single day together."

He picks up a strawberry. "Guess we'll have to go a few days with the phone instead."

"But—"

"Besides, Nathan needs his time with you too."

It's not like Drayton isn't sweet and thoughtful. He's completely thoughtful, all the time. But surrendering what he recently referred to as precious days together seems out of character. I'm not sure whether to be disappointed or not. Truthfully, I've also been looking forward to seeing Drayton camping. He is more of a hotel person, but I don't believe he wouldn't brave a tent and sleeping bag if it meant being tucked in beside me under the stars all night.

"Okay," I say. "Remember, I only have two weeks off work, and that means we have even less time."

"I still have to train all summer, so I'll just do it then. Besides, shouldn't you quit soon? You can't keep working there from California."

"It's hard for you to understand, my privileged love, but I need to save as much as I can before I go. My last day is August thirteenth."

"Quit sooner, I'll make up your wages."

"I promise, one day, when we're married and I have to retire from dancing because my body doesn't work anymore, you can fund my life. Not a moment sooner."

He gives me a quick smile, and then he moves over to me, puts a strawberry between his teeth, and leans in for me to bite the other side. I do, and then he grasps the sides of my face, kissing me while our mouths are full. I laugh and grip the neck of his shirt, pulling him closer.

"All I heard is that we're getting married one day," he murmurs against my mouth. "I can't fucking wait, baby. Oh, and don't ever tell me this body's not going to work. Impossible."

I promised myself I would ignore the little pangs over our impending separation. But it's so hard. In these moments, when he feels like the other half of me, as if we were created in perfect balance with one another, I don't understand how I'm supposed to go months at a time without feeling his arms around me or his mouth on mine. This was my choice, though; I was the one who convinced him he didn't need to choose a college near me and that we'd be fine doing long-distance.

Drayton leans back, his brow a little pinched as his gaze roams over me. "Baby, we had a deal."

"I know," I say. "I'm fine."

He looks at me a beat longer.

I lean back in and kiss him again. "This is why I was doing my best not to fall in love with you, by the way."

"Let's not have that debate again," he says, and then he pushes me onto my back and crawls over me, holding my head in his palm so it's not resting on the hard ground. And we lose ourselves for a little while.

~

A few hours later, Drayton and I are heading into the library, hand in hand. This is really the last place I expected us to end up. It wouldn't surprise me if he has some "make out in the stacks" fantasy that he wants to tick off his list.

"Gabby is working here for the summer," I say, peering at the checkout desk as we come through. The library has multiple floors, and I'm blanking on which one she said she'd be on.

"We're not here for her, Cheer," Drayton says.

"Yeah, I bet it's a much kinkier reason."

"If you think I want to fool around in the stacks . . . you're right. But later."

He's full of surprises today. We head up to the next floor, passing the open space with desks lining the windows and short round tables flanked by low chairs. People are tapping away on laptops, reading, highlighting notes, or putting tabs in their books. We arrive in the romance section, which holds shelves and shelves of books.

Dray pulls out his phone, taps on the screen, and then turns it around to show me a five-minute timer.

"Five minutes to find a romantic quote that best describes us. Go."

He kisses me hard and fast and then darts off, leaving me bewildered. It doesn't take long before I'm snapping into action, and I start frantically scanning the shelves for books. I don't read a lot, though, so I have no idea what to look for. Gabs would be a huge help right now. I start sliding books out and flicking through the pages, only skimming the second halves since I figure that's where most of the confessions are happening.

I go as quickly as possible, moving through the stacks and grabbing random books. So far, nothing is jumping out at me.

"Three minutes," I hear Drayton shout from somewhere nearby and wince at the volume he's using in the damn library.

I carry on, haphazardly grabbing at books without even reading the spines first. It wouldn't make a difference. I don't know what I'm looking for. Suddenly, I've found it. Smiling, I read the quote a few more times and put my thumb between the pages.

A few moments later, I hear, "Time."

I sigh at his complete lack of concern for his surroundings and make my way in the direction I heard his voice coming from. He's in the last row beside the windows, standing there with his elbow leaning on the shelf and a book hanging from his hand. His phone is set up on one of the shelves, recording. He likes to record our adventures, which is sweet.

"You got one?"

I wave the book at him. "Yep."

"You go first."

"No, you."

"Why?" he asks.

I shrug, not having a reason.

"Fine," he chides playfully and brings his book up to hold it with both hands. "'All I know is, one moment I was existing and the next, I was living. And I'd never known the difference until I met her.'"

My heart starts to flutter as he lowers the book and looks at me again, his suntanned biceps pulling his T-shirt sleeve tight, his tattoo looking as sexy as always, and now I want to fool around in the stacks.

"Read your quote before you jump my bones, baby."

I stick my tongue out at him and lift the book, scanning the words quickly to find the quote. I clear my throat.

"'I've lost enough in my life to know I can survive it. I've never loved enough to make me question that, until now.'"

When I peer up, Drayton has straightened up off the shelf and is staring at me with a longing I will never get used to. Though, there's a little sadness in it too.

"You have me, and you aren't losing me."

He crosses the space between us and wraps his arms around my waist. He kisses me as his hands move up my spine and into my hair, and then he's pushing me back against the shelf.

"Okay, that was fun," he murmurs against my lips. "Now we shake these shelves."

"Mmm," I gasp as his mouth moves onto my neck. "We are not going all the way back here."

"It'd be so fun."

I laugh against his mouth and let myself feel all of the love that comes with being adored by him.

CHAPTER 2

DRAYTON

Eleven weeks to go

Lying to Dallas doesn't come naturally to me. Sure, for a while there, I downplayed how I felt about her. I didn't let on that I'd imagined marrying her the first time I ever saw her wearing my T-shirt after I brought her home drunk.

I've been in love with her for as long as I can remember, and being honest has never been a question for me. Letting her think I'm going to Baylor for college and watching the sadness in her face whenever she thinks about it is killing me. It's also confusing. It wasn't that long ago that my girlfriend was acting like a long-distance relationship would be a piece of cake and I should quit considering colleges near her.

I let myself into her house on Saturday morning.

"I need a favor," I say to Nathan. He's on the sofa with a coffee, his phone in his other hand. "Tell Dallas you don't want me to go camping with you guys."

"I don't want you to go camping with us."

I grin at him. "I know you invited me."

He rolls his eyes, and I sit down on the sofa next to him. Dallas is here somewhere, in her room no doubt, getting organized to leave for California tomorrow morning. I can't wait to spend a week away with my girl.

"That was out of obligation," Nathan says.

"Yeah, well, Dallas asked me to go, and I had to pretend like I just don't like camping. I had to tell her no. I never tell her no."

"If you're not careful, that'll go to her head."

I shrug and lean back into the cushions, giving Nathan a look as if to say, And? He cracks a smile and shakes his head.

"You're good to her. I do appreciate that."

I give him a light slap on the shoulder. "I would do anything for that woman."

Except tell her that I have to spend a week doing assessment training at UCLA. I'll also be meeting my teammates (and getting to know who I'll be up against for starting quarterback), the coaches, and the assistants. I'm looking forward to it. I was thinking ahead when I initially checked out the campus. Even before we became official, I knew I wanted to factor Dallas into my future. It's hard to explain, but I had a gut instinct that she was the one. Plus, she was too driven and focused to change her plans for me, which I would never have expected. She's wanted CalArts for a hell of a long time. So either I changed course and followed her or we did the long-distance thing. Fuck that, I want to see my girl as often as possible.

I considered telling her that I can't go camping because I have to be at Baylor for assessment training, but that would mean she'd want to see the campus. I know her well enough to know I would not be able to avoid a FaceTime tour.

"I still don't see why you can't tell her," Nathan says, bringing his coffee up to his face. "She'd be pleased."

"Because it's a surprise," I say. "I've mentioned that."

He stares at me as if expecting me to elaborate. I can't—I just want us to spend the summer in the moment. Loving as if we're running out of time. Living as if it's our last summer. I don't know if it's cruel. It might be, but it can't be a bad thing that we're having the time of our lives so far. I have two passions in life: football and making sure Dallas feels loved. I'm dedicating my every waking moment to both.

"How long do we need to be camping for?" Nathan asks.

"A week."

He stands up and wanders over to the kitchen, flicking the faucet on and rinsing his cup. "That doesn't sound like a long time, but it is when it comes to camping. Especially for Dallas."

"What about Dallas?"

Dallas appears from the hall in a pair of denim shorts that hug her spectacular ass and a pastel-pink cropped T-shirt. Her hair is up in a loose bun, and I'm gifted with her sweet smile before she goes back to looking at her brother, brow raised.

"Nathan was telling me he doesn't think you can handle camping for an entire week." I get off the sofa and walk over to Dallas, slipping an arm around her waist and giving her a kiss on the head.

"A week?" she gasps.

Nathan gives me a subtle glare. "Might as well make the most of it."

Dallas peers up at me with her bottom lip pinched between her teeth. "That's a big chunk of our summer gone."

I love that she thinks that. A week isn't a massive amount of time, but then again, I'm the one who knows we're going to be together next year. My heart lurches again, and I wonder if I should give up this whole idea and tell her the truth. Then again, so far, I haven't outright lied. I've found ways to avoid telling her plainly that I'm not going to Baylor.

I had acceptances to both schools—and four others—by March but sent my intent to register letter to UCLA on the last possible day. Until a few weeks ago, I also had no idea where the hell I was going to end up. I had to get my dad on board before I told him about the letter I'd sent. As adamant as I was about doing what I wanted, the thought of his disapproval still weighed on me. Things have been getting better, though. He and I, we're getting past our shit.

"I did mention perhaps I should come," I say. "I know I said I wouldn't, but then I thought it could be fun and we'd get to do something new together. But Nathan said no."

Nathan leans a palm on the countertop and sighs, fed the fuck up. I almost laugh. I shouldn't stir the pot, but it amuses me. Dallas looks at her brother, head tilted in confusion. "You were the one who first suggested inviting him."

Nathan glares at me for a few long beats, and I wonder if he's going to rat me out. Perhaps I pushed him too far. Finally, he lifts his shoulders. "We need some sibling time. You're spending ninety percent of the summer with Drayton anyway."

"Yeah." Dallas relents. "I suppose so."

"It's no stress, baby." I give her another kiss on the head and lead her toward the front door. We should split before Nathan has a change of heart and decides to expose me. "I've got people I can visit and plenty to do to keep me occupied."

Another indirect lie. I do have people to visit and plenty to do to keep me occupied. In California.

As we reach the front door, I look back at the kitchen, where Nathan is watching me with exasperation, and give him a thumbs-up.

Dallas and I head back to my place to have lunch with my parents before we leave tomorrow. By the time we get back from California, they'll be gone, off to set up some business venture for Mom. We go inside, and Dallas and I both still at the raised voices coming from the living area.

I don't hesitate to follow the sound of obvious dispute, but my sweet, respectful girlfriend tugs on my arm.

"We shouldn't interrupt," Dallas says. "That sounds like Gabby's mom."

"Camilla loves me."

"Oh, babe." Dallas winces. "No, she doesn't."

I wave her off and take another step, only to be intercepted again.

"This is probably about the pregnancy," she whispers. "We don't need to go in there."

"What if your best friend needs your support?"

She stares up at me, her eyes narrowing, the internal conflict obvious on her face.

"You're playing on the fact that I want to go in there and save my best friend just so you can watch the drama."

"You know me so well." I press a firm kiss against her mouth and take her hand, dragging her toward the living room. Her steps are reluctant, but I know she wants to be in there as much as I do.

"This would never have happened under my roof," Camilla snaps.

She's standing in the middle of the room with my mom and dad, though there's a decent distance between them. Josh and Gabby are doing their best to sink into the couch and disappear. Josh is my best friend, but he became more of a brother when his parents moved to Canada. Mom and Dad agreed to let him stay with us so he didn't have to leave school or his girlfriend at the time. Neither of which worked out. When he dropped out, Mom hired him as a PA with the expectation that he was to work towards supporting himself and being a responsible adult. I don't think knocking up his girl was what they meant.

Dallas and I stand behind the couch, the adults not detecting us. Dallas reaches down and takes Gabby's hand, and the two exchange a small smile. I nod at Josh. He gives me a little two-finger wave before sinking further down.

I circle around and sit next to him.

"Well, that isn't necessarily true." Mom is doing her best to be gentle while my dad stands with his hands in his pockets, looking frustrated. "They obviously didn't use protection no matter where they were."

Good point.

Camilla scoffs. I get it, she's upset, but my hackles go up in defense of Mom. As if sensing it, Dad twists and looks at me, shaking his head. Message: Don't get involved. I'm still deciding if the message has been received.

"There would have been no sharing beds under my roof," she argues. "I didn't know she was spending nights here with no supervision, allowed to do whatever."

Dad tilts his head at her. "You didn't know where your daughter was spending her evenings, and that's our fault?"

Mom pushes her elbow back, giving Dad a gentle jab in the ribs. Steam appears to be coming out of Camilla's ears. This might be the first time the three of them have gotten together since the news broke. I knew Camilla was upset, but Dallas said she was handling it all right. Mom told Josh they were welcome to live with them. I thought the issue was sort of resolved. I guess being in the same room raised some grievances. I peer over at Dallas and notice a subtle glare aimed in Josh's direction as she leans in close to Gabby, who whispers something in her ear.

"How did this all start?" I whisper to Josh. I'll find out what the girls are talking about later.

He puts his hand over his mouth. "Camilla came with us to the ob-gyn checkup and was dropping us off after. She decided to come in and talk to Mom and Dad, and, I don't know, one comment led to another and it got tense."

"Dude, quit trying to blend into the furniture and stand up. Handle this shit. Have you even apologized to her once since it happened?" I whisper.

Josh scowls at me. "Why should I? It was a team effort."

"That's not the point," I say, keeping my voice low. "You need to be the epitome of a man right now. You're about to have a kid. Camilla needs to see you being fit for that role. Not hiding behind Mom and Dad."

He bounces his leg. "What do you know about all this?"

"It's about what people expect. Having confidence and taking charge and at least pretending to be in control helps build trust. Also, an apology goes a long way with moms. Believe me."

I've missed the last few moments of conversation, but I tune back in to hear Camilla expressing exactly what I was saying. "What are they going to do? Is Josh going to go off and lead the life he wants while Gabriella is stuck here raising a child? What about her future? She had plans."

Mom's shoulders deflate a little, and she looks at my dad with obvious distress. Suddenly, Josh stands up and steps forward. I feel a little surge of pride for the fucker. Until he speaks.

"I'm not an asshole."

Camilla looks at Josh with her brows pinched.

"What I'm saying . . ." Josh clears his throat, clearly nervous, and Dallas and I look at each other with subtle judgment—well, subtle from me, not so much Dallas. I love the kid, but that was not an opening line. "I'm not going to leave Gabby to handle this on her own. If her plans change, then so do mine, and we share the load. We have equal opportunity, and we make equal sacrifices. I'll work to support her, and if she can take classes to keep up with her dreams, we'll make that work. We're in a better position than some. We have a good support system, and I'm sorry we broke your trust. I am sorry. It's not ideal, but I won't leave her to do this alone."

That's better. Gabby's clutching her chest with tears streaming down her face. It seems she needed the reassurance too. Dad gives Josh a light pat on the back in support, and while Camilla still has her arms crossed, her face has softened. Just a little.

She nods. "That's good to hear."

Mom gestures outwardly at the room. "And the kids are welcome to live here. We have so much room, and it'd be no imposition."

Camilla sucks in a sharp breath, hardness returning to her features. "Gabriella should be at home with me."

"We'll talk about that, Mom," Gabby mumbles, wiping her face with open palms.

Finally, as if Mom is just realizing Dallas and I are here, she waves her hands at us, gesturing for us to get away from the sofa. "You two, out. Go and wait in the kitchen, we'll be there in a minute."

I sigh, standing up and taking Dallas's hand, leading her out of the room. "Well, all right. We'll be unsupervised, though. Someone might end up pregnant."

"Boy," Dad snaps, quieting the little snickers from Gabby.

Dallas whacks me in the arm. When we get to the kitchen, she blows out a breath and leans her elbows on the kitchen island, shaking her head a little.

"What was Gabs whispering about?" I ask, standing next to her.

Dallas looks at me with confusion.

"You two were whispering in there, and it incited some death glares in Josh's direction."

"It's girl stuff."

I should probably accept that answer. "Please tell me."

Dallas straightens up and turns to me. "Apparently, the ob-gyn scheduled another appointment for six weeks' time, and Josh asked if he has to go to all of them."

Why the fuck would he make a comment like that? "It might be to do with work. He was talking to Mom about needing more hours. Maybe he's worried about availability."

"Could be that, I guess," she says, still a little pinch of frustration in her brow.

"Mm-hmm, a bit more cash. Soon-to-be parents need it."

"Yeah." She shrugs, waving me off. "Yeah, sure."

Josh and Gabby come into the kitchen, and Josh rushes around with rigid shoulders, scanning the countertop. "Where are my keys?"

"Wait." Gabs sits down on a barstool next to Dallas. "You have to go now?"

"Yes," Josh breathes out with a huff. "I told you, I have work to do."

Dallas's eyes narrow again, and I'm sure it's his tone that's pissing her off.

"I'll go home with Mom, then." Gabby gets up again. "She's listening to Ellie talk about her own teen pregnancy. I feel like Ellie is doing her best to find a bright side for Mom."

Josh rushes out of the kitchen, and I follow him down the hall toward the basement door. "Dude, you good?"

He seemed fine five minutes ago when he was giving his speech. He stops at the top of the basement stairwell and pinches the bridge of his nose. "That was a lot to promise a person."

"What do you mean?"

He waves his arm in the direction of the living room. "I promised a bunch of shit that I don't know if I can deliver on. I have no fucking clue what the future looks like. I don't know if I can chase a good career and allow Gabs to do the same while we raise a kid."

"Allow her to?"

Josh sighs with frustration. "You know what I mean. We have to raise a child. A person. That's . . . a lot. I don't know how good I'm going to be at that or if I'll be able to provide enough or if it'll be realistic for both of us to get what we want in terms of a career. There's going to be sacrifice involved, and probably some resentment. This is fucked."

"You're freaking out a bit, man," I say, clapping him on the shoulder. "I get it. But what's done is done. You just take it one step at a time. Breathe. Communicate."

He nods, doing just that, taking a deep breath in and out. "Yeah. Right. It'll be fine. We'll be fine."

Hell, he might not be, but at least he's aware that this is all a big deal. That's a good start.

~

"This is delicious," Dallas tells Mom, directing a forkful of beef fried rice in between her plump lips. Anything this woman does is erotic to me. The four of us are sitting at the dining table, and so far, it's been quiet. Mom and Dad seem to have jittery nerves from their unexpected visitor.

"Mom didn't cook this," I say.

"Drayton," Mom chides me.

"What? You didn't."

Mom rolls her eyes. "I will take the compliment because I clearly know how to choose takeout. Thank you, Dallas."

Dallas smiles, and then her gaze darts to me and narrows as if I'm being told off.

I peer over at my dad pushing food around his plate, not eating a whole lot as if his thoughts are elsewhere. I wonder if it's about the fact that Josh and Gabby are having a baby. Mom and Dad handled the news well when they found out. They were teen parents, they get it. But it's probably not what they wanted for Josh.

"You good, Dad?"

He peers up, brows raised. "Mmm, fine, son. Dallas, how are your relocation preparations coming along?"

Dad apologized to my girl after we graduated last week, apologized for being a complete asshole to her. They haven't seen much of each other since then, but Dallas is still upset because she thinks my dad got his way about deciding where I go to college. That might be the hardest part of this charade. I want them to get along. These are two of the most important people in my life. I will always choose Dallas, in every situation, over every person because she is my future. But if she and Dad could find common ground and form something like a friendship, that would mean the world to me. He's going to have to put in the work, though. She's not easy to win over, speaking from experience, but she's sure as hell worth it.

"Good." Dallas nods, covering her mouth until she's swallowed her food. "I mean, sort of. I haven't done a lot just yet apart from researching the area more. It's going to be a huge change, but I'm excited."

"It's incredibly brave to relocate to a brand-new city." My mom leans back in her seat with a glass of water. "What are you most looking forward to?"

Dallas purses her lips thoughtfully for a moment. "Besides the school?"

Mom nods.

"The weather. The beaches, and the fact that it won't snow."

Dad nods in agreement. "That would tempt me for sure. It's summer now, but I'm already not looking forward to the winter."

"You grew up in Texas, right?" Dallas asks. "I suppose winters here were hard to get used to."

"I'm still not used to them. Hence Ellie and I travel as often as we can."

"What's your favorite place to visit?" Dallas asks, and my heart jolts at the effort she is making.

"Ooh, that's a good question," Dad says thoughtfully. "It's hard to choose when there are so many beautiful places to see. I love Canada. In the summer, of course."

"Of course," Dallas agrees.

"Northern Italy too, gorgeous." Dad looks more relaxed; he even smiles. "The Dolomites are fantastic. It's like being in another world up there, at the top of the mountains."

"I've heard that. It looks really beautiful."

"It is. Do you plan to travel?"

Dallas nods. "I would love to. I'm hoping that I can build my career in a way that allows me to see more of the world."

Dad points at her. "That's a good ambition and a good way to do it. People think traveling is just a luxury, and it is, absolutely. But it's also enriching. It teaches you so much about other cultures, history, language, art. It allows people to grow and to realize how big life is outside of themselves."

Mom and I share a quick look. It's lightning fast; we understand without words that this is a good moment. This is how I wanted everything to go at the first dinner I brought Dallas to. There are no undertones of hostility or tension. Sure, it's a little awkward: everyone is hyperaware that there was some tension. But this makes me happy. This is progress.

CHAPTER 3

DALLAS
Eleven weeks to go

Drayton and I are staying at the Homewood Suites in Santa Clarita, just a seven-minute drive from CalArts. It's beautiful. Big and modern with a pool and views of the hillside and Six Flags. Our room has a little patio, and I stand in the sun, watching the roller coaster going around the enormous loops. The sound of happy screaming doesn't travel this far, but I can imagine it.

"Should we go there instead of Disney?" Drayton wraps his arms around me from behind and rests his chin on my head.

"I don't think I'm into that. Disney looks more magical and fun to me."

"Come on, Cheer. You used to get thrown in the air. You can handle some roller coasters."

I turn around and look at him. "I was like six feet off the ground, max. Not . . . whatever that is." I wave a hand at the park.

He grins down at me. "We could do it together."

"I'll think about it."

He gives me a quick kiss and heads back into the room, lifting his shirt over his head as he heads to the bathroom. Our room is nice enough: a king bed, a small desk in the corner, a TV on the wall, and a kitchen with all the basic amenities. The shower switches on, and I stand there for a moment, waiting.

"Cheer," Drayton calls out. "Come and see this."

I laugh as I head toward the bathroom because I know exactly what he wants me to see.

~

The next afternoon, Monday, we do a lot of driving. We start outside of CalArts and just . . . drive. Drayton points out things he thinks will be helpful —a laundromat, cute cafés, gyms, grocery stores, the hospital, Home Depot. I'm not sure why I need to know where that is until Drayton explains I might want to get picture hooks for my dorm room. He's sweet. He thinks of it all. When we get to Valencia Town Center, we park the car so we can get out and walk around.

The sun feels so good as we walk hand in hand. We wander around Macy's and JCPenney and get burritos from a Mexican grill. It's a good chance for me to ask a few of the retail stores and fast-food places if they're going to be hiring in the next few months. I make a note in my phone of where to email my resume. Downtown is only seven minutes from campus, which is perfect.

After we've eaten, we head back to CalArts and visit the dormitory. It's about a ten-minute walk from the main campus, and as we walk the route toward my classes, I find it hard to believe this will be my routine in just a few months. It feels so right, even more so with Drayton walking beside me.

But he won't be here. That fact hits me like a blow to the chest. Right now it's fun and exciting, but he won't walk this walk with me; he won't even be in the same state. I blow out a quick breath so as not to let him in on the fact that I'm stewing again. These feelings are becoming more regular, and I wasn't expecting them to start so soon. I knew it would be hard when it came time to leave, but my excitement has always outweighed any other feelings.

"Stop here, Cheer," Drayton says, holding my shoulders and angling me so I'm in front of a building. He steps back, and I twist to look over my shoulder at whatever is behind me. It's the main entrance. We made it all the way here, and I was too in my head to notice. On the blue wall behind me are the words CALIFORNIA INSTITUTE OF THE ARTS. There's a vibrant garden with flowers and small shrubs and a sprinkler giving everything a light mist. Drayton pulls out his phone and starts snapping photos.

His excitement is infectious, so I raise my hands and smile and pose. Sometimes I can't get over how lucky I am to have someone like him. So wholly supportive. It takes my breath away.

He lowers the phone and looks at me knowingly. "I can see you mulling from over here."

He's so intuitive, it scares me sometimes. I wave him off. "Mulling. What a word."

Sliding his phone into his pocket, he makes his way back toward me. "You suit this place, baby."

"You'd suit it too," I mumble, resting my hands on his chest when he envelops me in a hug. "You could dance."

He takes my hand and pushes me away from him. I barely get a chance to find my footing before he reels me back in, and then we're dancing. I don't know what kind of dance it is, but it doesn't matter. He twirls me, and we step together, our bodies moving as we laugh.

"Consider this my audition, CalArts," he shouts at the top of his lungs, and my cheeks heat up as I drop my forehead to his chest. The campus isn't busy like it was the last time I visited, but there are people here. "You couldn't possibly reject all of this."

He holds my upper back and lowers me, not a sign of strain as he keeps me from hitting the ground. "What do you think my chances are?" he asks.

"You're better off trying to charm admissions, babe. That almost never fails."

"Are you saying all I have is raw sexuality?"

Still suspended where he's holding me, I grin. "Oh, absolutely not, but you do have it."

He kisses me, lifting me back upright.

Over the next few days, Drayton and I do all the tourist things we can. We go to Santa Monica Pier and ride the Ferris wheel. We buy a bunch of random souvenirs from the souvenir stands. We take photos in front of the water. We get into an argument over which direction we're supposed to walk to find our rental car. When he's right and I'm wrong, I distract him with a passionate kiss, and he's gracious enough not to rub it in my face.

We walk up to the Hollywood sign. It takes us all day, but thank goodness we're in shape. We walk Rodeo Drive and visit the Academy Museum of Motion Pictures. We go to the Farmers Market in The Grove. There are dozens and dozens of eateries packed into this funky sheltered space with tables and chairs and the occasional retail stand. We hop from eatery to eatery and get far too much food. Fresh-baked breads, seafood, Mexican food, doughnuts, and ice cream. We sleep well that night. We spend two days at Disneyland, one in each park. It's fast become one of my favorite places on earth, save for the crowds. Drayton and I buy a pair of ears each and wear them the entire time. We take thousands of photos and videos, and again, we eat too much food.

Drayton and I decide to visit Hermosa Beach on our second to last day. It's a gorgeous little beach town that rivals Santa Monica in my opinion. The stores are quaint, the food is beautiful, and the streets are perfect for walking. We get an ice cream from Creamy Boys, a brand from New Zealand. It's deliciously made with frozen berries and vanilla. The sun is hot, and the sea and air smell fresh.

"I love this place," I tell Dray as we walk through the pier, surrounded by people with children and dogs. On either side of the wide walkway are eateries and boutiques, bike stands and strung lights.

"It's got a good vibe," he agrees.

"Yeah, like it's close enough to LA, but it's got a calmer energy."

Drayton nods, and we keep walking down to the Strand, a long stretch between the sand and the street. We look around at the homes that back onto the beach, with big windows and gorgeous decks that look out over the water.

"I could live here," Drayton says.

"Can you imagine?" I sigh dreamily, looking at my man in his white shirt, the top few buttons undone to expose his chest and the contrast of his golden skin against the pale fabric. We unintentionally matched, though my white tank top is more casual.

Over on the beach, there are a few volleyball games happening on the sand, kids on the swing sets, sunbathers, and surfers — so many surfers.

"That over there," Drayton says, placing his hands on my hips and turning me toward the strip of multimillion-dollar homes. "That's where I can see us living. Like every day is a vacation, out on the deck with a cold drink, my girl bathing in the sun, a step away from the sand and sea."

I lean into him, feeling all gooey at his vision.

"I guess we better make it big time," I say, looking up at him with a dazed smile.

"I'll make sure I do," he says, giving me a kiss. "Just so I can make that happen."

If anyone else ever promised me something like that, I'd laugh and take it as a pipe dream, but with Drayton, it feels that little bit more real, like he means what he's saying.

We end up hanging around in Hermosa Beach until after dark. We have dinner at a little grill, sitting at an outdoor table, the night air still thick with heat.. We order loaded fries, steak skewers, and deep-fried shrimp, and it's all so good. When the waiter sets our food down, he smiles at me and props his hands behind his back.

"Can I get you anything else?"

I start to shake my head and then look across at Drayton with a raised brow. "Babe?"

He's staring straight at the waiter, a young guy with loose blond waves, a nose piercing, and hand tattoos. "Oh, I don't think he was asking me, baby."

The waiter's head snaps toward Dray.

"Hi." Dray gives him an evil grin. "Yeah, she's so gorgeous, it's easy to forget I'm here."

"Dray," I say as the waiter starts shaking his head. "Stop."

"I'm acknowledging your mesmerizing qualities," he says. "You should see her dance."

Reaching for the waiter, I give his wrist a gentle squeeze because he looks awkward and frozen. "There's nothing else, thank you."

As soon as he's gone, I give Drayton a flat look. "He was not hitting on me."

Drayton scoffs and stares at me in bewilderment. "You have the face of an angel. Head-turning, jaw-dropping, fucking delectable. I understand the attention, and I consider it a privilege to be the one that gets to kiss that mouth. I'm not going to pass up the opportunity to call someone out for hitting on you, though. It's too much fun."

"It's a good thing most girls aren't as forward as guys are, or I'd be dealing with it all day too."

"Nah," Drayton says, picking up a skewer.

"Oh, shut up, girls are staring at you all the time."

"I wouldn't notice," he says with a casual shrug of the shoulder. "Too busy staring at the prettiest girl in the world."

"Smooth."

He gives me a big teeth-baring grin.

After we've eaten, we walk the pier. We come to a live band playing gorgeous acoustic music, a women singing joyfully. Drayton throws some cash in their guitar case, and we keep going down to the beach. The stars speckle the cloudless sky, looking exquisite as they meet with the sea in the distance. We can still hear the music from down here.

Drayton, as he often does, sets up his phone in the sand, leaning it against his shoes, which he's taken off. I do the same, kicking my flip-flops off to let my feet sink into the cool sand.

He takes my hand, and we walk to where the water laps against the shore. Our toes touch the cold sea. It's refreshingly welcome.

"You danced today, Cheer?" Drayton pulls me into his body, one hand against my back, the other clasped around my palm.

"I have not," I admit. "We've been so busy."

"You'd fit it in if you got your cute butt out of bed before seven."

"Ick," I protest with a laugh as we start dancing, slow and romantic with our feet in the water.

"I guess we'll squeeze it in now," he says as my head rests on his chest. "Just a light dance—we'll save the real exercise for the room later."

"Mm-hmm, sure."

"Have I ever told you I love you?" Drayton murmurs against my hair.

"No, this is the first time I'm hearing it."

"Thank God," he says. "Because this is the perfect first moment."

He spins me out, my feet kicking up the water, and then he pulls me back in, just like he did when we were on campus earlier in the week. He lowers me, the ends of my hair touching the water, the stars behind his head.

"Dallas Bryan"—his nose touches mine—"I love you."

"Oh, baby." I swoon as if I'm lightheaded. "I thought you'd never say it. I love you too."

He lifts me back up, gives me another twirl, and then scoops me into a bridal hold, all within seconds.

"Okay, picture it: we're on our honeymoon," Drayton says as he starts running further into the water. My arms tighten around his neck.

"Drayton!"

"Crossing the threshold, baby." He laughs, running into the water, both of us going in. It's cold at first, and my short bursts of laughter push through the gasps as I stand up, the water to my waist. Drayton shakes his head, flicking water like a dog, his white shirt clinging to the ridges of his torso. Mine must be doing the same because Drayton lets his gaze roam over me hungrily as he walks through the water and sweeps me into his arms, kissing me with slow and tantalizing strokes of his tongue. I'm not sure how long we spend splashing each other, falling into the water, lying in the shallowest spot where water meets sand while we stare up at the stars, but it turns into one of my favorite nights of the entire trip.

~

By the time our last night rolls around, I'm exhausted. We're both exhausted. The TV is on the music video channel at low volume while we sit under the covers, room service spread out before us and our phones in hand.

Drayton absentmindedly runs his hand up and down my arm. "Baby?"

"Mm-hmm?"

"What's your ultimate goal as a dancer?"

I look at Drayton, phone falling into my lap. "My ultimate goal as a dancer?"

He nods.

"I'd like to get into music videos or be a backup dancer in concerts. Tour the world. But I'd also love to perform in a production like West Side Story or Hamilton. I want to be on a world-famous stage, just once. And then perhaps get into choreography a bit later on; I could do that until I retire."

Drayton looks at me for a long while, and then he gives me a small, slow nod. "We're both going to have busy futures, huh."

I swallow the sudden lump in my throat. "I guess so."

"Listen," he says. "I love you. I love you so much that I don't even know how to process it sometimes. There's no part of me that thinks we wouldn't survive time or distance. It just . . . it would never be the end for us. You're literally part of who I am, and I freaked out a little over wanting to choose a college close to you, but I need you to know, I could be on the other side of the world and it wouldn't change a thing for me."

I force back the emotion threatening to overwhelm me and smile. "You're right, though. What if in five years I'm touring the world for, like, I don't know, Dua Lipa, and you're in the NFL? Traveling, on the road all the time, and even when you're at home, you're training. What if our time off the road never aligns, and we don't get the chance to see each other for months and months? Is that the kind of relationship you want?"

"I don't want a relationship if it's not with you, Dallas."

I cup his cheek with sincere and pure adoration for him. "But you'll have needs, baby."

"You're my need."

"Are we just being young and hopeful?"

He puts his hand over mine and kisses my palm. "Would that be so bad? What's wrong with hoping we can make it work? It's better to give it our all than to give up."

"I love the fact that you refuse to accept my fears."

He breathes out a light laugh. "We've been doing this for a while, Cheer. You freak out, and while I used to let you run off and get all dramatic, we're not doing that this time. There is nothing that I wouldn't do to protect this relationship. I promise."

I push our food further down the bed and scoot in next to Drayton, curling into him. "You have more emotional maturity than some thirty-year-old men."

"You mean Nathan?"

"Hey, he's only twenty-five," I scold, doing my best not to sound amused. "Yeah."

Drayton tucks me into him, holding me even tighter. "Maybe we should set him up before we leave. Find him someone to settle down with."

"He's incapable," I sigh.

"Nah, he just needs the right one."

"Well, if he hasn't found her yet in Colorado, I doubt she lives there. He's sifted through the entire field. He's going to have to go out of state."

"I don't think that's a terrible idea," Drayton says, and I inch back so I can see his face.

"What's not a terrible idea?"

"Nathan getting out of Colorado. He should come to California with you."

My mind turns into a little wind tunnel as I sit up again and think about the fact that I've never even considered Nathan moving. Ever. It's so hard to imagine him anywhere else but in the house our parents raised us in. It's become his.

"He . . . no. He couldn't."

Drayton sits up too and leans back against the headboard. "How come?"

"Because Castle Rock is his home, and if he wanted to come with me, he would've suggested it."

"Unless he doesn't want to step on your independent toes?"

Pushing my hand through my hair, I give a little one-shoulder shrug. "There's that too. But I need to stop leaning on him at some point, right?"

"There's nothing wrong with a little leaning, baby."

"If he wanted to come, that would be cool. But I'm not going to ask him to uproot his life. Not for me."

Because I have a feeling he'd do it.

"Yeah, that's fair, but what if he wanted to do it for himself?" Drayton slides his hand over my thigh, and I'm momentarily distracted by the sheer size of it and the way it spans my leg. "Did he ever have his own plans to get out of Castle Rock?"

"I guess he probably did," I say. "He wanted to go pro, but I don't know which college he'd have ended up at. He got injured, and then Mom and Dad died so he took care of me. Shit, maybe it's selfish that I've never considered he might want to do something other than community college coaching."

"He's never said anything about having different goals?"

I think back as far as I can. "No. Once he came to terms with his injury, he settled on coaching. It gave him the chance to stay involved with football, and he does love it. He finds it really rewarding."

"Well, if he ever wanted to spread his wings, I bet my dad could make some calls, find some coaching positions at the colleges out here. Nathan is wasted on community college."

"There is nothing wrong with community college, you snob."

"I know, I know," he says. "It's not varsity, though."

No, it's not.

~

The next day, Drayton drops me off at home so that I can unpack, shower, and have a nap in my own bed. It feels like we didn't stop all week. I give Nathan the souvenirs I got for him: some fridge magnets, a key chain with a Santa Monica license plate, a mug. He loves coffee, so the mug seemed fitting.

I put half of the clothes from my suitcase straight in the wash and switch it on. I thought I would need a nap by now, but I'm not that tired, so I head out to the kitchen and find Nathan making a drink in the new mug I got him. The front of it has a picture of the Santa Monica Pier. I slide onto a barstool and rest my chin in my hand.

"How was your week?" I ask. "Did you wash that mug first?"

"Yes. Yeah, it was fine, quiet. No teenage boys waking me up at first light."

"Quiet, huh?"

My mind drifts back to the conversation I had with Drayton about Nathan. Will he be happy here on his own? It's been the two of us for so long, and while I've never thought of him as dependent, I wonder if it'll be hard when I'm gone. Will he miss me? I mean, of course. But I'm sure he won't be miserable. Does he want to go further in his career? Surely.

"Yeah." He picks the kettle up when it's boiled and pours water into his cup. "Training starts next week, thankfully. I'm starting to get bored."

"Our camping trip is Monday, surely you won't be that bored."

He smiles and sets the kettle back down. "No, of course not. A week of watching you in nature will be just what I need to keep me entertained."

I glare at him, and he laughs.

"No, I'm looking forward to it. I think the last time we went camping you were thirteen and it lasted two nights before you decided to throw a tantrum and demand a real shower."

"Yeah, that's probably because I got my period for the first time."

Nathan recoils. "You did? What? I didn't . . ."

"It was embarrassing. I didn't know how to say it, so I threw a diva fit instead."

Nathan looks genuinely mortified as he swallows hard. "Shit, I'm sorry you felt like you couldn't tell me."

"It wasn't you. It was . . . it's hard to explain."

Nathan never made me feel embarrassed about anything growing up. When I added pads and tampons to the grocery list, he didn't flinch. He simply asked me what sort I needed and made sure he got them. But that first time was an experience only a girl could understand. It was unexpected and in the worst place possible. I was mad at my body and mad at the situation. I felt like this huge, life-changing shift had happened, and it was entirely against my will, knowledge, or schedule. There was far too much happening in my head to even begin explaining it to my older brother.

He still looks upset, and now I wish I hadn't told him. "Nate, you've been a really good brother. You've given me everything. Even when you didn't really know how to. You made sure I was safe and happy and clothed and fed. That was never your responsibility, but you did it really well, and I'm grateful. I'll . . . miss you."

Nathan nods, clenching his jaw a little, emotion on his face. "It won't be the same around here without you. Like, who the hell am I going to talk to in the morning?"

"I've said this before, you might need to settle down and find a more permanent companion."

He laughs. "You might be right. It's just getting embarrassing at this point."

"Don't be too hard on yourself. You're only twenty-five."

"Hey, you're not meant to encourage it."

"Oh right." I adopt a more scolding expression. "Grow up, man."

"Thanks." He sips his coffee and lets out a content sigh.

"Can I ask you something?"

"Sure."

"What college did you want to go to?"

Nathan looks surprised. "Ohio State first and foremost. Notre Dame was a close second. Great colleges."

"You wanted to get out of Castle Rock then?"

He gives me a curious look. "I wouldn't say I wanted to get out of Castle Rock. I don't hate living here. I did want to go to a good football college, though. Even as a junior, I was on Notre Dame's radar. They told me that. That's where I'd have ended up, I believe."

"You've never really talked about that before."

Nathan shrugs, swallowing another mouthful of coffee. "No point. Didn't happen, life moves on."

"Yeah, but—"

"I've never seen the point in dwelling on something that can never be changed. That can never be undone. Just sounds like a way to linger in misery. I got hurt, going pro was out of the question. It is what it is."

I want to ask if he'd have gone to college anyway or if he'd have moved away if Mom and Dad hadn't died. Part of me is afraid to hear the answer.

CHAPTER 4

DRAYTON
Ten weeks to go

"Yeah, the flight number is . . . hang on." I drop my cell from my ear and swipe open the details for the flight Dallas will be on when she leaves for school. I forwarded it to myself one morning while she was showering in California and then booked a seat on the same flight.

I read the number out to the customer service rep, Renee. She sounds helpful. Friendly. Sometimes you can hear when a person is going to be no use.

"Okay, great," Renee says. "I have it here. So, you're in seat nineteen B. You were wanting to change seats?"

"Yeah, I couldn't select the seat next to my girlfriend because we didn't book the flights together, and it says the seat is taken so I thought you might be able to do some shuffling," I explain. "She doesn't even know I'm joining her. It's a surprise."

There's a long, silent pause on the other end. "Uh . . ."

I sit up straighter and sigh. "It's not weird. I'm not a stalker."

Josh walks into the room then, brow raised. I roll my eyes and wave him in, letting him know I'll be a second.

"No, see, my girlfriend is going to college in California, and she thinks I'm going to Texas, but I've been accepted into UCLA and so it's going to be, like, a surprise when she sees me on the flight next to her. It'll just be a buzzkill if we're not seated next to each other."

"Okay." Renee sounds relieved at the explanation.

"Surely this isn't the first time someone has tried to surprise someone else on a flight?"

I can hear her tapping away at her keyboard. "No, not the first time. There have been occurrences, though, where it was definitely not a welcome surprise."

"Oh, shit." I wince and look at Josh, sitting on my settee with his phone and a nervous jitter in his leg. "Yeah, I guess people are kind of fucking whack sometimes."

She laughs lightly. "Now, I have to move Dallas if I seat you together. Can I confirm her booking number and passport number, please."

I read out her information, all of which I knew I would need if I was going to pull this off. Nathan helped me with the passport. He sent me a photo of it while we were in California after a huge debate about his rule not to go through Dallas's room. He really lost it when I told him if he didn't want to stumble upon our stash of Kama Sutra pose photos, he had to avoid the back of her side table drawer.

It was a joke. Sort of.

"There we go," Renee says after a few moments. "You are seated next to each other in sixteen A and sixteen B. At the moment, there's no one in C."

"Fingers crossed it stays that way because there is going to be a lot of tongue when she finds me on that plane."

Dead silence on the other end of the phone.

"Probably some cussing and tears first."

"Can I help with anything else?"

"I ideally would like to get seated early. Like, before all the children and wheelchair users. I want to be in there before she can see me in the boarding area."

I glance at Josh to see him staring at me as if I disgust him. It happens from time to time.

"I can't help you with that part, I'm sorry. You'll have to discuss that with the attendants on duty that day."

"Got it, well, thanks for your help, Renee."

"Have a nice day."

Hanging up the phone as I stand, I feel a little relieved that I have one part of this plan checked off. I head over to the dresser beside the window, open the drawers, and start putting my clean clothes away.

"What's up, man?" I ask Josh. "Got the feeling you need to talk."

"I need a job."

I look at him. "I'm not fucking hiring."

He scoffs. "I don't know what to do. I do this errand job for Mom, but I need something . . . more. More hours. More money. Something I can progress in. You know? Work my way up. She tried to give me more hours, but there's only so much I can do as a glorified assistant."

"Is there a sign on my door that says career counselor?"

"Don't be a dick."

He's obviously not in the mood to jest. I abandon the clothes and sit back on the edge of the bed, facing him. "You're still freaking out a bit?"

"Wouldn't you? I'm going to have a child. Like, a real child. One that I have to keep alive and fed and clothed."

"That's the minimum requirement, yes."

He scrubs a hand down his face. His very pale face.

"Man, what were you thinking?" I ask, careful with my tone so he knows I'm genuinely asking and not just being a judgmental asshole. "It's not a secret that there are results to rawdogging it. They're two little pink lines on a stick."

"I can't explain it," he mumbles. "It was stupid."

I don't bother voicing my agreement. I don't want to kick a dog while he's down. I can't imagine being in his position, but honestly, I never would be. Not only am I not ready for that sort of responsibility, I would never put Dallas in that position. Her goals mean as much to me as they do to her.

"Ask Mom if you can get into the office?" I suggest. Her skincare line has a building about an hour away. "You could work your way up there. Manager roles and all that shit. You know she'll do whatever she can to help."

"I know." He nods and lets out a long breath. "She's setting up the basement to be a living space. Like a small apartment for Gabs and me. Camilla wants us to live with her, but there's not enough space there."

"Plus, she'll crush your balls, dude."

"What?"

"She won't let you do shit." I stand up and slap his leg. "I can see it now. She'll take over in the name of helping, and you'll be redundant. She has that air about her. Now, quit stressing. What's done is done. I have to go and see Dallas. We have a date."

"Again?"

I quickly pull my T-shirt off and grab a clean one from the pile, sliding it on. It's white. As are the sweatpants I'm wearing. "Yes, again."

"What the hell are you wearing? You're bright enough to blind me."

"It's part of the plan." I slide open my closet door and grab a box of supplies, gripping it with one hand as I swipe my phone off my bed. "Later, man."

~

"I said a white T-shirt and pants, babe," I say to Dallas, who is standing in front of me in a little white dress. "You look fucking sensational, but please change."

Dallas closes the front door behind me and follows me through the house as I head toward the backyard. "I don't have white pants. I didn't even know you had white pants."

"This is the first time I've ever worn them."

"Are we getting married?"

"Kind of looks like it."

Outside, I walk to the middle of the lawn, which has recently been mowed, and set down the box of supplies. The sun is coming straight down on us, so I scoot the box under a tree with my foot and then open the lid. It's full of paints, brushes, and sponges. Dallas peers inside the box while I set up my phone on the fence post and hit Record. I don't care how long it records for or what it captures. I just know how much these little moments mean, and I want to be able to look back on them one day.

Dallas peers up at me when I come back with a knowing smile. "Are we painting each other?"

"That was the plan," I say. "But I'm not ruining that dress."

She looks down at it and then shrugs. "It's just a Target dress. You can get me a new one."

I raise a brow. "Oh, can I?"

"You were going to offer anyway."

I reach out and grab her butt, dragging her in close to me as I give her a kiss. "I like it when you ask me for things. Ask me for something else."

She drapes her arms across my shoulders. "You're a little strange."

"Ask me."

"Hmmm." She squints, thinking. "Can we go to the lake for a weekend this summer?"

"Babe, that's so sentimental and sweet. Ask me for something materialistic. Or kinky."

She rolls her eyes. "You bought me a motorcycle for graduation. I could never ask for something more materialistic than that."

"That was just practical."

"Fine, get me an apartment in California so when you come and visit, we can play house."

She has no idea that I've been looking at apartments between UCLA and CalArts. Not to move into immediately. We both have dorm rooms arranged for the first year. But eventually. I wanted to see what our options would look like when the time comes.

"Done," I tell her, knowing full well what she'll say next.

"Oh, as if."

"You can have an apartment instead of a dorm."

She steps back from me with a grin. "Your dad would never let you spend that sort of money. I'm surprised you were able to get the bike. Which I still think is outrageous."

"Trust fund, Cheer."

She pops her hands on her hips and shakes her head. "Okay, anyway, are we doing this?"

"Yeah."

I crouch and take the supplies out of the box. I squirt out a few blobs of different colors on a paint tray, and then I do the same thing on a second paint tray. Dallas takes one from me, along with a paintbrush, and then we stand facing one another.

"Now, we paint," I say.

"What kind of stuff do we paint?"

"Literally anything." I reach out and put two pink dots where her nipples are.

She tilts her head at me and sighs. "That's so creative."

"It was the first thing that came to mind."

She swipes her brush through light blue and then starts painting on my chest. I watch, jolting a little when she glides across my nipples.

"Quit moving," she chides.

"It tickles."

When she's done, she's drawn a simple flower. We look at each other for a long minute.

"I don't know what to draw," she exclaims. "Besides, that flower is cute."

"You're cute. All right, my turn."

We take turns painting each other's clothes. Hearts, words, basic faces, birds, random stuff that's easy enough for two people with zero artistic skills. Eventually, we paint our palms and handprint each other. Dallas gets a real nice one on my crotch. I tell her to turn around and then I plant one on her butt.

"What is happening out here?"

We both look over at the back door where Nathan is standing, assessing our now brightly painted outfits, my hand still on his sister's butt. I let go and wave at him.

"We're painting, what does it look like?"

"Hey, Nate." Dallas starts painting her palm with a fresh layer of purple. "How was your day?"

"It was good. Hot. You two eaten?"

"Is it dinnertime?" Dallas asks.

"Almost. I'm going to do pasta salad. You hanging around, Drayton?"

"I'll be wherever my dessert is." I gesture at Dallas and laugh when Nathan flips me off and walks back inside.

~

Nathan, Dallas, and I sit at the breakfast bar inside and eat pasta salad and garlic bread. Nathan is pretty good at cooking; I'll give him that. Dallas and I are still wearing our paint-covered outfits. I keep grinning at the handprints on Dallas's breasts. Nathan isn't looking at either of us.

"How are your folks?" Nathan asks, still not looking up from his bowl.

"In Barcelona on business."

Now he does look at me. "Barcelona?"

"Yep. Mom is partnering with some retail store to sell her skincare line. That part of the trip will take like three days, and then the rest is purely tourist purposes."

Nathan nods. "Don't blame them. You ever been?"

"Several times."

Nathan looks at Dallas, and the two share a small grin.

"I know," Dallas mumbles with a full mouth. "Worlds apart."

It never really crosses my mind that Dallas and I have such vastly different lives. I just love her for who she is and how she smiles and the way she accepts people and loves them and her humor and her sense of adventure and her independence and her fierce nature and her refusal to take shit. There's so much to love about her, and I never think about how different our bank accounts look. But perhaps it's more obvious to her. Later, after we've eaten and we're in her room with her straddling my lap on the bed, I hold her thighs and ask, "Baby, does the fact that I have money bother you?"

"You mean more money than the average teenager?" Her hands make small circles on my chest. "No, not really."

"Not really?"

She looks at me for a while, thoughtful. "Where is this coming from? What I said at dinner?"

"I don't want to think of us as 'worlds apart.' You are my world."

She turns that delicious shade of pink and bites down on her lip. "It's kind of impossible to ignore sometimes. Like, the fact that I have to spend the rest of summer earning and saving every dollar possible and it still won't be enough when I'm at CalArts, but you joke about how I should quit because you've never felt the crushing burden of needing to work just to get through the week. It highlights that sometimes we're on different wavelengths, babe. But I don't hold it against you. It's not your fault that you have that privilege. It is what it is."

Fuck, I feel kind of awful when she puts it like that. "I don't mean to be ignorant. I would look after you if you let me."

She leans down, covering my torso with her body. "Yes, you would. Which is so sweet. But then I would really feel the imbalance with you. It would just shift our dynamic too much. For me. Right now, I can tease you about being a spoiled silver spoon boy and occasionally let you pick up the bill at dinner."

"Occasionally?"

She giggles. "Fine, all the time. I'm not too proud to let you pay for my food."

I tuck her hair behind her ear. "I do like feeding you."

"Yeah, now we're not talking about food."

I lean up and press my lips lightly against hers. "No, we're not."

CHAPTER 5

DALLAS

Nine and a half weeks to go

I kind of love camping. I'm not surprised Nathan does it so often. We're at a popular campground. There are hundreds of other tents spread out on the grass, full of lots of families, and common areas with kitchen facilities, toilets, and showers. We've been here for three days, and none of it has sucked. There are volleyball nets set up on a dug-out sand patch, and Nathan and I have joined several games with people we don't know. We splashed out and hired a Jet Ski and tube for an hour, taking turns pulling each other around the lake. We went for a short hike through the bush and up the mountain; the views from the clearing were gorgeous.

It's also been nice to have a new backdrop when I practice. A couple of little girls from a nearby tent come and watch me in the mornings, following my moves. It's adorable, and in just a couple mornings, it's become a routine.

Our tent is a two-bedroom. There's a zipped wall that separates our sleeping spaces and a little awning stretching out over the front so we can keep out of the sun while we cook on a mini grill and watch the lake.

I imagined camping to be a lot quieter and more secluded. I suppose it can be, but I think I prefer this. The noise doesn't bother me, and I like having access to showers. Despite keeping busy, I feel well rested, switched off from the rest of the world. Not that I'm out of touch. I can still text Drayton and receive his charming photos.

We brought a week's worth of food with us, snacks and fruit and meat to cook on the grill. Nathan has been handling that. He's in his element here.

The sun is setting, we've finished eating, and now I'm sitting on a camp chair in the fading light, watching the water. There are still people swimming, which usually goes on until after dark.

"I'm going to take these dishes to the basins," Nathan says, and I look over to find his hands stacked with the plates, utensils, and cups.

I stand up. "I'll do it."

"Oh, I can do it."

I take the dishes from him. "No, you cook and clean up and do everything else. I'll do it."

He hands them over. "Thanks."

The basins aren't far away from where we are, a short walk through the tents and past the Jet Ski rental. There's a long line of basins against the wall of the communal kitchen. You can wash up inside or out, but it's usually quite busy inside. There's dish soap attached to the wall, but you use your own scrubbing brush. I drop the dishes into a free basin and wash them thoroughly.

I'm almost done when I feel someone standing behind me. I peer over my shoulder and see a woman who looks a bit older than me. She's beautiful. Shoulder-length light brown waves, quite a bit taller than me, and a physique that makes me think she must do Pilates or yoga.

"No rush," she says. "Saw you were almost done."

I didn't even notice the fact that the basins are all taken. I smile and make quick work of piling my arms up with the dishes.

"I love that skirt," she says when I turn around to leave.

I peer down at my white skirt. It's a thin material, made for sliding over bikinis. I'm wearing it with my yellow bikini top.

"Oh, thanks," I say. "I got it on sale at this little boutique in Fort Collins."

"I live in Fort Collins," she gasps. "Which boutique?"

"It's a second-hand one. Spring Fling."

"I love that place." She drops her dishes in the sink and pumps a little dish soap onto them. "Do you live in Fort Collins too?"

"No, my boyfriend's aunt lives there. I've only been once. It's a cute place."

"It is." She uses a sponge to clean her dishes and talks over her shoulder. "I moved there almost three years ago for a job. I didn't plan on hanging around, but I fell in love with the town."

"What do you do for work?"

"I'm a physical therapist," she says. "I work with athletes, rehabilitate sports-related injuries and that sort of thing. It's a cool job, and you meet a lot of interesting people. There's the odd client who decides if I'm stretching his calf muscles, I must want my butt touched. But they get kicked off the list and have to see old Craig instead, who should have retired years ago."

We both laugh as she lifts her plate and cup out of the sink, and then I feel the presence of another person. The woman's eyes slide over beside me, and I look over to see Nathan. His gaze darts between the two of us, and he has a towel over his shoulder.

"I was just heading to the shower and thought I'd let you know where I am."

"Oh, just chatting to—oh, what was—"

"I'm Emma," she says, telling me more than Nathan. Her gaze keeps flickering over him quickly, but it's as if she's doing her best not to look at him at all.

"I'm Dallas. This is Nathan." I jab a thumb at him, and her smile is small, coy almost. "My brother."

That gets her attention. A brief twitch of her features tells me what I need to know, and then she stops shifting and doing her best to avert her attention. She extends her hand, and Nathan takes it, giving it a gentle shake. I'm waiting for him to start his best work, pickup lines, flirting, all of it. She's for sure his type. Tall, athletic build, sweet smile.

"Hey, nice to meet you," he says. "Right, hitting those showers."

With a quick finger gun in the direction of the bathroom building a few feet away, Nathan heads off in what I assume is probably embarrassment because he just used finger guns. I watch him go and catch the little shake of his head.

"You're camping with your brother, huh?" Emma asks, watching after him. I wonder if I should warn her that the longest relationship he's ever had is with his Sports Weekly subscription.

"Yeah. It's some quality time before I leave for college. He practically raised me, so we're close."

"Aw," she coos. "That's so sweet. I thought he was your boyfriend at first and felt so guilty for thinking he's hot. Like, so hot. Sorry . . . I can't believe I said that."

"It's fine," I say, laughing. "I could tell."

Emma's eyes go wide, and her sun-kissed cheeks turn an even richer red than they already were. "Do you think he could tell?"

"I don't think so."

She giggles like a girl with a crush, and I wonder if I'm going to see more of her around the camp now.

"Who are you camping with?" I ask.

"My sister. She's visiting from out of town for the summer. We grew up camping with our parents; it's one of our favorite things ever."

"That's really sweet."

She smiles. "It was nice to meet you, Dallas."

"You too."

I wander back to the tent with the clean dishes and give them a quick dry with a towel.

When Nathan comes back from his shower, he leaves his flip-flops beside the tent door and crawls onto his bed.

We've closed ourselves in the tent and opened the middle partition so we can chat a little before we sleep. Sometimes there are small parties on the lakefront, nothing wild, just music and campfires, but Nathan is usually too tired to do much after nine, and I don't want to wander around on my own.

I'm on my blow-up mattress texting Drayton, who is sitting in the kitchen eating crackers and dip in his boxer shorts while he watches Bondi Rescue reruns on his laptop. It's more detail than I asked for, but it also doesn't surprise me.

"Emma, the girl we met earlier," I say, and Nathan hums as he stares at the tent roof. "She thought you were cute."

"Mm-hmm."

"You could tell?"

He lifts his hand into the air and pinches his thumb and forefinger together. "A little."

"I'm surprised you didn't reciprocate. She's gorgeous."

Nathan sits up and folds his legs. "She is gorgeous. But you freaked out when we were in California and I made plans with a woman. I didn't want to ruin another trip by hitting on her."

"So you glitched and did finger guns instead?"

He winces, screwing his face up and falling back into his bed. "Don't."

I start laughing and throwing up finger guns, mocking him mercilessly. He flips me off, throwing his arm across his face.

"I do appreciate that you were thoughtful enough to consider me, though," I say. "I wouldn't be impressed if you brought someone back to our tent. The walls are thin."

He chuckles, and I think about the fact that ever since we had the conversation about his rotation of women in California, I haven't really seen him bringing anyone home. He's been more single than ever, and it means the world to me that he cared enough to listen to how I felt, but I don't want him to be alone. Especially not when I'm so close to leaving.

"Nate, I never wanted you to, like, stop dating," I say, and he puts his hands behind his head and looks over at me. "I was in a weird place when I did the audition. So stressed out, and I needed you to be there with me, and I reacted kind of nuts. I do love spending time with you, but that doesn't mean you have to be celibate forever."

"I know, kid. It gave me something to think about, though. I'm getting older, and I don't want to keep wasting my time or anyone else's. If I'm going to keep dating, it's going to be with the idea in mind that maybe I'll settle down. At the moment, though? I'm fine. I'm not suffering alone or whatever. Single is just a status, not a sentence. I'm good."

"Right," I say. "That's good."

Drayton's idea of setting him up comes to mind. I don't consider myself a meddler, so I dismiss it pretty quickly. But if we bump into Emma again, what's the harm?

My phone starts ringing with a FaceTime call from Gabs, so I swipe it open and grin into the camera.

"Hi."

"Hi," she sings, lying down on Josh's bed. It's dim, like the lights are off, but the glow of the television illuminates her face. "Are you surviving out there? Keeping the fire going? Catching food and wiping your butt with leaves?"

"Ha ha." I stick my tongue out at her and then aim the camera at Nathan, who is also lying on his bed with his phone. "Nathan's here too."

"I'm aware," she says as my brother gives a little wave and goes back to doing his own thing. "I wasn't going to tell you anything he shouldn't hear, don't worry."

Nathan eyes me suspiciously but decides not to comment on that.

"How are you?" I ask.

"I'm fine," she says. "A little tired, but I was at the library all afternoon and it's a lot of time on my feet. I tried to get Josh to give me a foot massage, but he rubs for like two seconds and then his brain switches off and he forgets what he's doing."

"I'm surprised you ended up pregnant then."

Nathan sighs with disappointment, while Gabs ends up in a fit of laughter. "You've been around Drayton too long," she giggles. "He'll be disappointed he didn't hear that."

I laugh with her, avoiding saying what I really think, which is that Josh should give her a proper foot massage, because what the hell? This woman is carrying his child. A foot massage should be the bare minimum. I don't know what it is, but Josh is bothering me more and more at the moment.

"Anyway." Her giggles subside, and she pushes her hair back from her face. "He's down in the basement gaming. I've texted him like four times to bring me a grilled cheese because I'm that lazy right now."

"Yeah, no, I don't think you're being the lazy one," I say, and she quirks a brow. "What's Drayton doing? I think last time he texted he said he was eating. He'd bring you a grilled cheese."

Gabs laughs lightly and starts to sit up. "Yeah, I think he's around. It's no big deal, though, I'll just go and make it. Ellie and Leroy aren't here, so

I don't have to feel weird about using their kitchen."

"You don't have to feel weird anyway." I stretch out on my side with a yawn. "Can you imagine if Ellie knew you were hungry and didn't just go in there and get something to eat? She'd be mortified. If you plan on living there, you're going to have to use the kitchen when other people are around."

"I know." The camera moves with her as she walks out of the dark bedroom and into the light of the upstairs hall. "Well, I'm going to go find Josh, get something to eat, and then go to bed because I'm wiped. You look so great, by the way. Suntanned and wavy hair. Beach babe."

I smile at her. "I love you."

"Love you, night!"

I hang up the phone and drop it with a huff. Men are pathetic sometimes.

The next morning is another beautiful sunrise, and I stand outside of the tent, stretching. It's quiet first thing. Of course, there are plenty of early risers wandering about, but no one is talking above a murmur. I'm not usually one to roll right out of bed if I don't have to, but Nathan gets up early, and I've come to enjoy this hour more than I thought I would.

As usual, I pop my AirPods in, pick a song, and face the water as I start to dance. It's not long before my little friends show up. Three little girls, sisters I assume. They all have auburn curls and pretty dresses on. There're never many words exchanged, just beautiful attempts to dance along with me. I even slow down a little so they can keep up. After fifteen minutes, the oldest one, who must be about eight, tells the younger two it's time to go have breakfast. They all wave and run off. It's the best start to the day.

Nathan comes out of the tent in his swim trunks ten minutes later. "How about an early cold plunge?"

"Uh, no." I take out my AirPods and put them back in their case.

"Come on, you've been telling me how surprised you've been by this trip. You'll be surprised at how good a cold plunge can make you feel."

I point at the still lake. "That is not ice-cold water. It'll be cold, super cold, but not cold plunge cold."

"Cold enough." He rubs his hands together and gestures his head at the tent. "Come on. You just warmed up with a dance. Get your suit on. We'll do it together."

I hate being cold. Hate it. It's part of the reason I can't wait to move to California: the beaches, the sun, the lack of snow. But . . . I do like a challenge.

"Gabby was telling me that there's research to show a specific part of our brain develops when we do something we don't want to do," I say. "It's good for us."

"I've heard that." Nathan gives me a clap on the shoulder. "Get dressed, let's do this before the sun comes fully up and it's too hot for it to count."

"Fine."

Five minutes later, Nathan and I stand in front of the water. It's like glass. I can see the pebbles at the bottom, and in the distance the rising sun reflects, creating a glow on the water's surface. I inch forward, and my toes touch the cold, cold water. Colder than it was in LA when Dray and I splashed around in the sea at night.

"Urgh." I make an awful noise of protest, and Nathan laughs at me.

"It's not that bad."

"You go first."

"No." He holds out his hand. "We go together. I know you too well, Dallas. You'll run off as soon as I'm in there."

"Pssh," I protest but take his hand because he's right.

"Three—"

"No!"

"Two." Nathan laughs. "One."

He drags me forward, and we run. Our legs kick up the water, and it splashes me, cold pelts that make me want to retreat. I'm gasping already, but Nathan is like a damn bull that I have no chance of fighting. I barely manage to hold my breath before the bottom drops off and it's deep enough that we can fall and submerge our bodies. My head goes under, and the cold closes in on me like a complete shock. I find my feet, shoot up out of the water, and gasp. It feels like I've had the wind knocked out of me as I sputter.

Nathan is laughing, rubbing the water out of his face as he stands there looking pleased with himself.

"F-f-fuck this," I stammer, shivering from head to toe.

"Well done, kid."

"Well done?" I ask, making slow movements back to shore. "You dragged me in here with an iron grip. I'm waiting for the dopamine hit, Nathan. Where is it?"

"It'll come. You're not hopping out, are you?" I hear his hand hit the water, and then my back is showered with cold droplets.

"Fuck off," I snap and then slap a hand across my mouth when I see some kids walking their dog a few feet from the water's edge. "Yes, I'm getting out. I plunged, I'm cold, and now I'm done."

"Boo."

There's a splash, and when I look over my shoulder, Nathan is underwater. My arms are tucked in tight to my chest, fruitlessly trying to keep warm. Still, I manage to crack a smile.

When I get back to the tent, I wrap up in a towel. My jaw is chattering a little, but it doesn't take long until I start to thaw out. The water is cold, but it's not a cold morning. I sit on one of the camp chairs with my phone and start a FaceTime call with Drayton. It rings and rings and rings, and when he finally answers, his entire face takes up the screen but he's still in the dark.

"Baby, good morning," he says with that early-morning rasp. "You're wet?"

"Your voice does that to me."

He barks out an abrupt laugh. "You are the love of my life."

"Guess what I just did?"

"Tell me."

"A cold plunge."

He raises his brows in surprise. "Voluntarily?"

"Well, if you count Nathan almost ripping my arm off when he dragged me into the water." I sigh with amusement. I can still see Nathan swimming back and forth. "I agreed to do it, but I might've chickened out if it weren't for his encouragement."

Drayton lets out a low whistle. "I'm impressed, Cheer. How cold are you? Lower the towel a little so I can see?"

My brow furrows for a moment until I realize what he means. "My bikini top is padded for that reason."

He juts his bottom lip out, pouting.

"What are you going to do today?"

"Uh." He tousles his hair and clacks his tongue. He could tell me he's going to spend the entire day by the pool and I wouldn't blame him. I want him to do whatever he wants to do this summer. As soon as he starts college and real life sets in, he's going to have very little downtime for a very long time.

"I will eat." He narrows his thoughtful stare. "Probably do some exercise and some light training. Might drive around a little. Definitely fucking miss you."

"I miss you too." I pucker my lips and kiss the camera. "You could come out here, you know. It's only a few hours. Quicker on the bike. I'll share my air mattress with you, and we can skinny-dip after dark. Our favorite. It's really not that bad out here. You'd like it."

Drayton's smile falters a little, and I see him swallow. "Nathan told me not to, baby."

"He won't care," I plead like a pathetic little girl because I do miss him. I miss him so much, and once again I wonder how I'm supposed live without him close. "Besides, there's a girl here who thinks Nate's so hot, and we could totally set them up."

He winces as if he's in real pain. It's just so unlike him to listen to Nathan. He respects him, but I didn't think he'd let it stop him from being here with me.

"It's a handful of nights, baby. Then I'll be—you'll be back, and we'll be locking ourselves in my bedroom for seventy-two hours."

"Sounds like a marathon." I force a smile and do my best not to feel disappointed. I want him to choose me, to be as desperate as I am to be together again. Part of me is frustrated he's not more distraught, and I know that's unfair. It's fine, I've been having a good time with Nathan. I need to quit sulking, even if I do feel like our time together is slipping through my fingers.

CHAPTER 6

DRAYTON
Nine weeks to go

I've been eager to get home ever since I got to California. It felt way more deceitful talking to Dallas and answering her questions knowing I wasn't even in the same state. I mean, I found ways around telling a direct lie. "I'm eating in the kitchen" — not my kitchen, just the kitchen. "I'm exercising today." Not a lie. I've been exercising every day. It doesn't feel good, though. No matter how I try to spin it, I still feel like a rotten bastard.

Especially when she asked me to come see her. She should never have to plead with me for time together. I would have been at that campground in an instant. That's all I ever want, and I almost fell the fuck apart when I had to tell her I wouldn't be there. She looked so disappointed. I hated making her feel that way. I should just tell her the truth.

We just finished our last training session, I've showered, and now I'm getting an Uber straight to the airport. I packed and checked out of the hotel this morning so I wouldn't have to fuck around and waste time.

I tap out a text to Nathan as I walk out of the campus gym and bid farewell to some of the dudes I've gotten to know over the last week. Most of them are solid. Good attitudes, focused, nice enough. I wasn't sure what to expect, but it's been good vibes for the most part.

Keep Dallas at home until at least eight, please, man.

I swipe back to the Uber app and see my ride is three minutes away from the stadium parking lot. I take a quick mental note of the license plate and model. Nathan texts me back as I take a seat on a concrete bench, my small bag between my feet.

Lucky for you, she's too busy talking to some dude to help me with the packing up, so we'll still be here for a while.

I scoff, not believing him for a second.

Some dude?! Is he hot?

I was kidding.

No shit.

My Uber is a minute away when Jace, a linebacker from the team, wanders over, a gym bag slung across his shoulder. He's tall and has that California beach boy vibe going for him even though he's from DC. We were at the same hotel all week, so we shared Ubers and hit the gym together most evenings.

"Can I jump in with you?" he asks. "I assume you're waiting for an Uber."

I stand up with my bag and slide my phone into my pocket. "Could've done, but I'm heading straight to the airport."

"Oh, true." He reaches out his hand, and we shake. "You're not hanging around for the dinner tonight?"

The team management arranged a dinner to see out our week together. Some big restaurant with a private function area and a menu that would enrage Dallas because there's nothing simple to eat on it.

"Nah." I wave to the Uber I can see coming across the lot, a sleek white sedan. "I have a girl to get home to."

"Ah." He cracks a grin. "A girl? First I'm hearing of her."

I wave him off but don't apologize for spending the entire week singing her praises. She's the reason I'm here. I never shut the hell up about her, and I don't care if that makes me insufferable.

The Uber pulls up, and I open the back door, sliding my bag across the leather seat before I follow.

"I can't wait to meet her," Jace calls out as I roll the window down after I've closed the door.

"You stay away from her, you pretty motherfucker."

It's almost eight when I finally get home after landing and getting out of the airport. I can't stand airports. No one has an ounce of patience, the atmosphere smells stale, and it's loud. Josh was waiting in the parking lot for me when I got out. I asked him to stop at Trader Joe's on the way home so I could get Dallas some flowers and snacks. I chose a bouquet of her favorite lilies. There are other flowers in there too, purple and yellow ones. I don't have a clue what they're called, but they look nice.

Mom and Dad require half an hour of my time the second I walk through the door. They want to hear how the week went, if I made friends, like I'm a fucking five-year-old. Mom's absolute joy when I tell her I made a friend is kind of sweet, though, so whatever, I'll give her that. She says something about not wanting to send her boy off to a new school with no friends.

One thing I'm good at is slotting myself in and making myself the center of attention. Conceited? I like to call it confident. The therapist I saw for six months when I was fourteen called it a coping mechanism in order to make sure I'm in charge of the impression people get of me.

Sometimes I think about that for a moment, and then I decide, ah well, it's not the worst coping mechanism a person can have.

As I'm about to head upstairs, Dad stops me in the foyer. One foot on the bottom step, I turn and face him. "You were happy with how the week went?"

Adjusting the bag on my shoulder, I nod. "It was good. Challenging, but that was the best part. The campus is cool too."

"It is a good campus," Dad agrees. "I had an idea I wanted to run past you."

"Okay."

"I wondered if you'd be interested in going to the Super Bowl together in February."

That's not what I was expecting. Last time we went to the Super Bowl, Abby was still alive. Emotion stirs at the memories it brings up, and I clear my throat. "Yeah, I would love to, Dad."

He looks pleased and gives me a light bump on the shoulder. "We'll make a week of it. Dallas is welcome too, if you want her to come. I doubt she's ever been to a Super Bowl."

"She hasn't," I say, but I wonder if this is something Dad and I should do together. As much as I love that he invited her, it might be nice for it to be a father-son event. Of course, I don't want to rob her of that experience either. "I'll talk to her."

"Great, it's been a long time since we've gone," he says, and I recognize the grief in his expression, no matter how hard he tries to hide it. "It's about time."

A swell of gratitude comes over me that he's asking for this time with me, that he wants to create new memories where the old ones still cause him pain. It can't be easy for him, but it certainly feels nice to be worth the effort.

When I finally get to my room, I shower and unpack as fast as I can because Dallas is going to show up at any moment, and it needs to look like I've been here the whole time. I set the flowers on the bed, along with some strawberries, chocolate-covered almonds, grapes, and chocolate dip.

I'm standing next to the bed deciding if I should run downstairs and grab some toothpicks when my phone buzzes with a text from Nathan.

The bird is flying.

I stare at the message for a minute and then respond.

What the fuck are you talking about?

Dallas is on her way. Don't you watch movies?

I can see the meaning behind his message now, but I still sigh and tell him he's a nerd. Josh would've understood immediately. He's the movie buff. I drop my phone onto my dresser and head downstairs to pour a couple of glasses of water. Mom and Dad are sitting at the dining table with a glass of wine each, talking about their time in Barcelona. I suddenly realize it's been like two weeks since I last saw them. Their absence clearly doesn't bother me like Dallas's does.

I lean on the kitchen island. "How was it?"

Mom smiles. "It was good, sweetheart. As it usually is."

"What are the two glasses of water for?" Dad asks.

"Dallas is on her way over."

"Ah," he says.

Mom swallows her mouthful of wine and asks, "She still doesn't know about UCLA?"

"Nope."

Dad chuckles and pours himself another glass. "Dangerous game you're playing there, son. She might not like the fact that you can spend three months lying straight to her face."

Mom winces, nodding in agreement. "I'd be furious."

"Yeah, well, no one ever accused me of being sensible. Though, I will say, it's making our time together that much more special. We're not taking this summer for granted thinking 'Oh, we'll be together in California.' No, we're making the most of it, and we'll always look back and think about how special it was."

"Aw," Mom coos. "That is very romantic, sweetheart."

"Just don't follow in Josh's footsteps and knock this girl up," Dad warns me just as the sound of someone walking into the room gets my attention.

Dallas stands at the kitchen threshold with pink cheeks and an awkward smile. When Mom and Dad spot her, there are a few small waves of greeting. I stand there and watch it all, a smile on my face. She looks beautiful, of course, a little dark-blue sundress clinging to her waist and flowing on her hips. I have never been more content to just admire a person in my entire life.

Dad stands up and slides his hands into his pockets. "Hi, Dallas."

"Hi."

"How was camping?"

Mom and I look at each other; she's biting the inside of her cheek, doing her best to fight a smile. I am not hiding a damn thing.

"It wasn't Barcelona," she says, and the three of them chuckle. "It was better than I expected. The lake was beautiful and, uh, there were showers, so that made all the difference. I even did a cold plunge."

"Great," Dad says enthusiastically, and then his smile fades a little and he palms his jaw. "I apologize for what I just said."

"No need." Dallas is quick to dismiss his comment as I head over to her with the glasses of water in hand. I give her a kiss on the head. "It's reasonable to make sure your son isn't knocking his girlfriend up."

"Come on," I say. "We've had this exact conversation in this kitchen before. We're careful. So careful. Too careful."

"I don't even want to know what that means," my mom sighs from the table. "Go on, get out of here. Lovely to see you, Dallas."

"You too," Dallas says. "I'd love to hear about Barcelona."

"Meet me down here for coffee tomorrow morning."

"She doesn't drink coffee, Mom," I call over my shoulder, heading for the staircase.

"A mimosa, then!"

Dallas giggles, following me upstairs. I tap my bedroom door open with my foot, and she walks in, gasping when she sees the surprise I have for her. She stands at the edge of the bed and picks the flowers up, her lips parted and her elation evident. I set the glasses of water down and then I spin her around, scoop her up, and hold her under the bum.

"I missed you," I mumble, staring at her mouth.

She drapes her arms over my shoulders, the flowers still in her hand. "I missed you so much."

She leans in and kisses me. Our lips part, and our tongues meet and slide together, over and over again. Each stroke of our tongues creates more desire. Dallas's thighs tighten around my waist, and her breathing gets a little harsher. My hands slide over her waist, up her spine and down again, along the smooth skin of her thighs and under her dress. I can feel her lace underwear as I move further over her ass.

I drop her backward onto the bed, avoiding the snacks, without breaking our kiss and start sliding her dress up and over her body.

"Time to prove I'm responsible," I murmur against her mouth, and she laughs, finally dropping the flowers.

~

"We need to formulate a plan," Dallas tells me, a sheet wrapped around her while she dips strawberries into chocolate and sits opposite me on the bed.

"A plan?" I ask, leaning against the headboard, an arm slung behind my head.

"Well, that pretty girl from the campground I mentioned, Emma. I know where she works, and I think we should set her up with Nathan somehow."

"Where does she work?"

"At a physio clinic in Fort Collins."

"Do you know which one in particular?"

"No."

I raise a brow at her. "You know what she does for work. You don't know where she works."

"We'll figure it out."

She scoops some chocolate onto her strawberry and eats it with a far-off look on her face. One I know all too well. She's in her own head, and something is bothering her. I have a general idea what it might be.

"What's on your mind, baby?"

She looks at me, staring for a long while before she shakes her head. "Nothing. I'm just glad to be back."

I have a feeling that's not all she's thinking, but I don't push it. Instead, I open my arms for her. She crawls across the bed, scooting the snacks out of her way, and snuggles into my arms. I kiss the top of her head and tighten my hold on her.

"Something I want to run past you," I say, and she nods, listening. "Dad invited me to the Super Bowl next February, and he said you can come too."

"W ow." I can hear the smile in Dallas's voice. "That's generous. Nathan would be so jealous."

I laugh.

"That's the sweetest offer," she says, kissing my chest. "But I think this one should be just for you and your dad. That'd be really special."

I take a deep breath and feel relieved that she was the one to suggest it. Never would I want to leave her behind or rob her of new experiences, since that means so much to me, but deep down, I did want this for Dad and me.

"We'll go together one day," she continues. "When we can afford to take Nathan."

We both laugh, but I don't say anything. It's too hard to find the right words to express my gratitude for her and how perceptive she is.

Sometimes I can't comprehend how much I love this girl. It's this indescribable emotion that makes my chest feel like it's expanding and filling. But not painfully. Not as if it's running out of space. As if everything else inside of me was designed to make room for this very specific feeling. As if it's human nature that a person comes along and makes this sort of difference in your life, and it's your body's way of saying that this is the most real and natural thing you will ever go through.

Later, when Dallas falls asleep during the movie we're watching, her head resting on my arm, I push her hair back from her face and kiss her nose. She doesn't stir at all. She looks so peaceful, so content.

"I have a confession to make, Cheer," I whisper, testing the waters. Her lashes don't flutter at all. "We'll be together in California. I'm going to UCLA. Full ride, baby. I love you beyond words, Dallas."

I wait for her to sit up and cuss me out. She doesn't. I kiss her nose again.

"There, told you the truth. Don't be mad at me later on."

CHAPTER 7

DALLAS

Nine weeks to go

It's Monday, and I'm back at work. I can't complain, I had a decent amount of time off.

It's that time of year, which means we're packed with tourists and local teenagers who are on vacation. There's not a lot of downtime, so my four-hour afternoon shift goes fast. I punch out at five, pull off my apron, and wave at Wren as she comes in to take the dinner shift.

"Who's managing tonight?" she asks, hanging up her bag and slipping on her apron.

"Jonothan," I say, and we both wince.

Wren tips her head back. "I want Ryan back. Jonothan is such an asshole."

She's right. With the diner's owner, Ryan, on leave, Jonothan stepped in as his cover, and the power has gone straight to his head. I appreciate running things efficiently, keeping the place clean, being fast, following all of the hospitality rules. The problem is, Jonothan has unreasonable expectations. I'm not being lazy; he's just the master of complaint. Drayton can't stand him.

"Have fun tonight," I say and slip out before we get caught talking.

~

I head out into the parking lot. Gabby is waiting for me in her car, and I smile when she waves through the windshield. We have a girls' night planned.

Drayton was more than happy to relinquish some of our time together. He even gave Gabby a bag full of snacks and sodas. I don't know what he's getting up to tonight, but I wouldn't be surprised if it involves catching up with his friends. I get the feeling he hasn't seen them much since summer started, and I should feel bad about that, but I don't. I'm selfish. I want all of his time.

I slide into the passenger seat of Gabby's car, and we hug. She's wearing a tight tank top, and I coo at the tiniest little bump on her stomach. It blows my mind that my best friend is growing an entire human.

"That's just the Chick-Fil-A I ate for lunch, you bitch."

We both burst into giggles.

"No, it's not." She blows out a breath and runs her hand over her stomach. "It's there first thing in the morning too. Can you believe it?"

"No, I literally can't."

She lets out a loud, exaggerated groan and starts the car, reversing out of the lot. We're having a sleepover at my place, as we usually do. It's the lack of parental supervision that Gabby prefers. There's no mom listening in on our conversations or monitoring when we sleep or what we're doing.

I'm sure that probably does get a little old, but sometimes, I wish my own mom was around to pop her head in and ask us what we're doing, if we're having fun, if we need snacks. Nathan said Mom was a fun host.

I don't remember her presence at my sleepovers all that well, but I do remember her warmth and her kindness, so it doesn't surprise me to hear she made sure they were a success.

"How was the camping trip?" Gabby asks, driving at a snail's pace through peak rush hour traffic. She has her windows down and her AC on. Which seems counteractive, but I don't tell her that. "When did you get back?"

"Last night. It was surprisingly good. I didn't think I'd like it that much, but it was peaceful, and the water was beautiful."

"And you've never been camping before?"

"Once, but I didn't last long before I wanted to go home."

She hums, signaling off the highway and onto the quieter roads of the neighborhood. "We went with the school once, weren't you there?"

"No, that camp was just after Mom and Dad died."

"Oh." Gabs gives me a sad smile.

"I met this really pretty girl there; she had a huge crush on Nathan."

Gabby laughs, turning onto my dead-end street. "Well, that's not hard to believe. Nathan is a total hottie."

"Ew," I protest. "Whatever, I want to meddle a little and see if I can get them to go on a date or something. Nathan said she was gorgeous, but he wouldn't pursue her while we were camping together. I told him I didn't mind if he did, but she was like gone after that. I don't know, she must have gone home."

"Oh, did you find anything out about her?"

"Just that she's a physical therapist in Fort Collins and her name is Emma."

"That's a good start! We can totally find her."

I knew my best girl would support the cause without hesitation. Gabs parks behind the car Nathan and I share, and I help her take the snacks and her sleeping gear inside. Nathan is sitting on the sofa eating a bowl of broccoli when we walk in. The greetings are brief as we beeline straight for my bedroom. When I open the door, I see that Nathan has already put the spare mattress and sheets down. I'll sleep down there considering Gabs is the one that's pregnant.

"Thank you!" I shout.

"Welcome!" he shouts back.

Gabby waits for me while I shower and change into a pair of PJs. It's not even six, but I like to be comfortable when I'm lounging about with no intention of leaving the house. Gabs is in hers too, the spare bed all made up when I come back. We set up a movie on her laptop, order burgers on Uber Eats, and spend the next hour gossiping.

"Look." Gabby sits opposite me on my bed while she peers down at her baby bump. "It's doubled in size."

"Can I feel?"

She tilts her head and stares at me. "This is mostly food."

"It is not."

She pretends to pout and then drops her arms to her side. "Sure, feel it up."

I reach out and run my hand over the little mound. I'm not sure why I expected it to be solid. It's not, it's got a little squish. "When does the kicking start?"

"Hmm, well, I'm only sixteen weeks. I think it starts after twenty. At the earliest."

"I hope I get to feel it kick before I leave."

"It?" she scoffs. "This is a girl."

"You found out?!"

"No." She shrugs. "I'm just guessing."

"I won't even be here for the baby shower. I should've been the one planning it."

Gabby plucks a sour worm out of the bag and pops it in her mouth.

"We could do an early one. Before you leave? I'll know the gender by then. We'll keep it simple and cute. I wouldn't want to have it without you."

I smile at her, grateful that she'd do that. There's still so much I'll miss, though. It's another thing that hits me in the chest. So much is changing and moving too fast for me to catch up with. I inhale a deep breath.

"What's wrong?" Gabs asks.

"I'm just . . . I'm starting to have all these doubts, and I'm second-guessing things I didn't think I'd second-guess."

"Like what?"

"Like if I made the right choice to go to college so far away."

Gabby raises her brows in surprise. "But you want to be a dancer? That's one of the best schools in the country. You've wanted to go there forever."

"But I'm leaving so much behind. You, Nathan—"

"Drayton?" Gabs guesses with a knowing smile.

I palm my face with both hands and let out a long groan. "It's pathetic, I know, but Gabs . . . I love him so much. I didn't realize I would ever feel like this. What if this is that once-in-a-lifetime love and we don't survive the distance? What if I go to this college and dancing doesn't work out? What if I don't get anywhere with it and Drayton and I broke up for nothing?"

"Okay," Gabs says thoughtfully. "Or what if you don't go to this college and you follow Drayton and you still break up? You'll have missed out on your dream school . . . for nothing."

"I could still dance if I don't go to CalArts. I could take a gap year in Texas and then apply to SMU again. That's close to Baylor."

Gabby shakes her head with a look on her face that says she's about two words from stuffing me in a box and shipping me directly to CalArts. I don't blame her. I'm aware that I sound ridiculous, but I feel safe enough around her to be as ridiculous as I want.

"I'm only thinking out loud," I say.

"If Drayton is your once-in-a-lifetime love, you two will be fine. Do not give up on your goals. Imagine if Dallas Junior heard you talking like this? Hell, imagine if Dallas from four months ago heard you talking like this? What are you even saying?"

I pinch the bridge of my nose. "It's stupid. The odds are stacked so high against us. Most couples barely survive college when they're at the same school. It feels like this inevitable crash waiting to happen, and I hate it."

"Even if that is your future," she says gently, "why don't you just enjoy right now? I don't think you'll ever regret your time with him. He makes you too happy. Relationships are hardly ever a waste of time, even if they don't work out, because they teach you so much. What you deserve, what you like in a partner, who you are as a partner. It won't be a bad thing. Even if it doesn't work out."

"I'm so confused. Did that baby give you super-wisdom? Where did that come from?"

She shimmies her shoulders with a pleased smile. "My therapist."

"You're seeing a therapist?"

"Started last week. I needed a little help talking about this pregnancy and my own total freak-out about the future. I raised similar concerns about Josh and me. Teen parents—like you said, the odds are stacked against us."

"Might help that you'll be living together and have a child to consider before calling it quits." Even if he won't rub her damn feet or make her grilled cheese.

"It might." She seems uncertain, and now I feel like I've been selfish and pathetic for talking about my issues when my best friend is facing much bigger battles.

"Is everything okay between the two of you?"

She inhales deeply, nodding slowly. "For the most part, yes. But Josh is being kind of weird. He's distracted and stressed out, and I get the feeling he wishes he could bail. He was handling it all well. Then we went and had an ultrasound and he saw the baby, and ever since then, he's been frantic."

"Drayton said he's looking for a better job." I explain what he told me in the hopes it takes the worry off her face. I don't want this sort of stress on her shoulders. "It might be that that's distracting him."

"Oh." She looks thoughtful. "I wish he'd just tell me that."

"Men aren't always the best at communicating."

"True. Except for Drayton. Who communicates way too much."

We both laugh at that.

"What else are you talking about with your therapist?" I ask, picking up my phone and swiping open the screen to the SMU homepage. I won't show Gabs. I'm not even considering changing course. I'm just . . . looking. "Have you talked about setting new goals or what the future looks like now?"

"A little," Gabs says. "But I'm not sure my goals have to change a whole lot. I can go to Arapahoe and do English Lit later if I want to. I can still write. I can do whatever. She made sure I know that."

I hope the doubt doesn't show on my face. "Who will watch the baby? Sounds like Josh wants to be busier with work, not more available."

"He'll earn enough to pay for daycare so I can go to school."

I keep quiet and flick through the gallery of the SMU campus. I've already gone through their curriculum. I've also calculated the distance between SMU and Baylor. It's an hour-and-a-half drive. But that's better than a four-hour flight. Again, I'm just looking.

"Besides," Gabby adds, "even if I don't go to school at all, it's no big deal. There's a lot I can do without a college education."

I put my phone down. "There is."

She eyes me narrowly. "I know you're all about that college life. But I'm really not worried. Life will work out, as it always does. I might even just focus on being a mom for a while. That wouldn't be a bad thing. I kind of hate the idea of having my baby in daycare full-time anyway."

"Are you soft launching the announcement of full-time motherhood to me?"

She holds up her hands as if she'll say no more. "I'll go where life takes me."

I bite my tongue, burying the pang of concern I have. Gabs is too smart to not do well for herself in life or to have to depend on the teenaged father of her child. Of course, I can't possibly understand how it feels to be in her shoes, but I do know a baby changes your circumstances drastically. I just hope she knows that too.

~

It's late when Gabs and I decide to go for a drive and get slushies from the 7-Eleven. Gabs had a craving, and I wouldn't get in the way of that even if she wasn't pregnant. She sits in the passenger seat, phone in her hand. The streets are quiet, dark, the streetlights casting an ambient glow on the car. I prefer driving at night. It feels less chaotic.

"Okay, well, I found like fourteen clinics in Fort Collins," Gabs says, the brightness from her phone illuminating her face.

"Fourteen?"

"Mm-hmm. Most of them don't have a list of staff on their website, either. Some of them do. So far, no Emmas. We could call the ones that don't have staff lists."

"That could take forever, and then what would we even do with that information? Book Nathan in for a session?"

She looks over at me and shrugs. "Sure? He has an injury, right?"

"It's like super old, and he hasn't been to physical therapy for it in years."

"He's overdue then."

The car falls quiet while I drive and Gabs investigates. I actually have complete confidence in her ability to find this woman. I still don't know what I'm supposed to do once she finds her, though. There would be no casual way to get the two of them in the same space. I pull the car into the small 7-Eleven lot and park in the only available space beside a tall pickup truck. It's after ten, but there are a few people here doing the same thing we are. I swear summer vacation turns half the town into night owls. Gabs gets a large cup, I go small. I hate having too much liquid before bed. The need to get up and pee drives me insane.

I lean against the counter after I've filled up my cup with watermelon, slurping on the straw while I wait for Gabs, who hasn't even decided what she wants.

"I kind of feel like cola," she says, moving the cup toward the dispenser before she quickly pulls back. "Ooh, but pineapple . . . and mango! I can't do all three. I should've bought three smalls instead."

I don't think much of the doorbell jingling; it's been going off since we arrived with people filtering in and out. It's the voice I hear hollering when he comes through the door that gets my attention. Gabs looks at me with amusement.

Drayton is talking to Josh, I assume, and perhaps more people from the sound of the group that just entered. It's possible he missed Gabby's car in the lot if it's still obscured by the pickup. I peer over the shelves and see Drayton making his way through the aisles with his cap on backward. Josh is there, and so are a couple of the guys from the team.

I'm shorter than the shelves, so I leave Gabs to her dire decision-making and quickly beeline for my man. When I find him, he's facing the other way, asking Josh if he wants Milk Duds or a Crunchie bar.

Before he can turn around, I slide my arms around his waist and feel him freeze up as I paste myself to his back.

"Oh hell n—" His objection drops off as he grabs my arm, I assume to remove it, and his tone changes drastically. "I'd know this hand anywhere."

He keeps hold of it as he spins around and peers down at me. "Hey, baby." He looks me over with his sensual smile, and then it fades and he starts frantically looking around. "Not to be a dick, but I'm feeling a little jealous about whoever has seen you in these PJs since you've been here."

Josh takes that as his cue and drops the Milk Duds back on the shelf. "I assume Gabs is deciding on a slushy. I'll go find her."

The last thing I wanted to do when we left was get into a whole new outfit. My PJs are a pink camisole and shorts with white lace edges. It's not that far off what I'd wear if it was the middle of a hot day.

"Well . . ." I step into him; he's still holding my hand. "You're the only one who gets to touch."

He grins as I stand on tiptoe in my slippers and kiss him. His hands slide onto my butt, and he squeezes. I can hear feet shuffling into the aisle behind me, and there's a low whistle.

"What's up, Cheer."

I break the kiss with Drayton, but he keeps me glued to him so all I can do is look over my shoulder at Derek and Maxon standing there with an armful of chips and salsa.

"Don't call her that," Drayton warns, leaning an elbow on the shelf, the other arm securely across my shoulders so I can't turn around. I wonder if that has something to do with the fact that I'm not wearing a bra. "You like having eyeballs, Derek? Get your eyes off her ass."

Maxon taps Derek on the chest and gestures for him to follow. "I wouldn't test him, bro," Maxon warns as they walk away. "Austin still isn't over the smack he got for fucking with her."

"You're very territorial." I peer up at Drayton again. "If they're such animals, perhaps you shouldn't hang out with them."

"Maxon is fine. Derek isn't an animal; I like to stare at your ass too. He's just not allowed to."

Gabby and Josh come into the aisle, and Gabby has two cups, one in each hand. I suppose the choice was too much for her.

"What are you guys doing tonight?" I ask, finally released from Drayton's clutches. Sort of. He tucks me into his side instead, and I take another slurp of my drink now that I can reach my mouth.

"Picking up girls at the 7-Eleven. What does it look like?" Drayton kisses me on the head. "Come home with me."

Gabby's jaw drops with outrage. Even Josh looks offended.

"We're gaming, dude, what the hell?"

"Girls' night, babe." I tap him on the chest and peel myself away from him. "I'll see you tomorrow."

His hand drags down my arm and grips onto my fingers, his bottom lip pouting. He's so damn beautiful. "But now I've seen you, and I would like to continue this little catch-up in bed."

"What? All of us?" Josh taunts with a shit-eating grin.

Drayton points at him. "You need to spend less time in bed, funny motherfucker."

I give Drayton one more kiss and then pull out of his hold and slip my arm through Gabby's, taking our leave before my insatiable boyfriend can tempt me to stay with him.

Forever.

CHAPTER 8

DRAYTON
Nine weeks to go

Dallas has become obsessed with finding this Emma woman in Fort Collins. She has no idea what her plan is when she does find her, but she has me making calls to different physical therapy clinics asking if I can have an appointment with Emma. Most of the time I get told, "Sorry, we don't have an Emma. I can book you in with someone else, though."

Oh, no thanks. I'm a fucking weirdo who only wants to be looked after by someone with the name Emma. Couldn't even tell you her last name. Just Emma.

After the fourth call, I watch Dallas clearing a table on the other side of the diner and think about how I'm going to tell her I don't want to do this shit anymore.

If the physio community talks, Emma is going to end up moving states to avoid being stalked.

Dallas wanders over to my small two-seater table by the window with a tray full of dishes and looks at me with this hopeful excitement that stops my sentence short.

"Anything?"

I shake my head. "No, my love. I will keep calling. There's nothing else I'd rather be doing."

She tilts her head knowingly and sighs. "Don't bother. It's so stupid. What is wrong with me?"

I feel like an asshole. "Nothing, baby. You just want your brother to be happy."

"Yeah, but even if I found her clinic, I can't just like ... show up. That'd seem insane. Like, insane. Forget it. He can meet someone himself."

Thank fuck.

"Dallas, tables!" her boss, Jonothan, shouts from the kitchen entrance, staring at her like she's a piece of shit. I straighten up and stare straight back. He notices and flinches a little, but quickly scowls and disappears again.

"Babe, don't," Dallas sighs. "He won't be covering for Ryan much longer."

"If he keeps talking to you like that, I'm gonna be a fucking problem."

"Maybe you should go." She leans in and gives me a quick kiss. "I have half an hour left. Go for a drive and come back."

"Go for a drive where?"

"Somewhere I don't have to worry about you assaulting my boss and getting me fired."

"Fine." I stand up and drop three twenties on the table.

"What is that?"

"My tip. Not the one you're used to, but it's the only one I can give you until later."

She bites down on her smile and shakes her head. "You didn't even order anything."

"The service was excellent, though."

I give her another kiss and leave before she can argue.

I end up driving to the community college where Nathan coaches. It's Tuesday afternoon, so he'll be there. There's a decent number of cars in the parking lot when I pull in. Some of them have moms sitting in the driver's seat with the window down, waiting for their little football stars to finish training. I wander through the gate, past the small row of bleachers, and out on to the field where I can see Nathan watching his team run drills.

"Hey, coach." I sidle up beside him.

"What are you doing here?"

"Dallas kicked me out of the diner." I cross my arms. "I was about to knock her boss's teeth down his throat."

Nathan turns toward me. "What'd he do? Wait, is this the temp one? Jonothan?"

"Yeah."

"Oh." He relaxes a little. "Dallas said he's an angry asshole."

"Yeah, well, he can be angry with no teeth. See how tough he sounds with a gummy lisp."

Nathan chuckles, watching the team again before he scrawls something down on his clipboard. "That still doesn't really explain why you're here?"

"Her shift finishes soon," I explain. "I just needed to go for a quick drive, and you were close."

"Right."

We stand there quietly for a little while, watching. I make a few comments on his players, and he tells me to keep them to myself because I'm not a coach. I do see him write down my notes, though, and I give him a smug smile.

As the time ticks on, I shift restlessly because what I really want to ask him is how he feels about being left here alone. Would he be interested in Dad looking for coaching positions in California? Would he move if Dallas mentioned it? Would it be worth mentioning it? The problem is, I don't know if Dallas would want me to intervene. I can tell she's struggling with the big move more than she thought she would, and I want to help, but my girl is so independent, I run the risk of pissing her off more than anything.

Nathan is about to blow his whistle and gather his team in when I start talking again.

"I can't tell Dallas I'm going to California."

Nathan cocks a brow at me. "I didn't think you were planning to."

"I almost caved," I admit, wiping the sheen of sweat off my forehead and spinning my hat forward. "Couldn't handle seeing her upset anymore. But I realized she needs to face this move on her own and know that she was strong enough to go through with it, even though it's been fucking hard for her. I think if she knew I was going, it'd make it easier, and one day she might look back and feel like she didn't do it for herself."

Nathan doesn't say anything for a while, but then he gives me a light slap on the shoulder, tapping it a few times. "Makes sense to me."

"You ever thought about leaving Castle Rock?"

He shrugs. "Not so much. I would've for college, but you know how that went. Otherwise, nah, I can't say I've ever had the same sense of adventure Dallas does. She started ditching town as soon as she could drive."

I know what he means. Dallas loves an adventure. She loves seeing new things and making new memories and learning about the places she goes. I love that about her. I love the thought of spending the rest of our lives doing that together.

"I guess I've thought about it more lately," Nathan says. "I don't hate the idea of being close to Dallas, but I don't want her to feel smothered either. I've always known she'd spread her wings. I've been prepared for this for a long time."

I should keep my mouth shut, but I don't. "I don't think she'd feel smothered if you ended up in California."

"She said something?"

I shake my head, refusing to look at him. The lies just keep growing. Although, I think he can tell I'm full of shit. "But if you ever do think about relocating, let me know. I think Dad would be more than willing to make a few calls, see what coaching positions are out there. Something a little more advanced."

Nathan looks thoughtful, nodding slightly. "I'll keep that in mind."

"I gotta head back and get Dallas," I say, clapping him on the shoulder.

"Another date planned?"

"Absolutely."

~

"I'm too short for this," Dallas tells me. "It won't work."

"You'll be fine, I'll hold you up."

"No," she argues. "I'll get hurt."

"I wouldn't let that happen," I insist. "Come on, it's me. You think I'd put you in that position?"

"You put me in a lot of weird positions, babe. But this one has to be the craziest. Like I said, I'm too short. It's impossible."

"Sit here. Hold on here. I've got you. Now ride."

Dallas stares at me with a glare from her seat on the back of my motorcycle, her hands wrapped around the handlebar, helmet on her head. I stand beside her, holding the bike up so she doesn't tip over.

"Come on," I challenge. "There's a bike waiting for you in California. You have to learn to ride now so you can get your license when you get to LA."

She blows out a breath. "It's not that I don't want to, but if I have to stop, I can't put a leg down. I'll ruin your bike, and that'd be awful."

I have a little more faith in her than that. I think she can ride around her dead end and back to me before she has to stop, but I guess we don't share that conviction. I've been over the basics with her: how to change gears, how much throttle to give it. She's a quick learner, but I appreciate that she doesn't want to damage my mode of transport. I'd be more upset if she damaged herself, though.

"Fine." I swing a leg over and sit on the back, spooning her. "I'm right here if you need to stop. Drive up to the dead end, turn around, and come back. You don't have to go fast."

I see her shoulders rise on a deep breath, and then she nods. "Can you start it for me?"

"Give it a go."

"Ugh," she grumbles, finding the footrest so she can use it for leverage. With her right foot secured, she lifts, giving me a wonderful view of her ass in a pair of tight jeans, and then she drops her left foot down onto the kick start. The engine whirs, but it doesn't start.

I smile when she tries a few more times. So determined.

"All right." I wrap an arm around her middle, drag her back into my body so she's sitting on my lap, and then kick down on the lever so the engine roars to life.

She scoots forward and reaches for the handlebar again. "I could've done that," she shouts.

"You're welcome."

She goes still for a moment and finally asks me to run her through the steps again. I do, along with a quick demonstration. She pays attention as I do a lap of the street, nice and slow so she can absorb it all, and then we're back at the start again. This time, when she reaches for the handlebar, she doesn't hesitate.

I hold her waist, and we move forward, a little too slow. The bike stalls. Dallas tips her head back and almost smacks me in the chin with her helmet as she groans at the sky. I start the engine again with a kick and tap her encouragingly on the thigh.

"Bit more throttle, baby. Just a little. You go too hard and the same thing will happen. Find that sweet spot."

She tries again, and this time, we move — slowly, but a little faster than before. I listen to the engine, waiting for her to recognize when she needs to gear up. The pitch heightens, and then she flicks the clutch and the handle and moves into second. It's not the smoothest shift, but it's still a shift.

"Yeah, baby," I shout, giving her a gentle, barely-there squeeze around the waist. I don't want to distract her.

She stays in second gear, going slowly up the road and around the dead end. I don't expect her to go faster at the moment. Getting used to the feeling of the bike is the most important part. Speed comes with confidence and experience. She'll get there.

When she brings the bike back to the front of her house, I quickly reach forward and put my hands over hers, bringing us to a stop and lowering my leg to keep us up before I kick the stand down. Dallas squeals with excitement and pulls her helmet off, resting it on the handlebar. She turns herself around so she's facing me.

"I did it," she announces proudly, as if I wasn't the one telling her she could.

I lean in and kiss her, cupping her neck. Our tongues glide across one another, and my hand moves into the hair on the back of her head, holding it tight. When I pull back, she's all sensual and giving me that look that accompanies her shirt coming off.

"I'm proud of you."

Her smile becomes a little more dazed as she leans into me, toying with the front of my shirt. "You always believe in me."

"I always will."

Dallas does a few more laps of the street, developing her confidence, picking up a bit more speed each time. Eventually, she lets me off the back so I can watch her, and hell, does she look fucking fantastic. We call it quits when the sun starts to go down, the sky is becoming a burnt orange, and one of Dallas's neighbors is watching us from her kitchen window with definite disapproval over the rumbling up and down the street for the last few hours.

As we head inside the house, we bump into Nathan, who is leaving. He arrived a while ago, watched Dallas for a few minutes, and then disappeared when my commentary on how damn good my girl looks when she rides got too much for him. He makes it too easy to mess with him.

"Nathan, you look radiant," I holler as I cross the threshold. "Where are you going?"

Nathan, wearing a buttoned shirt with the sleeves rolled up, some crisp slacks, and a pair of shoes that aren't Nikes, glares at me. "I'm going out."

Dallas is still holding the door open where we're all congregated and looks pleased with this information as she assesses her brother's outfit. "On a date?"

Nathan sighs and gives her a dismissive nod. "Yeah, just a date. Done it a million times before, not sure what the fuss is about."

"You look very nice," Dallas says. "Girls love the sleeves like this."

"Yep, I know." Nathan looks like he's getting doted on by his mother, and it's hilarious.

"Who's the date with?" Dallas asks.

Nathan shrugs. "No one you know."

"What's her name?"

Nathan, for whatever reason, clearly does not want to divulge much information. I clap him on the shoulder and shove him toward the door.

"Well, don't be late. We'll hold down the fort here, just the two of us, for how many hours exactly?"

"For fuck's sake," he mumbles and walks out of the house, waving to Dallas as he goes.

She shuts the door and looks at me, her eyes wide with excitement and her hands propped on her hips. "This is good," she says. "This is really good. I haven't seen him go on a date in months, and he's dressed so well. It must be, like, a real date. Usually when he's just going out for booty calls he wears his sweatpants and a T-shirt."

"Easier to get in and out of."

Dallas looks at me with disgust. "Didn't really need to hear that."

"As you can see." I take her hand and wave it over my sweat shorts and black T-shirt. "It's a universal thing. Let me demonstrate the ease and convenience."

"Oh, because I've never seen it before."

She follows me to her bedroom.

~

Dallas and I are cuddled up in her bed, a fan aimed straight at us. It's not stopping the sweat from forming between us. Body heat is no joke. We're going to need a cold shower soon.

"I'm going to plan a baby shower for Gabs," Dallas tells me, sitting up and slipping her bra and shorts on. She walks over to the window and slides it open. It's dark now, but the summer night air doesn't offer much in the way of cooling down.

I do my best to ignore the fact that she just let the street see her in a bra. She wouldn't care even if I mentioned it. She sits on the end of the bed in front of the fan and looks over at me.

"Want to help?"

"Plan a baby shower?"

She nods.

"I'll help. I don't know much about it, but you can direct me, and I'll give you my credit card."

She smiles and rolls her eyes. "First task, location. I need you ask your mom if we can use the backyard."

I laugh a little at the suggestion of asking Mom if she'll allow us to use the backyard. I've been hosting events by the pool since I was fourteen. Not often with permission, either. Some were followed by a grounding. Still, Dallas would absolutely not accept going ahead with plans if I didn't make sure it was okay first.

Standing up, I look around for my phone in the pile of clothes on the floor. I come across my boxer briefs first, slide those on, and then find my phone in the pocket of my shorts. I call Mom and put the phone on speaker as I wander over to Dallas and kiss her on the head.

"Hello? Drayton?" Mom answers sounding a little anxious, as she often does when I call. Unfortunately, I have a long history of calling from situations I should not have been in. "What's wrong?"

"Nothing," I say, standing behind Dallas, the fan on both of us as I run my fingers across her neck, through her hair, and across her shoulders. She does the little satisfied shimmy she does when I tickle her back and it feels nice. "I need a favor."

"Oh." Her tone relaxes, but then it turns into suspicion. "Sure."

"Dallas wants to throw Gabby a baby shower in the backyard. Is that cool?"

"Of course," Mom says, now purely relieved. "Yes. That sounds nice. She's planning it?"

"Yeah, Mom."

"I can hire a planner if that's easier?"

Dallas twists on the bed and looks up at me, shaking her head. My fingers are still running across her soft skin.

"Nah," I say. "She wants to do it herself."

"That's sweet. Let me know if I can help and when she wants to do it. I assume it'll be earlier than usual because she wants to have it before she leaves for college?"

Shit. I didn't even think about that. Dallas nods.

"Yep," I tell Mom.

"Okay. Yeah, that'll be great," Mom says. "Where are you at the moment?"

"I'm in a girl's bedroom."

"What girl?" Mom shouts so fucking loudly, I wince, and Dallas slaps a hand across her mouth, eyes shining with laughter.

"My girlfriend's?" I sound confused.

Mom blows out a loud breath. "You are so exhausting sometimes."

She hangs up, and I drop my phone onto the bed, laughing with Dallas.

"Well, at least I know she has my back." Dallas scoots around to face me and gets up onto her knees, throwing her arms around my neck. "Thanks for doing that. You work fast."

"Only when I have to." I grin and kiss her, holding her close as I lower her onto her back. My lips travel down her throat.

"I have a question."

My body hovers over hers, and I continue tasting her soft skin.

"You must have to go to Baylor this summer, right?" she says, and I freeze for a second before I run my tongue across her collarbone as if I'm not bothered by the question at all. "Can I come?"

I lean up and look at her.

"I've never been to Texas before," she says, her hands in my hair, legs looped around my waist.

"I don't have to go and tour the campus or any of that shit," I say, remaining calm. "I've done that a million times before. I know that place like the back of my hand."

"You don't need to go and do assessment training?"

More panic. "Nope."

"Oh." She deflates.

"You'll see Texas soon, baby. You have to come and visit all the time."

She nods, but her lips are pinched, and it looks like she has more to say. I'm not sure where the sudden interest in seeing Baylor has come from, but I'm not surprised. She loves to travel, and unfortunately, she hasn't done a lot of it. I'd take her all over the world if I could, and one day, I will.

CHAPTER 9

DALLAS
Eight weeks to go

It's been almost a week since Nathan went on his secret little date, and I have no idea if he's been on another one. We've been missing each other a lot. I'm either at work or at Drayton's when he's home, and when I'm home, he's at training or at the gym. I think. I don't know. When I tried to ask him about how the date went, he stonewalled me. Rude. All I want is to know he's happy.

I'm at home tonight, alone so far. Nathan is still at training, and Drayton has gone away for the night with Josh and some of the other guys. Gabby was going to come and hang out, but she isn't feeling well. I'm heading over there soon to check in on her. Her mom is there, but I still find it a bit weird that Josh left his sick, pregnant girlfriend for the night.

I might be thinking about it too hard, but I can't imagine Drayton doing that to me. Last time I was sick with a cold, he fussed so much. He slept over, he never let my water run out, he fluffed my pillows and made me comfortable, and when I tried to do anything at all, he stopped me and made sure he did it first. Save for going to the bathroom. He even vacuumed the house, which is my job because Nathan hates it and he does most of the other cleaning.

Whatever, maybe Gabs insisted Josh leave. She's trying so hard to keep things normal, to make sure neither she nor Josh feels like life is turning upside down. She hasn't said it outright, but I wouldn't be surprised if she's doing her best to cater to Josh's stress over becoming a dad and the pressure he feels. Which I get, but life is different for them now, and I don't see the point in letting him pretend it's not. When that baby is born, guys' nights will be fewer, and I know it's technically none of my business, but he better get used to it.

I decide to use this time to box up a few things—things I want to take with me to college but can live without for the rest of the summer. I can't take a lot because it's expensive to ship it, but there are sentimental items I don't want to leave behind. Nathan grabbed a few boxes from the college and left them for me in the corner of my room. I know it has to be done, and it's probably best to start now rather than leaving it until the last minute.

I put one of the boxes on my bed and then head over to my shelf in the corner of the room. I pick up the scrapbook Gabs made for my eighteenth birthday, full of our memories and moments. A couple of books Dad used to read to me at bedtime. They've been on my shelf my entire life, just display items now, but I can't imagine parting with them. I wrap them in some bubble wrap and carefully place them into the box on my bed, along with the scrapbook, some cheer medals and ribbons, and some little dancer figurines I've collected over time. My chest tightens a little.

My speaker softly hums out music in the otherwise quiet house as I wander over to the corkboard on my wall and look at all the photos. There's a ton of Nathan and me. Some old photos with Mom and Dad. Some new ones with Drayton. Gabs and me too, of course. I'm not taking the corkboard: it's too big, and I can get a new one. I start taking the pins out of the photos, gathering them up and holding them close to my chest. The corkboard becomes emptier, and my chest tightens a little more.

My gaze roams over a photo of Nathan and me at a carnival a few summers ago. We're standing in front of the Ferris wheel with our hands in the air and huge smiles on our faces.

A lump grows in my throat, and I look around the room as my vision starts to blur. I've barely put anything in that box, and still, the room looks emptier.

This is the only room I've ever known. It's the room my mom painted blue for me just months before she died. It's the room my dad found me sulking in when I didn't get my own way and he had to remind me that even though I'm his little princess, I won't always get what I want. It's the room Nathan consoled me in when our parents died and I didn't know how to get off the floor. It's like a montage of everything that's ever happened in this room is playing out in front of me, the good and the bad.

I didn't realize how much of my life was tied up in these walls until I started dismantling it. It starts to feel wrong, and suddenly I don't want to touch a single thing. I don't want this space to change; I don't want to leave it. This is my home, the place I've felt safest over the years, even when everything around me was crumbling. I can't even remember why I wanted to move to California in the first place. It seems so selfish now.

I sit on the bed, still holding the photos against my chest as I fall apart, tears streaming down my face.

I don't want to go. I don't want to leave Nathan and Gabs. I don't want to leave Drayton, and I'm tired of pretending otherwise.

Every adventure I've ever been on, I've returned. I've never had to pack up my life and leave everyone behind, and now I know I can't fucking do it.

I cry even harder, I'm not sure for how long, until I feel an arm drop around my shoulder and the bed dip beside me.

"Dallas, what the hell happened?" Nathan asks, panic in his voice. I look at him and see the dread in his expression.

"Nothing." I shake my head and wipe my face, not that it does much good because I still can't stop crying. "I'm okay, I'm just . . . don't worry, it's nothing."

"It doesn't look like nothing."

I realize I'm still clutching the photos to my chest, so I lower them to my lap. "I can't do this, Nathan. I can't go. I don't want to go."

A fresh wave of despair rushes through me, and I blubber so hard, I have to gasp for air as I drop my head onto his chest. Nathan holds me a bit tighter, rubbing my arm as he does his best to soothe me.

"I'm not brave," I wheeze. "I'm not this fly-with-the-wind girl I wanted to be. I don't want to leave my home or my people or this town. I don't want to start over anymore, Nathan."

He's quiet for a little while, and I don't care how pathetic I seem right now, this is how I feel.

"You can feel more than one thing at a time, Dal," Nathan says quietly. "You can be excited to start over and chase your goals while also grieving what you're leaving behind. You can make space for both of those emotions."

"There's no space for both," I sniff. "I don't wanna leave."

"What are you going to do if you stay?" he asks, pushing me up so he can look at me. "What's here that will make you feel happy and fulfilled?"

"You. Gabs and her baby. This room . . . the mountains."

"Drayton isn't going to be here for much longer."

"No, but he'll come back all the time and see me and his parents."

"Are those things going to make you feel happy and fulfilled forever? Or will you eventually want to build a career?"

I wipe my nose with the back of my hand and shrug. "Maybe."

Nathan stands up and gets me a tissue from my side table before he sits down again. I take it and blow my nose. "What career would you build here?"

"I don't know," I mumble. "Whatever, I'm sure I'd figure something out."

"But would it make you happy?"

"Maybe I don't need some big career to feel happy. Maybe I just need the people I love."

Nathan looks at me like he doesn't believe me. "That might be true for some people. But this goal of yours is all you've talked about from the time you were a kid. I get it, the change is creeping up, and it's big, so it's going to be hard. You might feel homesick, and you will miss the people you love. But achieving your goals is going to come with challenges. Big dreams always do. It doesn't mean it's not worth pursuing."

I know he's right. Deep down, I know what I've always wanted. I know that I still want it. I just didn't know it would feel so hard to leave.

"And listen," Nathan says. "If you go and you give it your all and you find out it's not everything you wanted, there's always a home for you here. You are allowed to change course and try new things and start over more than once. There are no rules."

I nod and wipe my nose again, sitting up a little straighter. I'll miss him so much, but he's right. I can make room for more than one emotion. I can feel it all, and it doesn't mean that what I'm doing is wrong.

Nathan rubs my back as I work on pulling myself together. "You were so sure about leaving, and so driven, you didn't prepare to feel what it's like when it's time to leave."

"I expected to be sad when it was time to go, but I didn't think it would hit me until I was gone. I had all of these ideas of what the emotions would look like, I just didn't expect . . . this. I blame Drayton. I told him falling in love before I left was a bad idea."

Not that it's just him I'll miss.

Nathan chuckles. "Actually, I think it was a fantastic idea."

I look at my brother. "What?"

"Not the fact that you're sad. But that you found someone who makes you so incredibly happy," he says. "You had one goal and one focus, and you were doing well, but after he came along, I started to see you living. Smiling and walking around with this energy that I'd never seen before. And he's so good to you. He pisses me off sometimes, but he loves you, and I will never have to worry about you getting hurt when it comes to him. No matter how far apart you live."

My smile becomes watery, but it's no longer because I'm upset. It's because it means the world to hear how important my happiness is to Nathan.

"What if . . . what if what you said about changing course after a year feels like a really good idea?" I say. "What if I decided to apply for SMU in the spring? I got rejected before, but getting accepted to CalArts and spending a year there might make a difference next time."

Nathan looks apprehensive. "To be closer to Drayton?"

"I've been thinking about deferring this year and moving to Texas—"

"What?" Nathan stands up and stares down at me. "You're kidding."

"I've only thought about it, in a moment of weakness. I wouldn't have gone through with it. It's like an intrusive thought. You imagine cutting your own finger off. You don't actually do it."

Nathan runs a hand through his hair, stress all over his face, and starts pacing back and forth.

"Relax," I say. "I haven't deferred."

"Yeah, don't," he warns, pointing at me. "You worked way too hard for too long to run off and spend a year doing nothing in Texas while your boyfriend goes to college."

"I agree. But what if I apply to SMU in the spring? It'd only be one year long-distance instead of four."

Nathan stands in front of me and props his hands on his hips. "You told him, very specifically, not to pick a college close to you."

"That's because I never thought I would do that for someone, but now I'm wondering if I would. Missing him is going to suck."

Nathan tilts his head in agreement. "Like I said, there's no rule that says you can't change course. If you decide to transfer to SMU, then that's fine."

"It's just something to think about."

Truthfully, I've been thinking about it more and more. I told Drayton I would never change my plans for a relationship, but that was before I knew what it was like to be loved by him. To have someone who would give me the world if he could. He once told me that where he went to college wouldn't matter to him as long as he gets to do what he loves and be close to me. I understand that more now than I did then.

~

Later that night, I'm at Gabby's, and the poor girl is in a state. She's exhausted, her nose is blocked, and her head hurts. She's in her bed with a fan aimed at her, a cold cloth on her forehead, and an ice pack across her chest. Camilla has made her a big batch of chili, which smells great, but Gabs hasn't touched a drop. I sit on the armchair in the corner of the room while a movie plays on her TV. Quietly, of course. I'm relying on subtitles for the most part.

"You need anything?" I ask for the fourth time. "More water?"

"What's the time?" she groans, eyes barely open.

"Nine-twenty."

"Ugh," she cries, but it's more like a croak. "I can't have more pain relief for another hour."

"Is it your head?" I stand up and walk over to her. If she's got a headache, the heat won't be helping either. I touch her cloth and pack and find they're basically room temperature. "Here, let me replace these. You drink as much water as you can. It'll help with the headache."

She barely moves when I take the cloth and ice pack and head out to the kitchen, the smell of cooking still lingering in the air. Camilla is loading the dishwasher as I open the freezer and rotate the items.

"How is she doing?" she asks.

"Feverish, it seems," I say. "It's hard to tell with it being so hot."

"Her body is fighting something, as it should."

"Being sick like this can't hurt the baby, right?"

"Not usually, no," she says, closing the dishwasher and drying her hands on a dish towel. "Thanks for stopping in, Dallas. You don't have to hang around. I'll make sure she's looked after."

"Oh, I know," I say, giving her a small smile. "But I need her to know I'm here for her."

She takes the cold cloth and ice pack from me and meets my eyes with a genuinely warm and affectionate look that's rare coming from her. Camilla isn't awful. She's just stern. "She knows. You've never let that girl down. But it's late, and I don't want you getting sick if it's contagious."

"Okay," I say. "Josh should be here."

"I agree. She sent him off, though," Camilla says. "She thought he'd be no use here. Sometimes a girl just needs her momma to look after her."

I haven't had a mom to nurse me when I'm sick in such a long time. It's the sort of thing I don't realize I'm missing until someone brings it up. But perhaps my mom sent me Drayton. He takes good care of me. Nathan does his best, he makes sure I have Advil and water, but he doesn't fuss the way Drayton did when I was sick. The memory makes me smile.

Camilla must hear what she said because she looks at me apologetically. "You're welcome here anytime you're sick and you need a momma to take care of you."

I laugh lightly, feeling appreciative. "Thanks, Ms. Laurel."

We pop back into Gabby's room to give her the cold cloth and ice pack, and she stirs from her sleep enough that I can let her know I'm leaving. Even in her half-conscious state, she tells me she loves me and blows me a kiss. Camilla walks me to the door, and I step out onto the porch, facing her.

"Do you think Josh is doing everything he could be?" I ask.

Camilla leans against the doorframe and crosses her arms, thinking. "I'm sure he thinks he's doing his best. I don't want to be hard on him, but that's my girl, and I'm worried. She has such a big heart, and she loves people with everything she has, to the point where sometimes she doesn't protect herself enough."

"She doesn't expect people to love the same way, either."

Camilla shakes her head. "She doesn't. She thinks, 'This is just how other people are, I know they love me in their own way.' As a mom, that can be hard to watch. Because deep down, I do feel she deserves someone who is as fierce as she is. She deserves someone who loves her as loudly as Drayton loves you."

It hasn't occurred to me that she'd notice things like that.

"I don't mean that she deserves Drayton," Camilla clarifies, a hint of worry on her face. "You understand?"

"Yeah, I do."

"This isn't what I would've chosen for her," Camilla says, a tremor in her voice and a glisten in her eyes. "She's so smart. I wanted her to apply to the big schools; I wanted her to write and travel."

Now I'm confused. "Gabs said she applied to Arapahoe because you wanted her close."

Camilla sighs and straightens up off the door, looking out at the quiet, dark street. "I think it was about staying close to Josh. She said it was about being close to me too, but in truth, she's comfortable in the familiar. She did express to me that she was worried you wouldn't understand, being so keen to get out of here."

I understand more than ever, but I'm a little hurt that she felt like she had to blame it on her mom instead of just telling me she didn't want to leave home.

"I just always wanted the best for her and her big brain," I say. "She still has a beautiful bright future, though. She's smart and driven, and she can do anything."

Camilla smiles. "She'll be all right."

~

When I get home, it's dark and quiet. I don't know if Nathan went out again or if he's asleep, but I don't bother finding out. I creep up the hall, a familiar fragrance hitting my nose as I go. It makes my heart beat a little faster as I reach into my room, find the light switch, and flick it on.

Drayton is lounging on my bed in his boxer briefs, his hands propped behind his head, his thin chain hanging around his neck. His thighs always make me weak, and his suntanned skin has a slight sheen to it due to the heat. He looks like a damn model. I've always thought that, though.

"Hello, lover." I slip my flip-flops off.

He leans up on his elbows. "I thought for sure you were going to be scared. I'm a little concerned at the ease with which you accept an unexpected guest lying on your bed in their underwear."

"I knew you were here," I say and start getting undressed out of my denim shorts and tank top. "I could smell your cologne."

"Too much?"

"No, it's not overpowering, I just know it well."

He grins, watching me with delight as I get down to my underwear and pick up my PJs from the end of the bed.

"No, no, no," he protests. "What you're wearing is fine. Come here."

I roll my eyes with a laugh and crawl onto the bed, over his body, and onto his lap so I'm straddling him. "What are you doing here? You're supposed to be off on an adventure with the guys, right? Something about a resort and hotel room poker games."

Drayton's hands run up my thighs as he watches me. "Josh felt like an asshole for leaving Gabs while she's sick, so we came back."

I narrow my eyes. "I just came from there, and he was not there."

"Baby, lower your weapons," he says. "He just dropped me off here like two minutes ago. I heard your car pull up as I was getting undressed. You probably passed him."

"Oh." I blink back the rage and suspicion and recall at least three cars passing me as I came home. "Good, I'm glad. But be honest, was it his idea, or was it planted by you?"

"Does it matter?"

"Kind of."

Drayton sits up, holding me around the waist as he brings our faces closer together. "All I did was mention that you'd texted me to say you were there helping out, and he said, 'I should've been doing that,' and we left. He wanted to be there the whole time. Gabs was the one who said he should leave."

My fingers slide into the soft mess of hair at the back of his head, and I nod.

"You got a little beef with Josh, baby?"

I shake my head and take a quick breath. "I just had a hard afternoon while I was packing up. I got emotional, and I don't know . . . I have to leave my best friend in the hands of her baby daddy. He has to be exceptional or I'm going to worry."

Drayton's hands slide up from my waist to my back, then down onto the top of my ass. He watches me with affection and desire and, most of all, love. Loud, loud love. "You'll always worry because you love her. But they're having a kid, they're doing adult shit, and they made decisions. You have to let them figure it out. Be there for Gabs, but don't drown yourself trying to get her on a life raft."

"That was very poetic."

"I've been practicing that speech the whole way home. I knew you were going to need to hear it. I can tell when you're taking on everyone else's shit."

"My hero."

"Mm-hmm." He grips the back of my neck now and kisses me. He kisses me hard and hungrily, and my hips roll against his lap. His other hand grips my butt, and he flips me over, throwing my back onto the bed before I have the chance to blink.

CHAPTER 10

DRAYTON
Eight weeks to go

We're more than halfway through June already, and I have no idea how the hell that happened. I've been giving Dallas casual little riding lessons most evenings. She's getting good, which doesn't surprise me. She picks things up fast for the most part.

I've just finished training with Samuel, the private coach Dad hired for the summer. God forbid I spend three months without one. I didn't argue: it keeps me conditioned, and I'll get to UCLA in the shape I should be in.

I wipe the sweat off my face with a towel as Samuel packs his cones into a bag. "Good stuff today, kid."

"Thanks, man."

"You hear if you got starting quarterback yet?"

I drop the towel around my shoulders. "No. I won't find out until I get there. I've got it, though."

Samuel chuckles. "What makes you so sure?"

"I was there during the assessment."

Now he full-on laughs. "Fantastic confidence, kid. Keep up the drills every morning. I want to see your time advance by at least a second or two on Monday."

"Yes, Coach."

"What are you getting up to for the rest of the afternoon? Plans with your girl?"

"Yeah, she doesn't work Thursday afternoons, so we're going to get lunch and see a movie."

"Nice." He claps me on the chest and slings his bag over his shoulder. "I'll see you next week."

~

Mom comes into the kitchen where I'm sitting at the breakfast bar eating a bowl of chicken and vegetables for lunch.

"Hi, sweetheart."

"Hi."

She opens the fridge. "This looks cleaner?"

"I threw out some shit and wiped it down this morning."

"Oh, thank you," Mom says, getting the milk out. "How's Gabby doing?"

I stare at her while she fiddles with the espresso machine. "Why would I have the answer to that question?"

"You're all friends. I assume you'd know if she's still sick."

I shrug and stab a piece of broccoli with my fork. "Dallas hasn't said, so I don't know."

"You haven't talked to Josh? He hasn't been home for two days."

"Mom." I sigh. "You know he has a phone, right?"

"Yeah, I just thought I'd ask since you're here. I'll call him later. I just didn't want to bother him. It feels weird mothering him now that he's going to be a father."

I guess that would feel weird. Mom has a little insight into what it's like becoming a parent when you're still technically under parental authority. It's a complicated situation, and I think she's doing her best to handle it well. I finish up my bowl of food and go to the sink to rinse my dishes. Mom is steaming her milk when I lean against the counter and call Josh.

"Hey, man," he says.

"Where are you?" I ask.

"I'm working."

"Oh, true." Everyone around me works. Perhaps I should get a job. "Well, where have you been?"

"Staying with Gabs. She's a lot better now, but her mom seemed to appreciate me being there, so I've been helping out as much as I can."

"Yeah, she's luring you into living there. Pretty sure I warned you this would happen."

I can feel my mom watching me as she pours her drink.

"Dude, it's not that sinister," Josh says.

"Gabs is good, then?"

"Yeah, she's just got a little cough, but she's back on her feet and back at the library. She's been talking about doing a library science degree and working at the same time. One of her managers suggested it."

"That's wonderful. You still job hunting?"

Mom moves closer to me now, coffee in hand, listening carefully.

"Yeah, I've applied for a few office assistant positions and a bank teller job. Things I have some experience in."

"Sounds good, man. Well, catch up later, dude."

"Oh, sur—"

I hang up and look at Mom. "Hear all that?"

She taps me on the arm with a smile. "Yes, thanks, sweetheart."

Mom wanders over to the kitchen doors and starts folding them back, opening up the room to become one with the back deck. The sun pours in and streams across the floor.

"Mom," I say. "Did the financial difference between you and Dad put a strain on the relationship at all?"

Mom looks a little surprised at the question as she settles into one of the wicker seats outside. I go and join her, sitting opposite.

"No," she says thoughtfully. "Not really. It was there. The difference. But it never became an issue. Perhaps because I got pregnant so fast. He had to become a provider for his children, that was his role, so I didn't feel strange about it. You know?"

"So . . . I should get Dallas pregnant?"

Mom almost chokes on her coffee. "Don't even joke about that."

I give her a big teeth-baring grin and sit back in my seat, linking my fingers behind my head.

Mom gathers herself. "What's this about? Is this a problem between the two of you?"

"I don't know," I admit. "She just pointed out that I don't ever have to worry about finances and that's something that's always on her mind. She doesn't like it when I tell her to quit her job and spend more time with me. I think it makes me seem out of touch or something when I offer to bankroll her life."

Mom nods and lifts her feet, tucking them under her. "I can see how that might bother her. I always worried that I was doing you a disservice by not making you work. But Dad wanted you to focus on football and school, and he felt if we could provide you with the privilege to focus, then that's what we should do. It's what his parents did."

"I mean, I worked hard in other areas, right?"

Mom takes a mouthful of coffee and nods. "Oh, for sure. You trained and excelled in football, which takes a lot of dedication. You kept up with your grades. You help out around the house. You've done a lot of volunteer work for kids' sports teams over the years. You're not a lazy person. You just have privilege, and it's good to be aware of that. Dallas has to work hard in school and in a job. It'll be harder for her, and it's okay to want to spoil her, but of course she doesn't want to feel like she has to depend on you. That'd be totally unfamiliar to her."

"Yeah," I mumble. "Needed to get some perspective from a past peasant, I guess."

"Rude!"

"I'm kidding." I stand up and give her a kiss on the cheek. "Love you, Mom. Super glad Dad knocked you up."

"Thanks," she deadpans.

Sliding my phone out of my pocket, I head back inside to get ready to leave. Dallas told me to wait until one so she'd have time to do some dance practice without distraction. It's twelve-fifteen, and I'm not sure what to do for the next forty-five fucking minutes. Before I even hit the first step on the staircase, I hear the keypad lock on the door whirring and peer over my shoulder to see Dallas coming inside with a large parcel under her arm.

"Hey, beautiful." I smile, walking straight to her. "What are you doing here?"

She's grinning from ear to ear, wearing a pretty, green sundress with her hair falling in loose waves around her gorgeous face. She kicks her flip-flops off and stands on tiptoe to give me a kiss. I tuck her hair behind her ear and stare at her for a bit because I fucking adore her face.

"You got something for me?" I gesture at the rectangular parcel wrapped in brown paper.

"Yes." She slips past me and heads into the kitchen. I follow close behind, watching curiously as she places the package on the table and waves at Mom, who is right where I left her.

"I thought I was coming to meet you?" I ask, stepping beside her and running a hand up her back.

"Yes, but this arrived this morning, and I've been waiting. I wanted to give it to you straight away."

I give her another kiss, feeling all warm and appreciated. Mom wanders in while I'm lifting the tape off the paper. She and Dallas share a quick hello, but my girl is practically bouncing on the spot, watching me with anticipation.

As I lift the paper back, I'm met with a familiar picture in a large wooden frame. It's the photo of Mom, Dad, and me at graduation, posed in front of a tree, classic and cliché. But this picture has been painted, and now there's a fourth person. Abby stands beside me, the two of us between Mom and Dad. She's wearing a graduation cap, and it's topped with a little halo. I feel like I've been winded, and I hear Mom gasp.

Abigail looks like an eighteen-year-old girl. She looks like her, but in a way we never got to see her. She's smiling, her arm around my shoulders, and the painting is so realistic, if you stepped back a few feet, you wouldn't even know it's not a photograph. My fingers trace my sister's face, and I bite the inside of my cheek as tears gather.

I feel Dallas's hand on my bicep as a tear slips down my cheek. I turn and gather her in my arms so fast she grunts with the impact; I hold her and do my best to pour my entire heart into this hug because I need her to know she has it. All of it. I thought she couldn't top the star she had named after Abby for my birthday. But this is something else entirely. Fuck, I love that she finds ways to keep my sister alive and included in moments that we have to endure without her.

I peer over at Mom, her own tears falling down her face as she stares at the picture. I kiss Dallas on the head and then go to Mom, hugging her sideways so she doesn't have to stop looking at the image.

"You don't keep a lot of photos around the house," Dallas says, wiping her face. "But I thought it could go in her memorial room or—"

"We should have more," Mom says, nodding. "We should put more on the walls."

It's my fault we haven't. I hated being asked where my sister was by guests or friends who visited. I begged Mom and Dad to keep all the photos in one room. But she's right. We should put more photos on the walls. I don't want to hide her. Dallas was right when she told me her death wasn't my fault. I don't need to feel horrific shame when someone asks where she is. I have to tell them about who she was.

"I have the perfect spot for that," I say, still holding Mom tucked under my arm. I look at Dallas. "Thank you, baby. Thank you doesn't even begin to cover it."

Her eyes are glassy as she smiles. "You don't have to thank me."

I do, though. I have a feeling this cost her a bit. If I know her, though, she wouldn't have blinked at the price. It would've been worth it to her because when she gives, she gives with her entire heart, and it's a privilege.

Dad walks in and notices the odd, emotional gathering going on around the table, raising his brows with confusion. Mom waves him over as I go back to Dallas's side and slip an arm around her waist.

When Dad approaches the edge of the table and his eyes scan the picture, I see the physical reaction he has, like a wave pushes into him and knocks him off balance. His eyes well up with tears immediately, and his chin quivers.

He covers his mouth with his hand, and Mom starts to quietly weep all over again.

"She—" Dad stutters and sucks in a sharp breath. "She looks beautiful. She's beautiful."

Dad looks over at Dallas. "You had this made?"

She nods, and Dad shocks the hell out of all of us when he embraces her in a hug. My hold on her drops, and Dallas doesn't hesitate to hug him back. It means the world to me, and the fact that my sister can bring this sort of moment into our lives overwhelms me. I can't even name the emotion. It's painful and beautiful and soothing and a storm all at once.

Dad steps back again and stands beside Mom. "She looks just like our girl. Just . . . as she should be. Now."

"There's this company that does the pictures, and they have a special software to age the person to whatever age you choose," Dallas explains. "I made the order straight after graduation. I thought it would take longer than it did. One of their top reviews was their speed, though."

"I might've heard of it," Mom says. "I've thought about doing something like this. I just never found the strength, I suppose. I wasn't sure how I would feel seeing her like this. But now I know. It hurts, but it's the most beautiful gift we've ever received."

I nod, agreeing, and half an hour later, the four of us stand in the entryway, admiring the photo on the wall. It's the first thing someone will see when they walk in. Our family.

"Are we even sure she'd have graduated?" I break the silence and get a smack in the arm from Mom. "Ow, I'm kidding."

"Well," Mom says as she tilts her head, smiling at the picture, "she did talk about going into sports journalism, so I assume so."

"She also talked about marrying one of my friends and securing herself a football WAG title, so."

Dad laughs. "She could've gone into sports journalism and become a WAG."

"She would've done anything she set her mind to," I say, looking at her smile.

I would do anything to see that smile in person. To have more time with her. I'd have given my life in place of hers, and even after all these years, there's still a desperate pull in my stomach to do the impossible, turn back time, change the outcome. For months after her death, I prayed every single night to wake up on that day so I could do it all over, stop her from walking home, bring her back to the now. I don't think I'll ever stop wishing I could've done things differently. But I've learned not to blame myself.

Dallas and I are sitting outside on the hammock, the sun on our faces. She's got her back to me, sitting draped between my legs. I did have a date planned for us this afternoon, but the heaviness of all the emotion made me feel more drained than I'm used to. It was Dallas's idea to bathe in the sun and just be still for a little while. She's so in tune with what I need without me having to vocalize it.

"Thank you again." I kiss the top of Dallas's head. She's scrolling through social media, liking videos of dancers and cute animals and movie clip edits and whatever other random shit pops up on her page.

"You don't have to keep thanking me, babe."

"I do," I insist. "I can't get over how fucking thoughtful that was."

Dallas drops her phone into the grass and twists until she's lying on her front. She rests her chin on my chest. "You do so much for me, all the time. I just want to give you the things you deserve, and I know that's small in comparison because I don't ha—"

I press my finger to her lips. "Don't, Cheer. We have to stop coming back here. You give me everything I need just by loving me."

"That's all I need from you too, and you continue to shower me with gifts and extravagance."

"Yeah, because I can."

She huffs out a little laugh.

"I have privilege, baby. Like you said. No point pretending otherwise. If I want to share that with you, I will because honestly, there's nothing more important to me than making you smile and spoiling the fuck out of you."

"Okay." She rests her cheek on my chest, relaxing. "I understand."

"Also, Mom suggested pregnancy so I have a valid reason to become your sole provider."

"Sure, she did."

I laugh and sweep my fingers through her hair.

CHAPTER 11

DALLAS
Eight weeks to go

"Three fries and two beef burgers," I repeat back, scrawling on my notepad. "Anything else?"

The three teenagers tucked into the booth look at each other and shake their heads. Freshmen, if I had to guess. They look so young. There are two girls and a boy on the other side. Since the three of them walked in, I've wondered if it's a chaperoned date. Best girls have to look out for each other. It reminds me of something Gabby and I would've done on a summer Friday afternoon.

"Won't be long," I tell them with a smile and turn around to see Drayton coming into the diner wearing a black T-shirt and sweatpants. His hands slide into his pockets as he scans the space before his sights land on me.

We walk toward each other, and he greets a couple of people from school with brief handshakes and head nods. I sometimes forget he was the most beloved person in the entire school. As soon as I'm in front of him, he kisses me. It's rarely just a peck with him. He grips my waist and draws me onto my tiptoes, his hand holding my chin. When he lets me go, I slip past him and keep walking with the order I need to deliver to the kitchen. He knows the drill, following me.

"I have plans for us tonight."

"Mm-hmm," I say, sticking the order slip to the kitchen window frame. Drayton stands at the counter, off to the side so he doesn't cut in the line of people ordering to-go. "What are the plans?"

"We're babysitting my cousins in Fort Collins."

I pick up two plates of BLTs and waffle fries, raising a brow at him. Once again, he follows me as I take the order to table five. "Lucy and Coen?"

"Yeah. Aunt Cass is going out with some girlfriends or something. I didn't ask questions. Apparently, the kids asked for me to watch them tonight."

I set the plates down and nod at the two girls, who thank me. When I face Drayton, he looks ever so proud of himself. "That doesn't surprise me. They adore you. But where's their dad?"

"Probably getting his ass waxed in Vegas." He waves his hand dismissively. "Who cares. The kids requested their favorite cousin and his girlfriend."

"They asked for me too? Specifically?"

"Well, no," he tells me honestly, and I laugh. "Cass was the one who suggested it. She knows we're a package deal. You'll come, right?"

"Of course," I say. "That sounds fun. Perhaps we can go for a swim once they're in bed, recreate our little escapade. We might even kiss this time."

"Great minds think alike, Cheer," he says, kissing me again before he backs up. "I packed you an overnight bag, we have to leave straight from here after your shift. I'll be back in an hour."

Nothing about him surprises me at this point. I'm not even concerned that he'll have forgotten something. I know he'll have thought of everything. Usually, I'd want to finish the last hour of my shift, but I tell him to sit down and wait a second as I head into the kitchen, fishing my phone out of my apron pocket.

I call Wren and ask if she wants to come in and cover my last hour so Drayton and I can head out earlier. If we leave now, we can hopefully get there by five-thirty. I imagine if Cass wants to go out, she'll want to make the most of it. Wren doesn't hesitate to pick up the extra shift and tells me she'll be here in two minutes. I also shoot Nathan a quick text to let him know I'm spending the night with Drayton so he knows I won't be home.

Wren wasn't exaggerating, either. She comes through the door two minutes later, pulling her hair into a bun. She obviously lives closer than I realized.

"Thanks for covering," I say at the time clock in the back room. She punches in, I punch out. "I have to go to Fort Collins with my boyfriend."

"Yeah, no sweat." Wren gives her apron a flick and then drapes it around her waist. "Literally, call me whenever you want to get out of here early. I need the cash. I'm thousands of dollars from my goal."

"What's the goal?"

"To have enough cash to leave town, perhaps the country, and live somewhere brand new. I'll need some money to support myself for a few months, maybe get a car, depending on the public transport, and then I want a backup fund in case I can't find a job or I don't like the place. I'll go somewhere else."

"That's quite a plan," I say as we head back out into the kitchen. "No college?"

"Not my buzz. I want to travel. I don't want to stay in one place forever, and I don't really see tertiary education as an upper hand in this country anymore."

"Right. Yeah, that's fair."

I think she's about to say something else, but Jonothan appears with a plate in each hand and a scowl on his face aimed at Wren. "What are you doing here this early?"

"I'm leaving," I say. "Wren is covering for me."

He looks between the two of us with a sneer that can only be akin to disgust. "You didn't think to run this past me?"

"We don't have to," Wren states. "She's not leaving you short-staffed, and she covered her own shift. Be mad about something else."

Jonothan recoils. "You can't talk to me like that."

"Have you heard how you talk to us?" I ask.

"I'm your boss."

Wren scoffs. "You're filling in while Ryan is away, who will honestly probably fire you when I tell him what an asshole you've been."

Jonothan gives us both another foul look and then shoves past us and goes into the kitchen. Wren and I share an amused look, and then I tell her I owe her one. I head over to Drayton, who is sitting at a two-seater beside the door, his head resting on his fist, his legs spread while he scrolls his phone.

"Should we go?"

He looks up, confused. "Now?"

"Wren's covering the last hour of my shift."

~

We get to Cass's house just before six and park in the driveway. I love her home. It's two stories, white with pale-blue shutters and planter boxes hanging from the windows. Inside, it has gorgeous, polished wooden floors, so many windows that let the natural light flood through, and beautiful wooden detailing on the staircase handrail. The bottom floor has two living spaces, a bathroom, and a kitchen that opens out onto a large deck. Cass lets us into the house with an enthusiastic hug, and we follow her into the bright, open kitchen with sage green and white walls and wooden window frames.

I always smile when I remember the first time I was here. Drayton and I snuck off from an away game, and he chose this house to skinny-dip in the pool. I didn't realize he knew who owned the house. Not until we were caught and she made us come inside, where we stood in this kitchen, wet and wrapped in towels.

Cass is a good sport, though, and she didn't tell Drayton's mom and dad. Not even after we were late getting back to the hotel and the school found out we'd left the premises. We were both suspended, but our skinny-dipping remains a well-kept secret.

"The kids have had baths, they're dressed for bed, and there's snacks in the fridge," Cass tells us. She looks fantastic: her tight blond curls are swept up in a loose bun, and she's wearing a dark-red, almost brown, dress with a square neckline.

"Dressed for bed?" Drayton asks, looking a little disgusted. "It's not even six on a Friday night."

"Yes, but I saved you from having to tell Luce that it's time to get dressed for bed. It's her least favorite part of the evening."

"She would never argue with me."

Cass scoffs and gives him a look as if to say Sure, pal. "Bedtime is seven-thirty. No later, please."

"You look beautiful," I say, and she clutches her chest with gratitude. "Where are you going?"

"Thank you. A couple of us from work are going to a comedy show." She waves a dismissive hand. "I think it's like a stand-up thing. No idea. There's free alcohol and appetizers. I didn't need a lot of convincing once I heard that."

"You got a ride home?" Drayton asks, his expression leaving no room for mistaking how serious he is.

"Yes, I do." Cass slips her phone into a clutch.

"A sober one?"

She gives him a deadpan look. "Yes."

Drayton tuts. "Don't look at me like that. Just making sure Luce and Coen will still have a mom in the morning."

"I appreciate the concern, Dray." She taps his arm and then steps into the black stilettos sitting beside the dining table, using the back of a chair for balance. "I have to go. It's going to seem cruel, but I'm not going to go upstairs and say goodbye to those two because it'll take another hour of settling Coen and convincing Luce that I'll be back. Ever since her dad left, she's in a panic that I'm just going to move out one day."

Oh. Shit. That's awful. Drayton must share my sentiments, but he chooses to express them a little differently.

"I'm still open to breaking his legs if that works for you."

Cass throws her head back with laughter. "I'll consider it. I'll have my cell phone on, call me if it's urgent. Urgent. Oh, and the guest sheets should be washed before you leave. I'm not dealing with whatever goes on in there."

"Sheesh." Drayton screws up his face at her while I cover a laugh. "We're not animals."

She starts backing out of the kitchen. "No, even worse, you're teenagers."

"Real nice, Cass."

She waves as she click-clacks across the floor and out the front door. Drayton watches after her and shakes his head. "She needs a therapist."

"She's cool."

Drayton looks at me. "You can be cool and still need a therapist."

"Yeah, that's true."

We head upstairs. The walls are lined with photos of the Lahey family. Faces I recognize, faces I don't. It's bright up here too, and at the top of the staircase, I peep out the window at the street. Cass is just getting into a car full of women who are clearly excited for their night out.

We wander down the hall past two bedrooms, and then we stop outside of what looks like a playroom. It's blocked off by a baby gate, and inside the walls are covered in decals of balloons and fairies and other characters I'm not familiar with. There's a show playing on the television mounted to the wall, toys scattered all over the floor, and the cutest dollhouse I've ever seen sitting in the corner. I would've loved something like that when I was seven. It's three stories tall and full of realistic miniature furniture and doll clothes.

Lucy is sitting next to it with a doll in her hand, which she starts to smack on the ground as hard as her little arm will allow. Drayton and I share a look of concern. Coen is stacking blocks on the other side of the room, occasionally glancing over at the television.

We've silently decided to simply watch, and I feel like an observer at a zoo. Not that these children are animals, but it's fascinating nonetheless. Neither of them has noticed us standing in the doorway. I can't imagine having this little awareness of my surroundings.

Lucy abandons beating the shit out of her doll and stands up with a sigh, like she's just done a hard day's work. Her nightie is cute, albeit ill-fitting for the rage she just displayed. It's a soft pink, covered in little bunnies with frills on the sleeves. Her long blond curls are in a braid that slips over her shoulder as she walks across the room, kicking things out of her path.

Finally, she looks up, and her whole body jolts with fright before she lets out a bloodcurdling scream. I have never heard anything like it.

Coen's whole body convulses with fright, and he starts screaming too, and then it's tears. Both of them are in fits of tears within seconds of Lucy noticing us.

~

"You good?" Drayton asks Lucy, who sits across from us at the table with an ice cream the size of her head. She nods with a big smile.

"Coen. Is that good, my man?"

"Yes, Dray-Dray." He grins, his entire mouth covered in cookies and cream.

It was about the only thing we could do to console them. Luce knew she wasn't in danger as soon as she registered that it was Drayton standing there, but she was mad. She didn't want him to come near her or talk to her. Coen kept crying, but he ran straight into Drayton's arms. It was his sister who'd scared the life out of him. He didn't even know what the screaming was all about.

It took some coaxing and the promise of an ice cream, but Lucy eventually agreed to calm down and come downstairs.

"What should we do tonight?" Drayton asks, and then he slips his phone out and looks at the time. "For the next hour before bed."

Coen makes some indecipherable noise as he fills his mouth up with ice cream.

"What about charades?" Lucy asks. "I like charades. We played it at school, and my teacher said I was very good."

"Dallas?" Drayton looks at me. "Charades?"

"You'll have to teach me how to play, Luce," I say. "I've never played it before."

Her jaw drops with shock. "Never?"

I shake my head. "Never."

"I will teach you." She nods, seeming pleased with the decision.

After the kids have finished their ice cream and Drayton has sent them to the bathroom to wash their hands, he looks at me, raising a brow. "You've never played charades?"

"Of course I have. I just needed some bonding material."

He chuckles. "That's cute, babe."

We gather in the living room, and I let Lucy teach me the rules of charades, making sure I ask her a few questions so she has the chance to explain it all to me. I can tell it makes her feel very important. Drayton sits on the couch with Coen on his lap, watching us with a soft smile.

When it's my turn to pick a card and act it out, Lucy is my biggest fan. Drayton guesses that I'm a couch potato pretty damn fast, and Lucy takes credit for giving me such excellent instructions. Coen is only two, so he's not old enough to act on his own, which means Drayton brings him in on his charade. I sit on the couch, Lucy sidled up nice and close as we watch.

Drayton lifts Coen over his head and runs around the room with him, the little boy in absolute fits of laughter. I'm supposed to be guessing their card, but I'm too busy watching how gorgeous Drayton is with children.

"A flying monkey!" Luce shouts, bouncing on the seat beside me.

Drayton stops on the other side of the room, bringing Coen down to his chest as he laughs. "How did you guess that?"

"Coen is the monkey, and you were making him fly."

Drayton shrugs, walking back over to us. "Yeah, you know what, fair enough."

He sits down beside me and kisses me on the cheek.

"Ew." Lucy turns red and screws up her nose. "Do you guys kiss?"

"Of course we do."

"Gross."

"Totally." Drayton humors her and lets Coen snuggle into his chest. He lets out a big yawn. "Tired already, kid? We haven't even played Monopoly."

Lucy gasps. "I love Monopoly."

"I know. Go and get it."

She bounds off, and I look at him, smiling. "You're a natural."

"Careful, Cheer." His tone turns teasing. "No babies for us. Yet."

I roll my eyes at him. I am in zero rush for that. But there's something beautiful about wanting to share that milestone with the person you love. I can totally picture Drayton and me together during that phase in our lives. It makes me a bit mushy, but it also reminds me that our futures look particularly busy, and we're destined to spend the foreseeable future with what might be very little time together. It feels like perhaps our only shot at lasting is if I transfer as soon as I can. But what if I end up falling in love with California? What if I make friends that I don't want to leave or I have incredible teachers or I find a great job that aligns with my classes? What if I adore living in LA so much that not even Drayton is enough to make me want to transfer to SMU? If I wasn't going in the first place, I'd never know what I'm missing. It feels like there are a thousand things to think about, and every day it's something new—a new perspective to send me spiraling and doubting every decision I've made up until now.

"Dallas," Lucy says as she walks back into the room with the board game, snapping me out of my thoughts. I push the trepidation down, choosing to ignore it for now. "You will be on my team, and Drayton and Coen will be on a team."

Drayton and I share a pleased look. I've won her over.

~

"You do not own that street." Drayton sits on the floor on the other side of the coffee table and stares at me while I hold out a hand for the rent on Park Place. Coen has drifted off to sleep in his lap and rests undisturbed while we play.

"Yes, I do," I say and look at Luce, sitting beside me on a stool. "We do own it, don't we?"

Lucy's brows pinch thoughtfully. I probably shouldn't encourage her to lie for me.

"When did you buy that?" Drayton asks.

"Ages ago," I say.

"You're a cheater, woman." Drayton stretches his neck, looking over at my pile of property cards. "You haven't paid for half of those. You're just putting them in your pile."

"Nuh-uh," I lie. "You just didn't notice me putting the money in the bank."

"I don't think you should be the banker anymore."

Drayton relents and gives me the rent for one of the best properties in the game, and I grin. He still doesn't believe me. I hand Lucy the cash to add to our growing pile, which she organizes neatly and then fans her face with.

"We have a lot of cash, Dallas," she announces proudly.

Drayton glares at both of us and takes his turn, moving over the spaces until he lands on a train station. "I'm going to buy this one."

"Oh no, you can't, we own that one," I say. "You owe me fifty bucks, because I own two train stations."

He stares at me flatly. "You own this whole damn board or something? You've just been not landing on them but somehow have the cards and a huge pile of cash?"

"I'm just really good at this game."

He starts to laugh, dropping his head into his hands. Coen shakes a little against his chest but remains fast asleep. "You're an actual nightmare."

"I have to be rich in at least one universe."

"Wealth does not become you, my love. You're a monster."

We both burst into giggle, and Lucy laughs too, though I'm not sure if she knows what she's laughing at.

The antics go on for a while until Drayton notices that it's just after eight and Lucy was supposed to be in bed half an hour ago. He promises her a sweet treat for breakfast if she goes upstairs and brushes her teeth without arguing. While she does that, Drayton puts Coen down in his little bed. It's low to the floor with a rail on the side so he doesn't fall out.

I feel all gooey as I watch him cradle Coen's head and set him down so gently that he doesn't even stir. He pulls the blanket over him and ruffles his hair before he meets me at the door and we go in search of Luce. She's finishing up in the bathroom and leads us into her bedroom, a cute little girl's space with pink walls and sheer white curtains. She climbs into her twin bed and snuggles down.

"You have fun tonight?" Drayton asks, tucking her in.

"Yes," she says. "You are the best babysitters ever."

I hear the plural in that and feel all sorts of delighted. Drayton gives her a hug good night, and then she stretches her arms out for me too. I'm honored.

"Good night, Luce." I give her a hug, her little arms encircling me. "I had a good night too."

CHAPTER 12

DRAYTON
Eight weeks to go

Dallas and I head downtown before the kids wake up so we can get the breakfast I promised Lucy. I'm a man of my word. Plus, I bet Cass has a hangover, and I like the idea of leaving with her children all hopped up on sugar. We park outside of a waffle shop. The coffee here is good, and there's orange juice and all sorts of other breakfast options too.

Dallas and I get out of the car and head inside. She tucks into my side while we stand back and look at the menu.

"The sundae waffle stack sounds good for Luce," Dallas suggests.

It comes with ice cream, berries, syrup, and a churro. It's the absolute last thing a child needs first thing in the morning. But it is a special occasion. Coen can share it with her. Cass can deal with the consequences.

We wander up to the counter, and I start ordering. Something for Luce, Cass, me, and then I look at Dallas, who is staring out the store window. "What do you want, Cheer?"

"Nathan!"

I turn to the dude behind the counter. "You have those here?"

He looks at me like he's sick of his day being wasted already and it's not even eight. I turn, looking in the same direction as Dallas, and spot her brother on the other side of the street outside of a café. He looks like he's paused in the middle of whatever he was doing to check a message on his phone.

"Baby, what do you want to eat?" I ask.

She looks at me, confused. "What?"

"Breakfast?"

"Oh, uh, I don't know," she says, her attention shifting between me and the store window. "Waffles? What is Nathan doing in Fort Collins at seven-forty-five in the morning?"

I sigh; she's no good right now. "She'll have the classic stack. Throw in a couple of strips of bacon too, and an orange juice, please."

"To-go or for here?"

I hear the door open and turn to find Dallas leaving. "To-go, man, thanks. I'll be right back."

As quick as I can, I head out of the store and catch up to Dallas, who's hit the other side of the road and is beelining toward her brother. "Dallas," I say. "What are you doing?"

"Finding out what he's doing here, what does it look like?"

I grab her arm and stop her in her tracks. She doesn't fight me, but she does look mildly frustrated.

"Why do you need to know?"

Her narrowed gaze wanders to the side. "Because it's weird and unusual, and I want to know what he's doing here."

"It might be private, and you and your brother are usually pretty big on respecting each other's boundaries."

Her shoulders drop a little. "Mmm, I guess."

"I'm curious too, babe, believe me. But let's not stalk him. You might find out something he's not ready to share."

"Yeah." She laughs with a little shake of her head. "Yeah, that's not fair. I'm just so curious. Like, he must've spent the night here, right? Otherwise, he got up super early. It's just odd. He's never mentioned he comes here before."

"Let's go and get our food and deliberate the possibilities over waffles," I suggest, tucking her under my arm. She puts up no argument, and we go back to the waffle shop, where our food is waiting for us. It's all bagged up, the drinks in cupholders. It smells so fucking good. Dallas hops into the car first, and I hand her the drinks, leaving the food on the floor at her feet. When I finally start the car, ready to reverse out of our spot, Nathan comes strolling past on the sidewalk, his arm draped around a pretty brunette.

Dallas gasps so loudly I'm surprised he doesn't hear it. I'm also surprised he doesn't see us. I guess there's enough of a glare on the windshield to obstruct our faces. Or he's just too caught up in the leggy girl who's got a smoothie cup in one hand and her other arm around his waist.

"That's Emma!" Dallas basically screams, slapping the center console and looking at me with all of the joy in the world. Even I'm a bit fucking taken aback at the news.

"The one from the campground?"

"Yes!" Dallas exclaims. "What the hell is going on? They're seeing each other. But how? This is insane. I can't. I literally can't."

I love it when my girl starts speaking in valley girl.

"But why wouldn't he tell me?" She looks at me, still smiling, but the confusion is creeping in. "Maybe he wants it to be a sure thing before he does. Maybe he really likes her."

"All that searching for her, and they were together the whole time." I start the car. "Guess you have good matchmaking instincts, Cheer."

"I knew they would look so cute together."

"So cute," I say, earning a withering look from Dallas for being sarcastic. "Babe, they look good. Like tall, athletic, genetic winners. Their children will be beautiful."

Dallas laughs, tipping her head back against the seat with a smile. "I'm so happy for him. He looked so happy, right?"

"He looked pretty pleased," I admit. We drive past them on the way back, and Dallas doesn't look too hard out the window, which surprises me. I guess she doesn't want to get caught.

"Now I have to pretend I didn't see him and that I don't know," she says.

An idea comes to mind, and I cast a quick look over at Dallas. She can see the devious thoughts written all over my face.

"What are you smiling like that for?"

"You wanna mess with him a little?"

She pretends to be hesitant and thoughtful, but I know she wants to. "Duh."

We get back to Cass's with the food and find her at the kitchen table with a coffee, last night's makeup still on her face and the kids watching cartoons in the living room. The French doors are open, and the deck is the perfect spot to eat breakfast. The sun is pouring down on the outdoor furniture.

"I'm going to set this up on the table," I tell Cass as I pass her, and she looks at the brown paper bags with interest. "Dallas, baby, can you grab the kids?"

Dallas wanders into the living room, and Cass follows me out on to the deck, where I start spreading out the boxes of food. She puts on a brave face when she sees all the sweet options, but I can tell it makes her want to throw up. I get some plates so I can share Lucy's portion with Coen.

THE QB, SUMMER AND ME

"You go too hard last night?" I give Cass a slap on the back, and she glares at me as she cuts up half a waffle for Coen into little bite-size pieces.

The kids finally emerge, no doubt not wanting to leave their cartoons. As soon as Luce sees the dessert on her plate, she screams, making her mom cringe.

"I didn't get you sugar," I tell Cass, lifting the lid of her breakfast. Hash browns, bacon, sausages. She sighs with relief and looks at me with total gratitude. I'm not a complete asshole. She needs fatty fried food. I don't know anyone who wants to eat sweets with a hangover.

We all sit down and eat. Cass shares a bit about her night, the comedy show, the barhopping afterwards, the impulsive decision to dance with whoever asked.

"I'm too old for this," she murmurs, leaning back in her chair, slowly chewing on a mouthful of food. "I physically can't handle the aftermath. This is going to last like two entire days."

"You're like thirty-two, relax," I say, sighing when Coen uses his ice cream–covered hand to hold on to my shoulder and stand on the arm of his chair.

"Oh, Coen, no, darling." Cass mumbles a half-hearted attempt at giving some direction to her two-year-old. "Don't stand on that."

"I got him," I say, holding the kid's shirt so he doesn't slip and break something. "You know, we do have to leave today. You're going to have to get your shit together in the next hour."

"Their dad is coming to get them for the night," Cass tells me.

"When?"

She checks her phone, and I peer over at Dallas, her food finished and her eyes closed as she leans back in her chair and relaxes in the sun with a content smile. Luce is shoveling waffle into her mouth; her ice cream, berries, and syrup have turned into a weird-colored liquid, and it drips off her food and onto her front.

"In two-ish hours," Cass tells me.

"We're out of here before then."

Cass chuckles, checking something on her phone. "You don't want to see Uncle Noah?"

"Nope, and besides, we need you for something tonight, so best get some sleep this afternoon. You're coming to Castle Rock."

Cass lowers her phone and stares at me with panda eyes. "Why the f—why would I do that?"

"Because I ask for nothing when I watch these two . . . usually. But this time I'm calling in a favor."

She huffs loudly and buries her face in her hands. "But I can't."

Dallas and I share an amused smile.

~

Dallas and I shuffle into her living room later that afternoon. We spent some time at my place so I could shower and change out of the clothes Coen got ice cream all over. Then we got caught up talking to Josh and Gabby for hours. I couldn't stop staring at the baby bump. Josh is going to be a father, and it's bending the hell out of my mind.

"Hey," Dallas greets her brother as she walks through the living room to take her bag to her room. He's in the kitchen scooping protein powder into a blender while he watches television. It looks like he's just come back from the gym.

Nathan nods in greeting as I slide onto a stool at the breakfast bar. How dare he lie to my love about what he's been doing? Am I also being a liar? Yes. Beside the point.

He doesn't ask what we got up to last night because Dallas sleeps over all the time. It was nothing out of the ordinary. Still, I want him to ask so I can tell him we were in Fort Collins. I want to see him panic.

Dallas comes back with her slippers on her feet. She hops onto the stool next to mine. "Guess what?" she says to Nathan.

He secures the cup on the blender but pauses before he turns it on, raising a brow at his sister. His gaze shifts between the two of us, and then it slowly turns to fear as he rests both of his palms on the counter and takes a deep breath. "What?"

Dallas chuckles. "Why do you look like you're freaking out?"

"You two look like you're about to give me some sort of news I don't want to hear about. You get married? Arrested?"

Dallas looks at him like he's fucking nuts. "You have to stop assuming I'm just going to elope."

Nathan points an accusing finger at me. "He would talk you into it."

"I totally would," I admit. "But I also want my girl to have a wedding and wear a beautiful dress. If that's what she wants. Is that what you want?"

Dallas looks at me, head tilted in thought. "I think so. Perhaps not anything huge. Something pretty and intimate. Beach vibes. I'd definitely want to wear a pretty dress."

Nathan clears his throat, interrupting my mental image of Dallas telling me "I do" while she looks like a princess. We both look at him. "Sorry to interrupt the wedding plans, but was there something you wanted to tell me?"

Dallas straightens up with excitement. "Yes. I've planned a blind date for you. She'll be here in like fifteen minutes."

Nathan's face turns ghost white as he recoils and stares with his eyes bulging out of his head. "You did what? Dallas. What?"

"She's gorgeous. A little older. Thirty-two. But I think you've gone older. She's hilarious. Such a good time. You'll like her a lot."

He looks like he's glitching as he stammers for words. "But, why would you do that? I don't want to go on a date with someone I don't know."

"You plan dates through Tinder all the time." Dallas does a damn good job of acting like she's confused about her brother's outrage. "It's kind of the same thing. You just haven't seen a photo or swiped right. But don't stress. I swear, she's beautiful. You will not be disappointed."

Nathan runs a hand over his face and palms his jaw. "Where did you even meet her?"

"She's friends with Drayton's mom." Dallas jabs a thumb my way.

Nathan's jaw drops, and he blinks with disbelief. "You set me up with a friend of your boyfriend's mother?"

Shit, he'd be really mad if he knew she was my aunt. To be fair, though, it's more truthful calling her Mom's friend. We all loved Aunt Cass so much, we kept her instead of my dad's own brother.

"I wouldn't have if it wasn't a match made in heaven," Dallas exclaims excitedly. "I don't usually get super involved in your love life, but I knew it would be perfect."

Nathan is pacing at this point; his smoothie still hasn't been blended.

"You should probably change, dude," I say. "She'll be here soon."

Nathan just stares at us as he runs his hand through his hair over and over again. The man looks stressed the hell out, and Dallas and I both know it's not over a blind date. It's over the fact that he's clearly got a girl he doesn't want to disrespect.

I keep expecting him to tell us the truth, but nope. He starts blending his smoothie, staring into outer space while he does it. Dallas and I share a quick look, and I can tell she's doing her best not to burst into laughter.

When he switches the blender off, the sound of knocking on the door becomes audible. Dallas gets off her stool with glee. "She's here."

Nathan stares at the front door while he chugs back his smoothie. Dallas swings it open, and Cass walks in looking a lot less dead than she did this morning. She's wearing the shortest fucking dress I've ever seen.

I do my best not to look like I'm grossed out by my aunt wearing what might as well be one of Lucy's dresses.

"Nathan, this is Cassandra." Dallas uses her full name in the hopes it'll throw Nathan off from recognizing the name Cass, which has come up once or twice. I'm honestly surprised the two of them have never crossed paths until now.

Nathan keeps a tight hold of his smoothie cup and comes into the living room, still pale, walking as if he's being dragged against his will. "Hey." He smiles, even if he does look like he's in pain.

Cass, however, looks pleasantly surprised and holds out her hand for him to shake. She's all goo-goo eyes and fluttering lashes. "Hi, it's nice to meet you."

Nathan pulls his hand back and gestures at himself. "Sorry, I'm not dressed to go out. I wasn't given . . . a lot of notice."

"Oh, that's fine," Cass practically purrs, looking him over. Dallas gives me a wide-eyed stare, as if to tell me this was not part of the plan, but it's fucking hilarious anyway. "Shower, dress, whatever you need to do. I'll wait."

Nathan gives her another tight smile. "Yeah, won't be long. Dallas, can I borrow you for a sec?"

He grabs her arm, drops his smoothie cup on the counter, and drags Dallas down the hall.

Cass whispers to me when they're gone, "Wait, but he's actually so hot."

I stand up off the stool and look straight at her. "You can't have him. My aunt is not dating my girlfriend's brother. Fuck no."

"It's not a big deal. We're only related by marriage . . . or previous marriage. Related by divorce? I don't know."

"He is seeing someone. Did you forget the entire reason we're doing this?"

She huffs with disappointment. "Sure, but I didn't expect him to look like that."

"Have you seen Dallas? She's like out-of-this-world stunning. Why would her brother not be in the same realm of attractiveness?"

She tilts her head. "Good point."

Dallas comes back down the hall with her hand over her mouth and her eyes alight with pure amusement. She giggles as she walks up close to us and lowers her voice. "He is freaking out." She blows out a breath to stop her laughter and looks over her shoulder. "He did say you're very beautiful, by the way."

Cass shimmies with excitement, and I shake my head at her.

"But he's trying to get out of it by telling me he's working on his celibacy." She rolls her eyes. "I told him you don't have to sleep together, just get dinner and talk. So, he's going to shower."

"I'm not opposed to sleeping with him." Cass shrugs her shoulders.

I give her a disgusted look.

"Let's not go that—"

Nathan comes out of the hall, not showered or changed. "Uh, I don't feel well," he says to the three of us, arms spread. "Think it was that smoothie. Cass, it was lovely to meet you, I'm so sorry, we'll reschedule."

He backs out of the room with a wave and disappears again.

"Well," Cass says. "He's loyal. That's more than I can say for the father of my children. I'm going to see Ellie; I told her I'd see her this evening at some point. It's the only reason I agreed to come all the way here."

Dallas and I say goodbye, and then we stand in the quiet living room. Dallas folds her arms. "I can't believe he didn't fess up," she says. "He is being so weird."

CHAPTER 13

DALLAS
Eight weeks to go.

I scrawl down the words party favors on a notepad with a question mark next to it. I'm sitting on Drayton's deck, planning Gabby's baby shower. I couldn't hang around at home after Nathan decided he'll do anything but tell me about his new girlfriend. I didn't trust myself not to pester him for more information.

I chew the tip of the pen, looking over the backyard, which is glowing with evening sun, and decide it's not really fair to expect him to tell me everything. There could be lots of reasons he doesn't want to tell me. I giggle to myself when I think about his face when we told him Cass was on her way.

I hear a few soft steps behind me, and then Leroy appears on the deck with a drink in his hand.

"Hi, Dallas."

"Hey."

"Where's Drayton?"

"He's just gone out to get some dinner. Ellie asked him to sort out food since she's gone out with Cass."

Usually, I would go with him, but he saw me curled up in this comfortable, cushioned outdoor love seat in the warm sun and told me to stay put. My notepad is full of ideas: I've been on a roll, scrawling things down, and I decided it was better to keep going with the flow. I have two possible dates: July eleventh, which gives me a little over three weeks, or July twenty-fifth, which gives me over a month. I don't want to leave it too late; I'll be getting busier the closer I am to leaving. I need to check with Ellie and find out what date she thinks is best.

"How did the babysitting in Fort Collins go?" Leroy asks as he takes a seat at the table.

I expect to feel a little awkward with it being just us, but I can tell he's making an effort to be kinder, more interested. After seeing his emotional response to the picture of Abby, I no longer feel a shred of animosity toward him. It struck me straight in the heart. This is just a father who wants the best for the child he still has with him. Plus, I know it would mean a lot to Drayton if we got along. His face whenever his dad and I converse tells me how pleased it makes him.

"It was fun," I say, twisting the pen around my fingers. "Those kids are cute."

Leroy chuckles and raises his glass to his mouth, looking out at the sun, which is slowly setting. "Yeah, they are."

I wonder what he thinks about the fact that his brother isn't being the greatest example of a father. I'm not going to ask, but I am curious.

It's quiet for a few minutes. Leroy is drinking what looks like scotch, and that gives me another idea. I quickly write down, Check if Gabs is wanting it completely dry or if she's okay with beer and wine being served. I have no idea what the norm is for beverages at a baby shower, but I'll find out.

"You working on something?" Leroy asks, gesturing at the notepad.

"Oh. Baby shower planning."

"Ah." He nods with recognition. "Els mentioned we were hosting that."

"I hope that's okay?"

"Of course," he says and stretches out his arm. "We have all that space. It might as well be used. I'm just impressed Drayton asked us this time. Usually we're told."

We both laugh, and I admire the space again. There's a long, wide stretch of flat lawn. There are several large trees scattered, two of which hold a hammock between them. They're always wrapped in twinkling lights too. The entire edge of the property is surrounded by tall fir trees to keep it private. The pool area, adorned with pool chairs and umbrellas, sits to the left.

It's the perfect space to set out tables with a number of buffet options. The deck is its own landmark, wrapping almost right around the house and complete with an entire outdoor kitchen.

"I appreciate it," I tell Leroy. "I haven't planned something like this before. I'm not even sure if it's customary to serve alcoholic options. That's what I was writing down."

Leroy looks thoughtful for a moment. "I guess that would have to be Gabby's choice? She's not legally supposed to be drinking anyway."

I gasp with amusement. "Oh my gosh, a baby before she's legal to drink. That's kind of hilarious."

Leroy chuckles. "I've been there."

I shut my mouth because I completely forgot he was also a teen father. It's hard to believe considering he had twins at eighteen and still managed to have a successful career in the NFL.

"It's all right," he says, noticing my abrupt silence. "It is funny. But I guess that's why I'm not overly stressed out at the situation. Look, Gabriella isn't my daughter, so it's a little different. But goals are achievable. Children or not. It just requires a lot of hard work and the right people to support you. Gabriella has that. She has good people. You included."

"Yes, but I won't be here," I murmur, the familiar wave of trepidation coming over me. The weight of my choices leaves me breathless.

"Your support will still count, I promise. My mom and dad died when the twins were babies. But they believed in me and loved me and wanted me to do well. It gave me the strength to keep going when it was hard."

I smile; that's a beautiful sentiment.

"And thank God for Els." He rests his elbows on his knees, the empty cup between his hands. "I would never have made it through without her. Never. I owe that woman the world. She did more than I could ever fathom so that I could stay in school."

There's such a genuine love in his voice and in his expression. Warmth floods me because this is the example Drayton has grown up with.

Leroy and Ellie have been through so much, and his dad has remained loyal and loving and grateful to the woman he shares his life with.

It makes me believe in our love just that little bit more. Drayton knows what it is to dedicate yourself to someone, to remain with them, to love them even when the world is dark and circumstances feel impossible.

"Besides." Leroy stands up. "There are worse things that can happen to your kids than teen pregnancy."

The pain in his face when he talks about his daughter is haunting. Unfathomable.

"Thank you again for that picture," Leroy says, looking at me. "It's beautiful and thoughtful. Since you came along, Drayton has really started to forgive himself for that night, which is all I ever wanted for him."

My chest tightens as I nod, hearing him but not having the words to respond. I don't think I really need to say anything anyway. He gives me a small smile and heads back inside.

~

Later that night, Gabs, Josh, Drayton, and I sit in the basement. The boys are gaming in beanbag chairs in front of the television, and I'm on Pinterest, adding inspiration to my baby shower planning board. Gabs is stretched across the sofa with her tank top only covering half of her bump and her feet on my lap.

She twists a piece of hair around her finger. "So, you saw him walk past with the same girl from the campground that you wanted to set him up with?"

"Yep."

"And he's keeping it a secret?"

"Yep."

"What are the chances of that?" She sounds bewildered, and then her brows pull together. "Isn't it kind of weird he doesn't want you to know, though? It's not like him to hide his conquests."

"Maybe it's because of what happened in California, when I asked him to stop being such a man whore. Not in those exact words," I say. "But to that effect."

The sound of gunfire comes from the television as I swipe the screen of my phone absentmindedly.

"Though," I pipe up, "I did tell him I wanted him to find someone and be happy. I just, like, don't get it. Usually, I wouldn't care this much, but it's the weird secretive side of it and the fact that he ended up with her of all people. I need answers. It's such a random situation."

Josh keeps his back to the couch and his focus on the television when he says, "Why don't you just ask him?"

Drayton scoffs. "Captain obvious with the impeccable advice over here."

Josh elbows him. "Sometimes the obvious gets overlooked by the drama queens back there."

Gabby recoils so hard she ends up with two chins and her jaw dropped. We look at each other and then at him and then at each other. It's as if Josh can sense he's put his foot in it because he twists and looks over his shoulder at us before turning back to his game.

"Idiot," Drayton mumbles, tapping his controller.

"I want to be told, Josh," I say as if I'm speaking to a child. "I want to be worthy of an actual conversation. Not have to force a confession out of him. Do you understand?"

Drayton laughs and lets out a little holler. "Walk him like a dog, babe."

I can't see Josh's face, but I'm sure his eyes are rolling into the back of his head. Gabs keeps quiet, no doubt stuck between wanting to defend her man and remaining loyal to me. I probably shouldn't put her in that position, but for some reason unknown even to me, he's really pressing my buttons at the moment. It's like he's giving me the ick and he's not even my boyfriend.

"Josh," Gabs says with a pleading tone, "can you please get me a slushy?"

"From where?" he asks.

"I don't know."

"Well, we don't have any here."

Gabby scrolls her phone. "Yeah, I know."

"So, you want me to go out?" he asks, sounding like he'd rather not.

"Yeah."

He lets out a long sigh, and I see Drayton shoot a glance over at him. He makes no move to get off the game for at least the next five minutes. Gabs and I keep scrolling on our phones, and she doesn't mention it again, but I keep waiting for him to get up. Even when he dies, he makes no move to leave, he just reloads into the game.

As the minutes tick on, my patience dwindles.

"Josh," I finally snap. "Are you planning on going to get Gabs her drink?"

He pauses the game and tips his head back.

"It doesn't matter," Gabs says, not looking away from her phone, though I can tell she's bothered. "I don't really need one."

"You sure?" Josh asks.

"Dude." I stand up, irritated. "I'll go, then."

"Baby." Drayton looks back at me with his brow raised. Gabs protests too, insisting she's fine.

"It's not like it's hard." I slide my phone into my shorts pocket and search for Gabby's car keys. "Your pregnant girlfriend wants a drink, like just go and fucking get it. She's growing your child. Like, just get her the drink."

Drayton is up off the beanbag now and takes my hand as he walks past me, pulling me along. "Josh, go and get the woman her slushy."

There's no room—or even time—for argument as Drayton leads me upstairs, his warm hand wrapped around mine. He takes me into the living room and sits us down on the couch. It's quiet up here. I have no idea where his dad is, but it is late, he could be in bed. I suppose Ellie is still out with Cass.

"Time-out." Drayton slips his arm over my shoulder and pulls me into his body. "What's going on, baby?"

"I don't know."

We hear the front door close with a loud bang, and my frustration starts simmering again.

"You seem so irritated by him all of a sudden," Drayton says. "Is it because you don't feel like he's doing enough?"

I rub my temples. "I don't know, Drayton. I honestly have no idea."

He kisses the top of my head. "If I had to guess, I'd say you're mad at him for knocking up your best friend."

Am I? I think I might be.

"But she had a part in that too," Drayton reminds me.

"Yeah, I'm aware." I stand up off the couch and walk over to the window, looking out over the large driveway illuminated by solar lights in the shrubs and on the trees. Josh's taillights are disappearing.

Drayton comes up behind me, and his chest is flush with my back as he rests his chin on my head. I feel bad for disrupting the evening with a tantrum. I sift through my thoughts, desperate to understand what bothers me so much about this situation.

"You can be mad, baby," he whispers. "I know how much Gabs means to you, and I get that you're worr—"

"There you are."

Drayton and I turn at the sound of Gabs walking into the room.

"I've been upstairs looking for you."

"What's wrong?"

She folds her arms, looking a little pissed. "I wanna talk to you."

Drayton taps me on the ass as he wanders off. "I'll be upstairs."

When it's just the two of us, Gabby shifts her feet and chews on her lip, obviously feeling awkward about whatever she has to say. Which leads me to assume she's mad at the way I handled things.

"What's going on?" she asks.

"What do you mean?"

"You've been so weird about Josh lately," she says, a gentleness in her tone that wasn't there when she came into the room. "Like, whenever we're all together you look at him like he's an asshole, you barely talk to him. You shut down the conversation whenever I talk about him, and Mom said you were, like, complaining to her about him."

Camilla, you bitch.

"Okay, well, I wasn't complaining," I say, feeling defensive. "I just said that I thought he should be doing more. You were half dead, and he was off having a boys' night. You're pregnant. His priorities have to change."

"He came back, and you know that."

"Yeah, after Drayton told him he should."

She raises her brow and scoffs. "He said he'd already thought of it, Dallas. And besides, I didn't have a problem with him going. Mom was looking after me. There wasn't a lot for him to do. He shouldn't have to miss out on everything from now on."

"That's not the point," I exclaim, throwing my hands up. "He doesn't get to act like he has no responsibilities anymore, and he shouldn't act like a twat when you ask him to do something for you."

She sighs. "I wouldn't want to go out in the middle of the night to get someone a drink either."

"It's ten. It's also the foot rubs, not making you food, not communicating. Stop defending him."

"Stop villainizing him," she practically shouts. "He's the father of my child, and I do love him. I get that he's not Drayton. Like, sure, you struck gold and landed a man that would do literally anything for you, and he goes above and beyond, which should be the standard. But not everyone ends up with that, and it doesn't make Josh bad. I guess it just makes other people exceptional."

"I'm sorry, but I don't think settling for 'not bad,'" I say with air quotations, "is how it should be. The man you have a child with should be exceptional, and if he's not, then he should learn. It's really not hard."

"It's a bit fucking late to change who I'm having a child with, isn't it, Dallas," she snaps. "And not everyone wants someone who is a stage ten clinger and has no other interests outside of his girlfriend."

I recoil and stare at her. "Oh, that is rude. I didn't say Josh has to change who he is. He just needs to step up and provide the support you deserve. Do you not understand that I'm in your corner here? Like, I want the best for you. How is that a problem?"

"He is doing his best," she says. "He's looking for a better job, and he's here. He's taking care of me. I'm not some poor, neglected pregnant girlfriend. I don't understand what more you want from him?"

"I want his life to change as much as yours is going to."

She stills at that, her anger smoothing out as if she's been stricken by thoughts she's never considered. I'm not even sure I considered them until now. But it's true. My best friend's life is going to change in a direction she never planned for, and I don't want her to do it alone. I want him to have the exact same fate.

"You think this is going to be totally negative, don't you?"

I open my mouth, but nothing comes out.

"You think I have no future now and I'm going to be miserable with a child and never do anything meaningful, and you want him to suffer the same way. That's what you really wanted to say."

"Gabs, no," I say, feeling total regret over how this conversation has gone.

She holds up a hand to stop me. "Don't plan my baby shower. There's no point in asking you to plan a celebration for something you so clearly see as horrible."

She walks out of the room, and I deflate. I'm on her side. I'm always on her side. I never meant to make her feel like I'm not.

CHAPTER 14

DRAYTON
Eight weeks to go

Dallas comes upstairs and finds me in my bedroom. She has that look on her face. The one that tells me she's got a whole lot going on in her head, and none of it is making much sense. I carefully put one of my framed photos into the box I was packing and walk over to where she's just sort of paused in the middle of the room.

"What happened?" I ask.

Dallas brings her attention to me. "We had a huge fight, and she told me not to plan the baby shower."

I blow out a breath, a little surprised, but also upset for Dallas because this is the last thing she'd want to happen before she leaves for college. She wanted this summer to be full of celebration and happiness. I stretch out my arms and bring her into me, cradling her head against my chest.

"I'm guessing she was defending Josh?"

I feel Dallas's shoulders shrug. "What's your perspective on him? Do you think he's stepping up enough?"

Fuck, it's going to be our turn next if I'm not careful. Not that Dallas ever expects me to sugarcoat shit. If I have something to say, she hears it. She might just give me an earful before she processes that I'm right.

"I've talked to him. He wants to better his career and be able to provide for her, and he's scared of letting her and the baby down," I explain. "Could he get off his ass a little more when it comes to the small stuff? Yeah. But I don't think that means he doesn't care."

Dallas is quiet for a while, and then she tips her head back and looks up at me. "You've made me this way."

I bark out an unexpected laugh. "What?"

"You're perfect. No one else can compare. Gabs deserves someone like you."

"You don't want to share me, Cheer."

She rolls her eyes with a huff and then drops her forehead back onto my chest. "I told her I wanted his life to change as much as hers is going to, and I think what I really meant was I want him to suffer as much as she's going to. She called me on it. She thinks that I think her life is going to be miserable."

"Do you think that?"

She pulls away from me and sits on the end of the bed, rubbing her hands across her face. "Maybe I did, originally, without realizing it. But I talked to your dad earlier, and he reminded me about what he was able to achieve when he was a teen father. Which is great, but it sounded like your mom made a lot of sacrifices to help him get there."

I sit next to her. "She did. But she knew what she was supporting, and when the time came for her to do something, my dad took on more at home so she could work on developing her business. They took turns, and now Mom has made this name for herself while Dad is retired. They call it seasons. Their seasons have had different focuses, but they've always had each other."

Dallas is quiet, thoughtful; there's the tiniest hint of a smile in her eyes that no one else would notice, but I do. I notice all of her micro-expressions, and right now, she's considering something that cuts through all of the ache her mind is bringing her. I'm dying to know what it is.

"What's on your mind, Cheer?"

She looks at me. "Just how lucky I am to have you."

I lean in and kiss her, and then I say something that is no doubt going to ruin her mood even further. "Baby, you have to ease up on this whole situation. We've had this conversation. Gabby's life is her own. Josh isn't a total deadbeat, and unless you want to push your best friend away, you have to stop trying to change what's already done. I know you want the best for her. You wanted her to take her big brain to college, and you don't want her life to slip by before she's had the chance to live it. But this is her situation to make the most of now. Just love her and let her do her thing."

Dallas's eyes start to glisten, and she purses her lips together to stop her chin from quivering. "I'm so exhausting, Drayton. Do you not get tired of talking me out of emotional turmoil?"

I cup her chin and meet her beautiful eyes. "If I didn't want to deal with your lows, I wouldn't deserve your highs, baby."

Her chin quivers as a tear slips down her cheek, and I brush it off with my thumb.

"Besides, I love the fact that you care so fucking much about people. I do, I love it. I think you just have to work on how you show it sometimes."

"I wanna be offended by that," she sobs. "But you're right."

I laugh and quickly hook an arm around her waist, dragging her onto my lap. "It happens so rarely."

"I've been thinking," Dallas says, sniffing. "Would it be crazy if I transferred to SMU in the spring?"

Shit. "What?"

"I could do a year in California and then transfer to SMU to start next fall. We could be closer."

It takes me a second to figure out what to say, and the hesitation is enough to make Dallas's eyes narrow.

"Yeah," I say, because it won't matter soon, not when she knows I'm joining her in California.

She stares at me for a moment. "You don't seem sure."

"I'm very sure," I say. "Sounds like a plan."

"Sounds like a plan?" she parrots. "I kind of expected more excitement at the idea of me moving to Texas."

There's probably some sort of way I'm supposed to respond to this situation, but I'm hung up on the fact that Dallas is telling me she'd want to move to Texas to be closer to me. How is this the same girl who blew up at me for even considering a college in California? The upcoming separation must really be fucking with her, and that is weighing on me big time. I don't know what to say; there's too much to sift through.

"This feels like the kind of idea that would've made you ecstatic," she says, brow furrowed. "You're being so . . . indifferent."

"I'm just surprised, Cheer. You have a plan, and I was never going to change that. Are you worried we're not going to go the distance?"

"No," she snaps.

"Neither am I," I say. "Baby, if we ended up at closer colleges, I'd be the happiest man alive. But you're going to love CalArts. You've been dreaming about it forever. I'm not going to hold out hope that you'll want to leave once you get there."

Her gaze is full of confusion and a little bit of hurt. I feel awful, but I know it won't last. As long as she chooses the path she's always wanted, and she does it for herself and gets on that flight, it'll all be worth it.

"We'll see, I guess," she mumbles. "No point thinking about it right now." My head is spinning as I stare at her. She's considering giving up

CalArts, for me. It shouldn't make me as happy as it does, but damn, it's nice to know she wants to be as close to me as I do to her.

~

The next morning, Dallas gets her period. I'm not at all surprised. I could tell it was coming. She keeps a basket of supplies in my bathroom, so she's all set, but she gets sore. Cramps and headaches. She curls up in my bed, and I get her a heating pad, even though it's hot as hell outside. I turn the AC down so low that Mom comes and finds me and asks why I'm turning the upstairs into an icebox. All I have to do is tell her that Dallas is cycling down the red brick road and she nods with understanding.

I end up putting on a hoodie while we watch a movie, and for most of the morning, we don't leave my bedroom. It's after twelve when she finally sits up and pushes her nest of hair back from her face.

"I should get up," she sighs. "I should go find Gabs and fix this shit."

"You want me to go get some lunch?"

She tilts her head back and forth. "I could eat. What are we having?"

"Red meat. I'd suggest my red meat, but that doesn't have the iron you need right now."

Her little laugh is tired. "Both thoughtful and suggestive in one sentence."

"Steak burritos?"

"That sounds good."

Dallas showers while I head out to get lunch. When I come back, Gabby and Josh are leaving. The three of us stand in the foyer, the brown paper bag of food hanging from my hand.

"How's it going?" I ask.

Josh furrows his brow a little. "Fine. You?"

He doesn't know the girls are fighting, I can see it in the way Gabby is staring straight into my soul with a warning look. I'm not sure why she hasn't told him.

"Dallas find you?" I ask her, and she shakes her head. "Oh, she wanted to tell you something."

"We're going out for lunch," Gabby says, slipping her arm through Josh's. "She can tell me later."

Josh looks between us with a little confusion as Gabby pulls him past me and toward the front door, which I'd left half open for them. I guess she's still pissed if she doesn't want to hang around and hear Dallas out. Whatever. I'm not getting involved. I don't want to see my girl upset, but I have to take my own advice and let them fix this on their own.

Dallas is sitting on my bed when I get upstairs, dressed in denim shorts and a little white tank top. Her damp hair is in a braid down her back, and she looks a little more alive than she did earlier.

I put the food down next to her, grab her braid, pull her head back, and kiss her.

I love kissing her. She's got the lips of an angel. Which is the title of a song I played once in her presence, and she told me not to ever subject her to that again. I wasn't sure why until I actually listened to the words, and it was basically an ode to cheating. Dumbass move.

We eat our burritos while we watch Clueless, because Dallas said she's in the mood for something that doesn't require brainpower to follow. Mom pokes her head in the door at one point.

"Dallas, honey, how are you feeling? Do you need anything?"

Dallas covers her full mouth. "Oh, I'm fine, thank you. Drayton is taking good care of me."

Mom looks pleased as punch.

"How was your night with Cass?" I ask. "She drag you into anything wild?"

"No." Mom chuckles. "We had some wine and enjoyed a live band. It was very tame."

"You're probably lucky she was still hungover from the night before," I mumble.

Mom looks amused until she sees what we're eating and walks further into the room. "Are those store-bought burritos?"

I sigh. "Mom, I wasn't going to ask you to make me homemade burritos in the middle of a Sunday afternoon when I know it's your self-care day."

"But I do them so well." She pouts.

"Yeah, yeah, I know. It's your signature dish. How dare I buy the one thing you can cook."

She waves me off dismissively and heads back out of the room.

"You should spend more time with Dad in the kitchen, Mom," I shout after her. "You might learn something."

I get ignored.

Dallas and I finish our food, and Dallas cleans up the trash. "I'll take this downstairs and then find Gabs."

"She's gone, baby." I take the trash out of her hand and start out of the room. "She went out with Josh as I was coming in."

"Oh, okay."

I turn around when I realize she's not following me and find her packing up her tote bag, shoving last night's clothes into it. "You going home?"

"Yeah, can you give me a ride?"

I look at her like she's silly for asking and then slip her bag off her shoulder when she comes toward me, carrying it for her. Downstairs, I throw out the trash and check that I've got my phone and keys, then we head out to the Jeep that Josh and I share. He uses it when he's not with Gabby.

When we get to Dallas's house, I park on the road and look at her before I turn the engine off. "Do you want me to leave you here, or can I hang out?"

Now it's her turn to look at me like I'm silly. "You can come in."

"I don't want to assume. You might need some alone time."

She smiles at me. "I needed to get some shorts that aren't denim. My stomach is killing me."

"You should've said." I switch off the car. "I would've given you something else to wear."

We get out of the car, and I meet her at the sidewalk.

"Your clothes are enormous on me."

"Yeah. It's adorable."

Dallas walks inside first, holds the door open for me to follow, and then, when my back is to her, she slams it so fucking loud, I almost drop to the floor to hide from the threat to life. I spin around and stare at her.

"What the fuck?"

She blinks at me, saying nothing for the next few moments, and then she shrugs. "I guess Nathan isn't here."

I watch her walk past me down the hall, and then I pinch the bridge of my nose. Menstruation is always a good time with her.

"Baby," I say, leaning on her doorframe while she sifts through her drawers, "you good?"

She pulls out a pair of blue sweat shorts and looks at me, confused, a little smile on her lips. "Yeah?"

I'm not so sure.

"Can you turn around for a sec?"

Oh, right. She won't change in front of me while she's on her period. I don't argue, facing the hallway for a few seconds until she tells me she's done. All of a sudden, we hear the toilet flush, and we both go still. A moment later, the bathroom door swings open and Nathan comes flying out, a little panicked. When he sees me, he relaxes. Sort of.

"Who the fuck is slamming the door?"

I consider taking the blame because Dallas is not herself at the moment, but she pokes her head out of her bedroom and waves at him with a shit-eating grin. "Me. The wind caught it."

Nathan props his hands on his hips. "What wind?"

Dallas doesn't bother responding. She disappears back into her room, and I mouth period to Nathan. He nods with understanding.

I should mention that she's also fighting with Gabs. Oh, and the fact that she knows he's not telling her about Emma. I'm part of the problem too because I wasn't enthusiastic enough about her suggestion to transfer next fall. My girl probably feels like all the control she usually has over her life is flying out the fucking window and she's hormonal. When it rains, it pours, I guess.

I go into her room and close the door. Dallas is sitting against her headboard with her knees up and her phone in her hand.

"Dray," she says when she can feel me watching her. "I know. I know I am losing it right now. I'm being a monster. I'm just ..."

Her breathing picks up, and she throws her phone down onto the bed to bury her face in her hands. I don't necessarily get it, but I've seen it before. I sit down next to her and wrap her in my arms.

"I have to work in a few hours," she mumbles.

"Call in."

"I can't. I need—"

"You need to take care of yourself, Dallas. Wren will cover your shift. Call in."

I'm relieved when she listens because this isn't about not wanting her to work so I can have her all to myself. This is about the fact that her brain is no doubt jam-packed full of bullshit that she's struggling to process, and she can't give her job what it needs right now. It's not long after she calls in that she falls asleep on my chest. I hold her tight and let her sleep.

~

Dallas and I sit at the breakfast bar later that evening eating beef bowls. Nathan is watching television. Neither of them has said a lot to each other, but I can tell Dallas has been doing her best to correct her internal storm so it doesn't seep out.

Dad texts me for the third time since I've been here and asks why I haven't worked out today. I do my best to prioritize training every single day, but I haven't had time to fit it in. I figure I'll head off soon. Dallas could probably use some time to get her own shit done. She likes having me around, but she probably needs to talk to Gabs.

Nathan walks into the kitchen to rinse his bowl and casts a quick look at his sister. "Haven't seen you much these last few days. What have you been up to?"

It's a friendly enough question, but Dallas lifts her head and gives him what I see is an evil smile.

Shit. Here we go.

"Oh, around," she says. "We've been planning the baby shower at Drayton's, and the other night we spent the night in Fort Collins."

Nathan's reaction would be obvious to the blind. His brows fly up, and he nods. "Fort Collins? Huh, random."

Dallas looks confused. "Not really. Drayton's aunt lives there. We were babysitting his cousins."

He swallows with a forced smile. "Cool."

"Mm-hmm. Yeah, and then on Saturday morning, we went to this super delicious waffle shop on Main. So good. I highly recommend it."

Nathan stares at his sister; she stares back. I watch them both as if I'm watching the timer on a bomb tick.

"Main?" He sucks in a breath. "On Saturday morning? Yesterday morning?"

Dallas continues to stare, and I'm not even sure she's blinking. I'm curious as to which one of them will break first. Dallas didn't want to force a confession, but I'm going to assume her mood left no room for pretending this evening.

Nathan presses his lips together and inhales a long, deep breath of defeat. "I was . . . also on Main yesterday morning."

Dallas drops her jaw open, sarcastic surprise all over her face. "You don't fucking say."

Nathan's shoulders drop with a sigh. "You saw her?"

Dallas opens her mouth like she's about to unleash absolute hell, but I put a hand on her thigh under the breakfast bar and give it a gentle squeeze. It stops her in her tracks, and she pinches her mouth shut. Her entire frame slumps, and she swallows hard. She doesn't want to do it like this.

"Yeah," she says calmly after a few moments. "I did."

"Emma, from the campground," Nathan clarifies.

Dallas's spark ignites just a little, and she scoffs. "Was there a rotation going on that morning?"

Nathan glares at her, and she retreats.

"Sorry."

"We're . . . dating," he admits.

Dallas's lips quirk, fighting a smile. "Why didn't you tell me?"

Nathan runs a hand through his hair and then throws his arm up. "I don't know. I wanted to, but I also wanted it to be a sure thing before I did. I really like her, Dal. She's . . . kind of perfect, and I didn't want to introduce her into your life if it wasn't going to last."

"Sure. But how did it happen?"

I keep eating now that the situation has defused and listen in. I'm also curious.

"I bumped into her the next morning after our cold plunge, and we got to talking. I asked for her number, and we've seen each other pretty much every day since."

Dallas laughs lightly, and I look at her, soaking it in. It feels like forever since I've heard that sound. Realistically, it probably hasn't been more than twenty-four hours.

"You're never going to guess what I've been doing since that campground," Dallas says, and Nathan raises a brow, curious. "I've been searching for that woman so I could set you guys up. I literally had Gabs and Drayton calling physio clinics in Fort Collins."

Nathan laughs. "What? Really?"

"I thought you guys would be so cute together. I just want you to be happy."

"I know, kid." Nathan holds out a fist, and they bump.

I feel like I'm witnessing one of the weights on Dallas's shoulders lift.

"So," I say. "When can we expect a niece or nephew?"

Dallas giggles, and Nathan flips me off.

"We're really good sitters. We have references from Cassandra, my aunt. You met her yesterday."

Nathan's eyes go wide, and he points at us. "I knew you two were up to some bullshit with that setup."

CHAPTER 15

DALLAS
Seven weeks to go

Nathan and I talking yesterday was exactly what I needed. Not that it happened the way I wanted it to. I'm a little unstable when it comes to my period. I can't explain the temper I get. It feels like there's a dark cloud in front of my face. Everything is a big deal. Everything bothers me. It's not fair, and I tell myself to calm down, but my reactive reflexes are honed. Not to mention it feels like there's a huge weight on my shoulders. Gabs and I haven't talked, my future is confusing me, and Drayton's reaction—or lack thereof—to my suggestion to transfer has thrown me off. All summer, he's been nonchalant about the fact that our time is running out. It seems like he's already prepared to go our separate ways and be done with it. The fact that he didn't jump for joy when I suggested enrolling at SMU is so unlike him. For the first time, it made me feel irrelevant to him.

Deep down, I know I'm probably overreacting. Drayton only ever does things in my best interest, but still . . . it hurt. It hurt. I let it go, though. I don't trust myself not to overreact at the moment.

I'm back at work this afternoon. It was nice to take the afternoon off yesterday, but I need to keep working as much as I can. Wren is on too, covering for someone else this time. I love that she picks up whatever shifts she can. We clear two tables during a small lull between lunch and dinner. There's only about four people in here, but that will change in the next half hour.

"Are you feeling better?" Wren asks, putting dishes into her tray.

I spritz my table with cleaning product. "I have my period," I admit. "It was not a good afternoon."

"I'm all for women taking care of themselves during that time of the month."

"Yeah, I would not have been able to put my best customer service foot forward yesterday. I was such a mess. My best friend isn't talking to me right now."

Wren wipes her table down. "Oh, that sucks. I hate fighting with friends, it's the worst. Can it be fixed?"

"I hope so." I fill up the cutlery basket with clean knives and forks and set it in the middle of the table. "You're not into the whole college thing, right?"

Wren laughs, raising an eyebrow. "No, I'm not. I know you are. Is that what your fight was about?"

"Not exactly," I say, and we both head into the kitchen with our dishes. "I'm just curious, from your perspective, do you worry at all about not going to college? Like how that might impact your future long-term?"

Wren purses her lips with a small breath. "I'm afraid to answer this without offending you."

"You won't. I know a lot of people don't go to college. I'm just interested in your take."

Wren and I move toward the kitchen door so we can see the dining room while we talk. "Well, college used to be the main hub for learning. It was where professionals shared their knowledge, and the information wasn't readily available like it is today. We're in a generation where knowledge is at our fingertips. Anyone can learn anything at any time, and they can do it without the pressure of trying to complete a thousand papers in one week and crumbling under the weight of an impossible task load."

"I get that," I say. "I've learned so many dance techniques or perfected certain moves because of YouTube. I still want to go to college and work under the best instructors and have the degree that puts me in the running for more opportunities."

"Yeah, it depends on what you want to do with your life. Personally, I don't want a big student loan debt, and I don't want to live to work. I want to travel and paint and work enough to cover the bills and still find time to relax on a beach or go to a festival with friends or ski or whatever. I want to live, and I just don't value college for that. Some people do, and that's fine, but I'm not motivated by climbing career ladders."

What she's saying makes sense. "Gabs is pregnant, and I'm struggling with the fact that her boyfriend will never experience the same sacrifice as she will."

"They never do," Wren sighs, and we both watch a small group of girls wander into the diner, here for their afternoon sundaes, like clockwork. "Plenty of moms out there have done well for themselves, though."

"Oh, for sure, she can do whatever she puts her mind to. She's so smart," I say as Wren and I walk slowly over to the group of girls. "I handled expressing my concern all wrong, I guess. Her boyfriend pissed me off just for existing without the same repercussions as her, and now she's mad at me for being mad at him."

Wren laughs again. "I get exactly what you mean. It's so easy to be mad at the injustice of societal standards. It takes two to tango, though. Your friend will be fine, I'm sure, especially with someone like you in her corner. You'll just have to accept the fact that she has a baby daddy now, such is life."

We share a small smile, and then I push it all to the back of my head and focus on getting through the rest of the shift.

~

The next morning, I sit on the couch, my attention switching between my phone and the music video channel. I've found so much inspiration on this channel. I watch the background dancers, the singers, the production that goes into it. Music videos are a dying art; this channel itself seems like it's barely hanging on. But I would love nothing more than to do just this one day. Backup dance in a music video. Be on set, learn the choreography with other dancers.

I huff out a breath and look at my empty screen, Gabby's name in the recipient box.

Hey, are you at home?

I still believe I'm not entirely in the wrong. Sometimes Josh seems lazy. But perhaps that really is just my perception of him because Drayton spoils me with his attention and his acts of service. Is it so wrong to think that should be the standard?

I put my phone down and wait for a while. Gabs and I have fought before, and we always fix it, but it feels heavier right now. I'm leaving soon. We'll see each other less. A lot less. I don't want our last two months—or less than two months—to be spent with this weird tension between us. Even if it means apologizing to Josh.

I don't like the idea of that, but I'll do it.

My phone starts to ring, and I think it's Gabs for a moment until I see a number I don't recognize.

"Hello?"

"Hi," a cheerful, feminine voice greets me. "Is this . . . Dallas?"

"Yep."

"Hi, Dallas, it's Carol here from Part-Time Party. You requested a quote for some balloons and decorations, I believe?"

Gabby's baby shower. The one she told me to stop planning. "I did. Yes."

"Great, so we have that here," she tells me, and I can hear a mouse clicking. "So for fifteen large helium balloons in the pastel-yellow foil, it's going to be fifty-five dollars. The ten pastel-yellow regular balloon bunches will be twenty-six. Then there's the tabletop packages, which include a tablecloth, a centerpiece, a small bouquet, and napkins. Six of those come to 187."

"Uh, great." I think for a moment. That's a fair bit of cash for a small amount of decor. "I'll just go with the helium balloons for now, please."

There are dollar stores in town where I can get cheaper balloons and crafts and tablecloths and whatever else I need to make my own tabletop decor. It'll be a bit more work, but it'll save money. Ellie would be baffled. She loves a planner to take the work off her hands, and honestly, I don't blame her. Paying for convenience if you can just makes sense.

"Okay, great! I can send through an invoice, and once that's all squared up, we'll get the items ready for you to collect in store on the date you've selected. What email address should I send the invoice to?"

I give her Drayton's email address. He'd genuinely be furious if I spent that kind of money on balloons; he already told me he'd foot the bill. Although, I plan on getting a lot of it myself when I go to the dollar store anyway.

I ended up selecting July 25 as the date for the baby shower. That gives me a month, which I'm going to need to get the decorations scraped together. Plus, there's always a chance it'll take Gabs a little longer to forgive me.

When the call ends, I look at my screen and see a response from her.

At the library working. Why?

Want to talk. Do you wanna come over after work?

Her response is almost immediate.

No. If you want to talk, you can come and see me.

At work?

Shit, she is pissed. Which is fair. I remember when I first told her I'd be applying for CalArts and she got upset with me for planning to leave. To me, it felt like such a lack of support, which pissed me off. She knew I wanted out of this town, and it felt like she was making it all about her.

She wasn't, of course; she was going to miss me, and all she wanted to do was express that. Guilt creeps in when I think about how she must feel if she believes that I have no hope for the quality of her life or that I think the child she's carrying is going to be a curse. She can't change what's happened now, and even if I do wish things were different for her, I don't have to act like I'm so much better because it didn't happen to me.

Yes, at work.

Seems like an odd place to have a conversation about reconciliation, but whatever. I'll prove I want to fix things if that's what she wants. I ask her for directions to the area she's in and then head off. Nathan has the car. I have no idea where he is, but the sun is out, and it's not a long walk.

When I get to the library, I sigh at the AC blasting the second I walk through the doors. I underestimated how hot it would be to walk twenty minutes in peak summer sun. I wander upstairs and pull my hair into a bun. Strands of it are damp with sweat and sticking to my skin.

Gabs is in the adult fiction area. The same space Drayton and I were in when we had our little date here a few weeks ago. At the checkout desk, I ask the woman behind it if she can point me in the direction of Gabby. She lifts the desk flap on the counter, lets me in, and directs me through the door of the staff-only area.

I'm hesitant when I walk inside because I'm not staff and this feels weird.

I spot her almost immediately, though: she's standing at a large table covered in books with a handheld scanner, swiping it over the book barcodes and placing them in a big tub on wheels. On the outer edge of the room is a long desk stretching across three walls. There are several computers stationed there, more books, personal effects belonging to staff, posters on the walls, coffee cups, and handbags. It's just us in here, though.

"Returns?" I ask, and she looks up, nodding.

I walk over to the table and stand on the other side. She looks beautiful. Her long dark hair is in a bun, bangs frame her face, and she's wearing a tank top and a pencil skirt. Of course, the skirt accentuates her bump, but with her lithe frame, it works. She looks professional, at ease, and totally in her element, surrounded by books.

I lean both hands on the edge of the table, and the room falls silent apart from the beep of her scanner and the thud of books landing in the tub. I need to say something, but I don't even know where to start. I clench my jaw and grasp for words.

"You were right," I say, and her gaze flicks up toward me for a moment. "I didn't realize it, but I kind of assumed things were going to be hard and . . . unpleasant for you from now on. It's kind of understood these days that a lot of the hard work is left to the women, and the men's lives don't have to change all that much."

Gabs continues scanning, but her face is thoughtful.

"I just let it get to me way too much when Josh did even the slightest thing that I considered wrong," I continue. "But it wasn't fair to add stress to the situation by being such a bitch about it all. I swear, I have only ever wanted you to have everything you deserve, but I do support you, and I love that baby already. I don't think she's a curse or whatever."

Gabs puts her scanner down and looks at me, sadness in her gaze.

"It will be hard," she says. "It's going to be harder than anything I've ever done. But I don't want to believe my life and opportunities are over. That's how you were making me feel. Like nothing good could ever come out of this because I'm just not capable of making it happen. I mean, you were still pissed that I applied for community college!"

"No." I sigh and think carefully on my words. "No, I understood choosing to stay close to home, and there is nothing wrong with community college. I think in my brain . . . I just don't feel like it's fair that I get to go off to this great college and dance and follow my dreams when you're so much smarter than me, and you deserve that ten times more than I do. It feels . . . selfish of me. Genuinely. You belong at, like, Harvard or something."

Gabs's shoulders drop, and she lets out a little huff of laughter. "You're not selfish. You worked really hard on that dream, and you deserve it. I was never that driven. I want to do something I enjoy. I can do writing and English Lit at community college and still be close to home. Our goals have always been different, Dal. But you get it into your head that everyone should be aiming sky-high or something, and it comes from a good place, but you need to chill out sometimes."

I wince and nod because she's right.

"I love this job." Gabs looks around the room. "Like, genuinely love working here. I've been offered the opportunity to do a library science degree part-time while I'm working, and I can study from home after the baby is born. It's perfect. I can still write, I can get qualified in a job that I'm having so much fun in, and I don't have to incur a crippling student loan debt. It's going to be hard work, but that's not a bad thing."

"No," I say, smiling at her. "It's not a bad thing. I'm so sorry I was so awful and have the worst way of expressing my good intentions."

Gabs laughs and walks around the table with her arms spread wide. She pulls me into a hug, her bump between us. "I knew we'd be fine," she murmurs into my hair. "You just needed to feel the absence of my love in order to understand what you'd done."

We both giggle, and when she pulls back, I nod. "It's true. I can't last a day without you. And I'm proud of you. You suit this job, and I absolutely believe you are capable of doing anything you want. I promise, that's how I feel, and I'm sorry I made you think I feel differently. It's your happiness that matters to me. Are you happy?"

"Most of the time, I really am. Do I have moments of struggle? Yes, but I'm not unhappy."

"Then that's all I need to know."

She smiles at me. "You didn't stop planning the shower, right?"

"July twenty-fifth. It's all on."

"Yes." She lifts both fists with a little pump and walks back to her station. "Good. Well, I have to work now. If you see Josh, be nice."

"I promise."

She blows me a kiss.

I have Drayton pick me up because I don't want to walk in the sun again. My period is still going strong, and at this point, I just want to shower.

Drayton drives with his hat on backward and his elbow on the doorframe, one hand on the wheel, the other holding my hand. He's in a tank top and sweat shorts with a pair of compression shorts on underneath. He looks like he's been exercising. He's so hot.

"What were you doing at the library?" he asks.

"Talking to Gabs."

His hand squeezes mine a little. "You sort things out?"

"Yeah, we did," I say, smiling over at him. "Hey, I'm sorry about Sunday. Being a little . . . unstable."

"No apology needed, baby." He brings my hand to his mouth and kisses the top of it. "Your hormones don't play fair. I'm sure it fucking sucks to be the one going through it; it's no big deal for me to cushion it a little."

Sometimes I'm sure I don't deserve him.

"I got an invoice earlier," he says, and I give him a guilty grin. "Don't look at me like that. I told you I'd cover it. It was a lot less than I expected. You cutting down on costs and doing shit yourself?"

"Yeah. I can find and make things."

"But you don't have to."

"I want to."

He sighs and pulls onto my street. "Stubborn."

We pull up at home, and Drayton leaves the car running as I climb out. "I have to head back to Samuel and finish up training,"

"Oh, I should've realized you were training." I stand outside of the car with the door open.

"Cheer," he says, and I purse my lips, giving him an apologetic look. "Don't even start. You know I would never not pick you up."

"I know." I crawl across the passenger seat and lean over so I can give him a kiss. As he often does, he deepens it, holding my nape and finding my tongue with his. He draws it out with a few quick pecks across my nose and onto my cheeks.

"I'll find you later, baby," he says as I climb back out of the Jeep. "Oh, and Mom and Dad have booked the lake house for the fourth of July. If Nathan wants to come too, he's more than welcome."

I have no idea what Nathan's plans are, but I tell Drayton I'll talk to him and head inside. He knew I wanted to spend some time at the lake this summer, and I'd be willing to bet he talked his parents into arranging it.

When I get inside, I pause because Nathan is standing in the living room with his arms around Emma, his mouth over hers. I close the door, and the two of them part. Sort of. Their faces part. He keeps her close to him, though. He looks so genuinely happy, and it makes me smile.

"Dallas," Emma exclaims, pulling out of my brother's grasp and walking toward me. She gives me a hug, which I don't love, but whatever, it's nice of her. "Nathan told me about the fact that you've been looking for me."

"Oh." I look at Nathan with a sarcastic smile, and he grins with guilt. "I was searching with good intentions, I swear."

"I know," she says with a light laugh and a beaming smile. She's as beautiful as I remember. Tall, defined muscle, and incredible quads. "Nathan and I were just talking about the three of us going out for an early lunch. Are you free? You should invite your boyfriend too; I'd love to meet him."

"I was about to call," Nathan tells me. "But we don't have to invite Drayton. He doesn't have the sort of social awareness I like to dine with."

"Oh, be quiet," I say. "I'll ask him. I don't know if he'll be free for another hour, though, and I have work at one. But let me shower and dress and then we'll head off."

Drayton lets me know he most definitely does not want to miss out on lunch and tells me to give him half an hour. Which is perfect, because I need that time to get organized anyway. He offers to pick us all up, and when he arrives, it's in his dad's Range Rover, which I assume is because there's more legroom in the back than the Jeep. He's thoughtful like that. Nathan doesn't seem thrilled about the arrangement as we pile into the car, with him and Emma in the back.

"Hi," she says, sliding over for Nathan to follow. "I'm Emma."

"Drayton," he responds as I do up my belt in the passenger seat. He looks at me with pure admiration. "Didn't expect to see you again so soon. You look beautiful."

He leans across and gives me a kiss before pulling away from the curb.

The drive to the restaurant is uneventful. Drayton asks Emma about her work, where she lived before she moved to Fort Collins (which was Nevada), and how she's liking Colorado so far. I'm sure Nathan is sitting in the back seat waiting for something horrific to come out of my boyfriend's mouth.

We go to a little restaurant that serves simple foods with a gourmet twist. Pizzas, pastas, salads, loaded wedges, garlic breads. I'm not a huge fan of overly fancy menus where the food doesn't even sound real. Nathan will eat whatever as long as it's got protein in it.

The restaurant is garden inspired. It looks like a greenhouse with plants and shrubs and tiled floors with a water feature in the corner and lots of windows to allow light. We sit at a round four-seater table that reminds me of an old iron patio set, including all the intricate patterns in the seats.

We order, and then we start talking.

Emma tucks her brown hair behind her ears. "How did you two meet?"

Drayton, who is leaning back in his chair with his hand on my thigh, says, "The way she handled balls really impressed me."

Emma's brows fly up, and Nathan's head drops with disappointment.

"I caught his sloppy football throw," I correct with amusement. He's such a dick sometimes. "He was so impressed at the fact that I can throw, and then he crashed into my car, on purpose, to get my attention."

Emma laughs lightly and looks between us. "Is that the actual truth? Like, crashed into your car on purpose?"

"Yes, it's true," Nathan deadpans. "He's a dramatic fool."

He lifts his shoulders. "It worked."

I hum with disagreement. "I wouldn't say that was what did it. I mean, it did get my attention, but I thought you were an idiot."

Drayton waves me off. "You wanted me."

I roll my eyes, but he's not wrong. As irritated as he made me, I was ridiculously attracted to him from the moment he knocked on my door.

Nathan looks over at the kitchen, as if our food can't get here fast enough. Drayton makes him so nervous, and it shouldn't be so funny, but it is. He makes it even worse when he decides to give Nathan a little finger gun wave when Emma checks her phone. Three times in a row, getting goofier and goofier each time. Nathan realizes he's making fun of him for the first time he met Emma and looks over at me with a withering glare that I can barely see because I'm too busy dying of laughter.

I don't think Emma realizes what's going on, but eventually I smack Drayton on the leg to quit it.

Emma rests her elbows on the table and looks at me after she's put her phone down. "Nathan tells me you're off to CalArts for college soon. That's so exciting and such a huge move."

"Yeah," I say as our drinks are delivered to the table. We thank the waitress, who lets us know the food won't be long. "It is huge. I've been wanting to go to this school for so long, though, and I feel really lucky that I get to."

Emma looks between Drayton and me. "I'm sure it'll be hard going alone, though?"

"I don't think going alone will be the hard part," I say. "Leaving the people I love and not seeing them as often will be the hard part. I'm not used to going more than a few days without being around Nathan. I mean, he raised me. So that'll be weird. Drayton, I can live without."

"Oh, ha ha," he drones, slipping his arm around my shoulder and leaning into me so he can kiss my cheek. "You're hilarious."

I chuckle and lean into him too. At this point, I really don't think I could live without him, in some form at least. It's still on my mind that I offered to transfer to SMU and Drayton didn't seem too excited at the suggestion. I'm doing my best to pretend like it doesn't matter and remind myself how much he loves me. He might be right about crossing that bridge when we come to it.

"At least she doesn't have to worry about her brother now," Drayton says, leaning back in his chair, his arm resting on the back of mine. "You know, we talked about getting you hitched before we leave so you're not alone."

Emma covers her giggling mouth with her hand and looks over at Nathan, who shakes his head at both of us.

"No, no." I jump in and wave a hand across Drayton's face to hush him. "I just worried about him being lonely and thought it'd be nice if he found someone, which he did, and I'm glad."

Nathan folds his arms across his chest. "Yes, because I don't have friends or a job or anything else to keep me occupied apart from my little sister."

"That's not the same as a companion," I argue, watching Emma's cheeks redden. "Anyway. You're great, so I'm glad he asked for your number."

"Aw, thanks," Emma says, and when Nathan looks at her, his whole face softens.

"Suppose there's no need for Dad to make those calls to coaches in California now," Drayton says, and the three of us look at him, confused. Or, in Nathan's case, exasperated. "Oh, I just said Dad could help him find a job there if he wanted to move and be closer to Dallas."

Drayton and I had talked about that, but I didn't realize he'd mentioned it to Nathan. I wonder if Drayton is really worried about the fact that I'll be in California alone or if he's just stirring up drama to see how Emma reacts. Because that is most definitely something he'd do.

Emma looks over at Nathan, curious but not upset. "You've thought about going too? I love California. It's beautiful."

"The more, the merrier." Drayton grins.

Nathan shoots him a glare. "Can it." He turns his attention back to Emma. "I mean, not really. I thought about it. Ish. I hadn't made any solid plans or come to any conclusions as to how I feel about it, and then . . . well . . . I met you."

I'm not sure how I feel knowing that Nathan thought about moving too. It's sweet he'd want to remain close. I definitely wouldn't be opposed to it. Plus, the opportunity to coach college football would be huge for him, career changing, if that's where he wants to go in life. But it's also sweet that he's met someone who means enough to keep him here.

"Wow," I scoff jokingly. "Who cares about me then. I'll go alone. I'll be fine."

Nathan barely spares me a glance. "Yeah, I know."

The food gets brought to the table, and as the waitress sets it out, Nathan and Emma share a tender moment, leaning in close to one another while they whisper. This is what I wanted for him. Happiness.

JULY

CHAPTER 16

DRAYTON
Six weeks to go

Dallas is lounging her fine, bikini-covered body out in the sun on a pool chair. We're at the lake for the Fourth of July, the water is a stone's throw from the pool house, it's hot as fuck, and so is my girl. I sit on the seat next to her and stare, because I can and it's a privilege.

She's scrolling on her phone with her sunglasses on, and then her face screws up.

"What?"

"What?"

She lowers her phone, staring at the sky in confusion for a moment. "Wha—"

"What?"

She brings her phone back to her face and scrolls a little again. "I'm confused. What?"

Fuck me. "Girlwiththegreatracksayswhat."

She looks at me. "What?"

I throw my hands up. "Yeah, exactly. What, woman? Tell me."

"Oh." She waves the phone in her hand. "I swear my seat for the flight to LA has changed."

I remain cool. So cool. "Oh . . . weird."

"I could've sworn I was in thirty-four A, and now I'm in sixteen B."

"You don't fly much, but this happens sometimes," I explain, which is actually another not lie. "Someone with a car seat or something might book a flight, or like a family with small kids that need to be seated together, so they'll shift people around."

"Oh." She shrugs, unbothered. "Whatever. It doesn't really matter where I sit, I guess."

"How come you were checking up on that?"

"I just wanted to check in on the flight, remind myself of the boarding time, that sort of thing. Keep it fresh in my head."

"Fair."

Dallas stretches out her hand for me to take, her smile all sated. "Thanks for bringing me here. It's beautiful, and this house is . . . insane."

I gesture for her to scoot over and then lie down next to her, putting my arm under her head. She never has to thank me for doing shit like this. It brings me an immense amount of happiness. I kiss her cheek, her nose, her lips. She smiles, and I kiss her again just so I can taste it.

We decide to go for a swim in the lake. It's fresh and cool, and I carry Dallas with her thighs around my waist while I wade into deeper water. I can see Mom and Dad on the lake house deck; Josh and Gabby are here somewhere too. Dallas is noticeably kinder when it comes to Josh at the moment. I'm not sure if it's just for her best friend or if she's gained a new perspective.

Dallas looks at me as the water gently laps around our chests. Her hair is all wet and sexy, and her beautiful face glitters with water drops. If I dropped her right now, she'd disappear under the surface. We're out too deep for her short little legs.

"I saw the box of things you're packing up to take to college last night before we left," she tells me.

"Uh-huh."

"There's not a lot in there." Her tone is curious, and I'm not sure where this conversation is going, but she's definitely got a direction. I can tell when she's making her way to a point.

My fingers graze her lower back under the water. "I'll pack more. I still have time."

"Dray," she says, playing with the hair on the back of my head. "How are you feeling about leaving home?"

Now I see where this is heading. I shrug. "I'm feeling like it's . . . inevitable. I've always known I'd go to college."

"You don't seem all that bothered. Like you won't miss home." I hear the undertone of her statement. She's wondering if I won't miss her.

I wonder if I've been far too casual about our impending "separation." If I really were about to spend the next however many years in a different state than the love of my life, I'd be tweaking the fuck out, and she's probably aware of that. The fact that she told me I'm being indifferent the other week is still lingering between us. She hasn't brought up SMU again, but I responded all fucking wrong.

"I'm in denial," I say, not wanting to wade into a dangerous conversation that would force me to lie with no way to twist my words so it can be by omission. "I'm in the moment, Cheer. This is summer, and we had a deal: school doesn't exist right now. I'll fall apart later."

She looks at me with those damp lashes of hers flickering with slow blinks. "Are you going to miss your mom and dad? Josh? You don't talk about it much, and I want you to remember that you can. You carry so much of my weight."

I jostle her in my arms. "You're not that heavy. The water is doing most of the work."

"Dray," she chides, tightening herself around me even more, our faces just inches apart. "You let me lean on you for so much, all of my moods and fears and worries. I just want you to know I've got you too. If you're nervous about leaving or you're anxious about missing your family, I want you to feel like you can talk to me."

I love this girl so much. I lean in and kiss her, and then I press my forehead to hers, and I feel like my heart is beating out of my chest.

"Dallas, you're the only person in the world I'd ever bare my soul too," I murmur. "You have my entire heart, and I feel safe when I need someone to hold me together, knowing it's going to be you. Please don't ever doubt how much I trust you."

With her forehead still pressed to mine, she takes a deep breath and gives a barely-there nod. "Okay."

"We had a deal," I remind her again/

One I forced her into, where we don't talk about what's to come, we just enjoy being in the moment. It was so I could safeguard against having to lie all the time. I still think it's important she has the courage to make this move for herself, though.

When I first had this whole idea, she hadn't shown an ounce of concern over leaving. I knew she'd miss me, but she was still all for CalArts. I thought it would be easy to pretend I was going to Texas, and then she shifted and started looking at me like the thought of being apart was too much for her to bear. It's not that I want her to wallow in sadness, but I want her to remember how excited she was to go to CalArts in the first place. She probably has every right to be mad at me for pursuing her and making her fall in love with me. She didn't want attachments before she left. Though, I'd argue she'd have had a hard time leaving Nathan and Gabby too when the time came. I know her, she has a big heart. It was never going to be easy.

She leans back, hands still clasped behind my neck, and puts on a brave smile. "Yeah, we're in the moment. Nothing else exists right now."

"Just you and me, baby." I kiss her, tongue dipping into her mouth and hands moving down onto her ass.

She breaks apart and looks toward the shore. "Well, us and your parents on that deck right there, so let's keep it—"

I kiss her again, and she laughs into my mouth, her hand coming up to cup my cheek. This is a moment I could exist in forever. The love of my life wrapped around me in nothing but a little bikini, her torso pressed to mine and her entire grip tight around me, as if she can't get close enough. Where else in the world would I ever need to be?

~

It's dark, there's a small fire crackling on the deck, the doors are open, and the screen doors are closed to prevent mosquitoes. Dallas is in the kitchen with a little sheer dress thing draped over her bikini. She's cutting up fruit and sliding pieces onto skewers, along with marshmallows. There's a bowl of chocolate dip beside her.

The lake house has an open plan on the lower floor. There's one step down from the living area into the kitchen and dining space, which is huge, with wooden cupboards and dark granite countertops. The dining table could host the football team, and the tall ceiling has large wooden beams stretching across it. Mom and Dad share the house with four other families. Of the group, I think we're the only ones who really use it.

The speaker is thudding with music, drowning out the parties going on further down the lake at the neighboring houses. From the deck, we can see bonfires, sparklers, fireworks, and silhouettes of people dancing on the shore. Gabby and Josh are sitting outside by the fire pit, and Mom and Dad are watching a movie in the living room, cuddled up and being all fucking cute with their wine and bowl of chips.

"I just got a message from Derek," I tell Dallas, coming up beside her and slipping my hand under her dress . . . thing. My hands coast along her back, over the tie of her bikini. If we were alone, I'd pull it undone for sure.

Dallas peers at me as I lightly rub her back. "And?"

"He and some of the boys are down the way at one of the houses."

She raises her brows with a knowing smile. "So go?"

"I thought we all could. I'm not going without you. If you're not into it, we'll hang out here." It doesn't bother me at all. I want to be where she is.

She thinks about it for a moment. "Yeah, we can go. Gabs might not want to, though."

I point at her platter of fruit skewers. "All done?" She nods and steps back a little as I pick the platter up with one hand and grab the bowl of chocolate dip with the other. "Leave the mess, I'll clean it up."

She drops the handful of fruit skins she's already collected into the trash and follows me out onto the deck where Josh and Gabby are tonguing each other. "Fuck, that's gross," I joke.

"You're one to talk. You might as well have been having sex out on the lake earlier. It was pornographic," Josh says from where he and Gabs are stretched out on one of the deck chairs that might as well be a bed.

Dallas drops into a single seater, but I pick her back up after I've put the food down on the table and sit down with her in my lap. "I was having sex," I lie. "I don't give a fuck."

"We were not," Dallas sighs as Gabs sits up and grabs a skewer.

"You two want to come down to Derek's?" I ask as Dallas dips a skewer in chocolate and hands it to me. I give her thigh a tap in thanks. "He's like four houses down."

"Will there be alcohol and, like, drunk people?" Gabby asks with chocolate on her cheeks.

"Nah, I think they're all sober and sitting around the campfire singing songs."

Gabby pouts at my sarcasm. "I don't want to be around drunk people.

I miss it too much. Plus, I'd look ridiculous at a party with a baby bump."

Josh finishes off a skewer and drops it onto the fire. "You'll be fine. You can't even tell when you're wearing a big enough T-shirt."

"That's true," Dallas adds.

Gabby thinks about it for a while and then settles back onto the chair, snuggling up. "No. You go, Josh. I'll hang out here with the other parents."

Josh doesn't immediately decline that idea, and I look at Dallas, who is staring daggers at him. I'm not even going to defend him this time.

As if sensing he's one wrong word from being kicked in the face by my girl, he shakes his head. "No, I'll hang out here with you. I'm not going to leave you here."

Gabby peers across the fire at Dallas, and the atmosphere becomes a little awkward. I guess. I don't particularly care if there's a lot of obvious unspoken tension. Dallas would be within her rights to call him out if he did decide to leave Gabby here alone.

"Fine, I'll come too." Gabby stands up and stretches. She's wearing a big T-shirt already, and the others were right, you can't see the bump all that well. "You'll be sober, right, Dallas?"

"Yeah," Dallas says, standing too. "I can't stand being hungover."

~

I'm not going to blame Dallas for being drunk right now. I tasted the cocktails she was drinking, and they were sweet and delicious but fucking potent. I'm positive she didn't mean to end up like this.

I watch her bonding with a random group of girls who were already here. Also dancers, except dancers who actually danced in a dance studio because they grew up in Denver, where there was plenty of that available. Dallas is hanging on to every word about their experiences and their future endeavors at Julliard.

She's standing at the bar, which is the fanciest damn bar I've ever seen at a house party. Who the hell serves a full cocktail menu at a lake house banger? She talks so animatedly when she's drunk: her hands join the conversation, her cheeks are flushed, and her glassy eyes are wide. She's not absolutely trashed, but she's heading there, that's for sure.

"Nah, man, he's going to UCLA."

I tune back in to the conversation I was having with Derek and three other dudes I've never met before.

"Oh, true." Derek's friend Kaden nods, holding his beer, a seven-hundred-dollar pair of sunglasses on his face in the middle of the night. "Good school that."

"California, man." Derek let it be known he was jealous when I told him I'd be going there.

We're only a few feet from Dallas on the other side of the bar, but I don't think she heard him. This place is packed, loud, and everyone is shouting just to be heard. I whack Derek in the chest. "If you tell one more fucking person I'm going to UCLA, I'm going to bury your head out in the sand. Just your head."

Kaden, Jordan, and the third guy, who I think is named Jesse, look confused. "Is it a secret?"

I'm not telling them the whole story in case one of them thinks it'd be funny to go and tell Dallas and then the whole night gets spoiled when I end up in jail for losing my temper with them. "Something like that," I say.

I peer over at where Dallas is standing and sigh when I see some pretty dude with dark hair and a great jaw talking to her with a look I know all too well. He's smitten. He's locked in, awe on his face while she tells him something. I mean, I don't blame him. I look at her like that too.

The conversation around me resumes without my attention because I'm too busy watching this dude flirt like he does it for a fucking job. I might fall in love with him.

I startle when Gabby appears beside me with a bottle of water in her hand, Josh nowhere to be seen. "Should I go intervene?"

I laugh lightly and slip my hands into my pockets. "I trust her."

"Oh, that's not the point. He is definitely thinking he has a chance, and she's way too oblivious to realize he's trying to take her upstairs. I heard her telling him about Nathan's ACL injury when I grabbed a water. Does that look like a man who's listening to a sports injury story? Or a man who is thinking about putting her in seven positions in seventy seconds?"

I look at them again, frowning. Yeah, she's right. He is picturing my girl naked, and I don't like that.

"Where's Josh?" I ask before I leave Gabs standing here on her own.

"He's in a card game."

I look at her and can tell she's over it. We've been here for the last four hours. Seems like enough. "I'm going to get Dallas, and we'll head off?"

"Oh, sure." She nods. "I'll tell Josh."

I walk over to the bar, step around to the other side, and come in behind Dallas, wrapping an arm around her middle while holding eye contact with the dude attempting to woo my woman. His face admits defeat, and he nods in greeting as Dallas stumbles and I keep her up.

"She didn't tell me, man," he says and holds up his hands like he's surrendering after a crime.

"Tell you what?" Dallas tilts her head, her back pressed against my front.

"You didn't tell me you had a man." He looks at her differently now, like she's wronged him. I don't fucking like it.

"Oh, I do." Dallas slurs a little and taps the arm I have around her front. "I do. He's him. This is my man. I didn't tell you? Oh. I didn't mean to not . . . I jus—"

"Did you ask?" I cut Dallas off and keep staring at the dude because while I thought it was amusing before, I don't like his fucking face and the entitlement on it.

"She should mention it if someone comes and talks to her," he bites out. "I would think you'd agree, man. She's your girl."

"You were talking to her for five minutes." I keep hold of Dallas, who's a little unstable on her feet but can't budge me off balance at all. "About what? Did you ask her if she wants to fuck? Or for her number? What was so deceiving about her conversation?"

He turns red and shrugs. "I don't remember what we talked about."

"Nathan," Dallas giggles. "You said you recognized me from when I was at Nathan's game once, because your brother was on his team, and you asked how he was because he got hurt."

I try not to smile because even though my girl sounds drunk as hell, she's so fucking cute. "So she's just supposed to tell you to fuck off over a question like that?" I ask. "She can't have the respect of a normal conversation with another dude because . . . why?"

"Oh, come on." The guy won't look at me now, and I think we have the attention of people close by. "We know what girls are like."

"Because you came over and decided you wanted to take her upstairs. Anything outside of that possibility and she becomes less of a person to you?"

He clenches his jaw. "Hey, if your girlfriend wants to dress like she's available and entertain other dudes, that's a you problem."

Oh, fuck this. I gently push Dallas out from between us and step forward. She grabs the back of my shirt.

"Oh, shit, here we goooo." She giggles as this little shit bag backs up, and so do the girls behind the bar. "Drayton—"

Josh steps in beside me and puts a hand on my chest. "Let's head out, dude."

"Get the fuck out of my way," I say.

"Yep." Josh moves aside.

"Tell me that again," I warn, about ready to quit talking to this moth-erfucker. "Tell me, I fucking dare you."

He broadens his shoulders and looks at me. "Or what?"

I huff out a humorless laugh. "Apart from the fact that you're a prick, she is drunk." I tip my head at Dallas, who is standing beside me, her hand still gripping the bottom of my shirt. "And I don't feel like leaving you here to be a fucking predator all night."

I grab the front of his shirt and hit him so hard in the face, he's lights out and crumpling to the floor in seconds. There's a gasp from around us; however, the rest of the party is still in full swing, people none the wiser as the music drowns out the drama. A few of the girls crouch down beside him. He's alive. He'll be fine.

"Lock him in a closet or something," I suggest, taking Dallas's hand and leading her straight over the prick on the floor. I hope she steps on him.

She follows along as I weave through the crowd and keeps her other hand wrapped around my arm. I expect Gabs and Josh will follow if they want to.

Outside on the grass, away from the noise, Dallas tugs on my hand. "I wasn't doing anything," she slurs, sounding worried. "I wouldn't."

I stop and turn to her; her face is downturned and sad, and I push her hair behind her ear. "You did nothing wrong," I tell her. "Don't think about it."

She nods, all wobble and drunk smiles. "Okaaaay."

~

Eventually, after Dallas has finished emptying her guts into the shrubs outside, I've helped her brush her teeth, and she's in bed snoring, I head back downstairs to get a bowl and a glass of water. I'd really like to believe she's finished throwing up, but I'd prefer to be prepared.

I'm filling up a glass when Dad appears at the steps and comes down into the kitchen in his sleep shorts and T-shirt.

Shit, he probably heard Dallas asking me if she smells like vomit over and over again.

"Morning, sir," I say, grinning like I don't have a care in the world.

"Very early morning." He smiles back, and now I'm scared.

"Don't suppose you being awake is a coincidence?"

"Definitely wasn't the sound of your very drunk girlfriend hurling outside of our window."

That fact didn't cross my mind once. Picking up the big bowl and the water, I nod, brows raised, and smile. "Great. Good night, then."

"Hang on," Dad says, holding out a hand as I attempt to walk past him. "What happened to your hand?"

I assess the red swelling and dark bruising across my knuckles and shrug.

Dad gives me a flat stare. "Should I expect the police to show up here?"

"No." I roll my eyes like he's being dramatic. "Some asshole was hitting on Dallas, being a creep, and acting like she was asking for it."

Dad's expression softens with understanding. "He go out cold?"

I laugh, caught off guard by the question. "Yeah, lights out."

Dad nods, looking thoughtful. "Sometimes people need to learn a lesson."

"I don't play around when it comes to her," I say. "She feels safe with me, and I want to keep it that way."

Dad claps me on the shoulder and smiles. "You're a good man, son. Your mother may not be so understanding, but that's for you to deal with."

I chuckle, feeling pleased with his compliment. "Yes, sir."

"All right, get some sleep."

I give him a quick nod. "Night, Dad."

CHAPTER 17

DALLAS

Six weeks to go

I'm lying on the couch in the living room, a glass of water on the side table, which Drayton pushed up next to me, a straw in my mouth, like I'm a hospitalized patient that can't lift her own damn head.

I'm not sure if I can, though. It's killing me.

Drayton sits beside me with my feet in his lap, scrolling his phone. I had no intention of getting drunk last night; those drinks were deceitful.

I'm dehydrated, for the most part. After we got back to the lake house, I spent half an hour throwing up in a bush while Drayton kept my hair back and my head aimed at the ground so I wouldn't vomit on myself.

Pathetic.

He never complains, though.

I think about the altercation he had with that guy last night. It's a bit of a blur, but I remember most of it. I remember how hot my man is when he's defending my honor. I twist a little so I can look at him. His gaze flicks to me, and he raises a brow in question.

"What's up, baby? You feeling okay?"

"You're hot."

He cracks a smile, dropping his phone beside him. "What makes you say that?"

"I was thinking it, so I said it."

"I like to live by that code also."

I laugh lightly, but it's kind of gurgled and sounds more like I'm half dead. He indeed loves to say exactly what he's thinking.

He picks my hand up and kisses it, and I notice the bruising across his knuckles. I'm not going to ask him what he was thinking or act like it was uncalled for. I know well enough by now that Drayton will not stand for predatory behaviour in any form, and even though I completely missed the cues last night, he didn't.

Gabby and Josh join us in the living room with a plate of breakfast each, filing in and sitting in the seats where the sun is coming in through the windows on the other side of the room. We acknowledge each other with small smiles and waves; Gabby looks at me with sympathy, but I hope this serves as a reminder of what she's not missing out on. I feel like shit.

Leroy and Ellie wander in next, and I quickly adjust myself into a seated position, hoping I don't look too hungover. I tuck in next to Drayton, and he rests his hand on my thigh, picking his phone up again.

The six of us sit spread out in the living room, everyone else eating quietly; the smell of warm bread, bacon, and coffee stirs my stomach awake. I don't even like coffee, but it smells like a café in here.

Ellie watches Drayton for a few moments, chewing her food, and then she points at him with her fork. "Why is your hand bruised?"

"Probably because he punched someone in the face last night." Josh grins when Drayton cuts a look across the room at him that I would not want to be on the receiving end of.

I think Josh will take whatever chance he can to pull one over on Drayton, simply because Drayton will never hesitate to publicly embarrass him.

Ellie gasps. "What? Why? Why are you always hitting people?"

Drayton looks confused. "He deserved it."

"Who?"

Drayton shrugs with boredom. "Some little fuck flirting with Dallas."

It was a little more than that, but I keep quiet.

"So you hit him?" Ellie seems flabbergasted. I don't think she knows I was drunk and the dude was not well intentioned.

Drayton slowly nods. "Like I said, he deserved it."

"No, that doesn't mean you can just go around punching people." Ellie aggressively cuts into her toast and egg. "Even if they do deserve it. That's not how life works. There are consequences."

"Yes, I know, I delivered a consequence last night. I'd do it again."

Leroy looks like he's trying not to laugh as he chews on his food and keeps his head down.

"If I deserved to be punched in the face," Drayton says with complete confidence as he rests his arm on the couch behind me, "I'd take it like a man."

"Oh, no you wouldn't," Ellie argues. "You'd fight back."

"I never said the guy couldn't fight back. He just didn't get up again."

"Oh geez," Ellie cries out and throws her hands in the air, knife and fork still in her grip.

Honestly, I find her son incredibly hot, but I can see why she worries about him.

The room falls quiet again, Ellie furiously eating, Leroy doing his best to pretend he's not amused. I like this side of him, he's so much more . . . human than he was when we first met.

Gabs and Josh take their empty plates to the kitchen and then disappear. I stand up and stretch, and when I look down at Drayton, I see him looking me over with his bottom lip between his teeth. Animal.

"Wanna get something to eat with me?" I ask.

"You on the menu?"

I give him a deadpan face and don't look around the room to find out if his mom and dad heard that, because I'm sure they did.

"I'm going to get breakfast," I tell him, and he stands up too, slipping his phone into his pocket.

"Feeling better today, Dallas?" Leroy asks as we go to leave. I stop in place and stare like a deer caught in headlights.

"Uh, hmm?" I look at Drayton for help and see the amusement in his face.

"All that throwing up last night. You must've eaten something bad."

My cheeks warm up, and now it's Ellie's turn to hide her laughter. I think I'd be more embarrassed if I wasn't used to Drayton's total lack of filter.

"Must've," I say as Drayton rests his hand on my lower back and guides me toward the step down into the kitchen.

"Quit heckling my girl," he calls over his shoulder.

We spend the rest of the day, and the next, lounging by the pool, swimming in the lake, playing board games, watching movies, and eating. Gabs reads like three books while we're here, and then we have to head home, back to work and real life. I love the lake. I want to make sure we come back every summer if we can.

~

I'm unpacking my bag, most of my clothes going into the washing machine, when Nathan wanders down the hall, passing the washroom and then backing up and peering in. He leans on the frame and crosses his arms.

"You just get back?"

"An hour ago," I say, pouring too much detergent into the drawer. "Oop, shit. Oh well. How was your holiday weekend?"

Nathan declined the offer to come along to the lake, which didn't surprise me. He and Emma went camping . . . again. The two have been seeing each other for just a few weeks, so it surprised me she didn't have prior plans with her friends or family. Then again, I don't know anything about her personal relationships.

"It was good," Nathan says as I switch on the machine and wander past him, out into the kitchen. "We just hung out with a few of Emma's friends and her sister. She's real close with her sister."

"Oh, so there was a group of you?"

"Yeah." Nathan drops onto a stool at the breakfast bar while I start pulling out sandwich ingredients from the fridge. "She had plans lined up, so I just joined in."

"Was that fine?" I ask. "Like, did you get along with everyone?"

He nods. "Yeah, it was cool. Most of her friends are newish to her too, being that she's only lived in Fort Collins for a few years. But her sister flew in from Nevada."

"Is she nice? How old is she?"

"She's twenty-three," he says. "Yeah, she's nice. I don't think she likes me, but she wasn't awful."

I laugh as I spread out some bread on the board between us and start buttering it. "Why wouldn't she like you?"

"I don't know." He shrugs dismissively. "She made some comment about body counts and then looked at me like I deserved jail time. I've been pretty honest with Emma about my past, but I didn't think she'd tell her sister."

"Of course she would." I look at him like he's a few screws loose. "That's a sister thing. I mean, I know I don't have an actual sister, but I consider Gabs to be like one, and I tell her everything. Everything. Even when I know she'll disapprove, I still tell her and vice versa. She's like my sounding board for all the thoughts I have all the time. It needs to go somewhere. I actually feel blessed to have found that in a person."

Nathan watches me with an almost pained look on his face, lips pinched tight. "I don't understand how girls have, like, projectile word vomit all the time. Why does it need to come out?"

I start laughing as I top my sandwich with shredded chicken. "That reminds me that I got so drunk at the lake by accident and I vomited for, like, half an hour in the shrubs outside and Drayton's parents heard the whole thing."

Nathan screws his face up at me. "Gross, dude."

"Yeah, anyway," I say, cutting my sandwich in half. "Girls just talk. You've heard me and Gabs enough, I thought you'd know this."

"I just didn't think she'd tell her sister that I used to get around. That seems unnecessary. Wouldn't she want her sister to approve of me if they're that close?"

I bite my sandwich and shrug, watching him with a full mouth while I chew. "You should ask her," I suggest after I've swallowed my mouthful. "My guess is, Emma was worried about whether she could trust you, and she was voicing those concerns to her sister, but she likes you too much to actually call it off. Now her sister knows the truth, her advice was ignored, and she's never going to trust you herself. If she lives in Nevada, who cares?"

Nathan's brows rise with contemplation. "That's definitely a theory."

"Do you want me to invite Emma to Gabs's baby shower?"

Nathan looks confused at the abrupt change in topic. "Uh, I don't know. Would that be weird? She doesn't know Gabriella."

"I'm asking so I know for sure just in case you get offended in a couple of weeks that I didn't invite her."

He sits there, brows pinched, more thoughtful concern on his face than the situation calls for.

"Never mind. I'll invite her closer to the time if she hasn't decided to listen to her sister and make a run for it."

Nathan glares at me. "I'm not going to mess around on her."

"That's good."

~

I walk through Target with a cart and drop things into it that I can use to decorate Gabs's baby shower. Little yellow ceramic jars to hold the bouquets. Ellie said she has a friend whose garden is abundant with flowers we can pick. Some cute white tablecloths with a border of yellow daisies on the edge. Lots of balloons. Some small gift bags. Paper plates. A dozen or so baby bottles that I'm going to fill up with yellow jelly beans and use as decor. It's not a cheap shopping trip, but I dip into my savings and figure I'm saving money by doing it like this rather than hiring someone to do the decorations for me.

I also grab a few bits and pieces for the special evening I have planned for Drayton tonight, a date I've been planning for the last week. He's been so sweet, keeping me entertained and distracted as often as he can, and I want to return the favor. I want him to feel as loved as he makes me feel.

It intrigues me, how calm he's been about the end of our summer being just over a month away, but it also doesn't surprise me that he's compartmentalizing and choosing to ignore it. That's not a foreign coping mechanism for him. I feel guilty for accusing him of being indifferent about us; I know him better than that. But doubt is like a plague. It sneaks up, and I'm constantly trying to push it back down.

When I go out to the parking lot, the sun is high and reflecting off windshields. I head to the car and dread how hot it's going to be when I open the doors. The first thing I do is turn on the car and the AC before I pop the trunk and start loading in the bags.

At home, I put the items away, say goodbye to Nathan, who has kindly agreed to go to Fort Collins for the night so I can have the house to myself, and then start setting up.

It takes me about two hours, and that's with no breaks. But I'm so proud of what I've put together. I send Drayton a quick text message while I stand in the middle of the now decorated living room.

You can come over now.

Be there soon, beautiful.

I quickly switch the stereo on so it hums out a quiet instrumental tune, the same sound that drones in the background of the video games he plays with his friends, and then I run to my bedroom.

The sound of Drayton's bike comes up the street as I'm finishing the last details of my outfit, and I stand facing the mirror, looking over the little khaki tank top, camo-patterned skirt, and knockoff Docs I'm wearing. He's going to love it.

He can't let himself in because the door is locked, so I go back to the living room and wait, listening to the sound of his motorcycle pulling up and switching off, and then I hear footsteps approaching. Quickly, I swing the door open, and he pauses on the step, his jaw dropping open and his gaze moving over me.

"I'm into it," he drawls. "I don't know what's going on, but I'm down."

I laugh and reach for his hand while he continues to stare at me. Inside, I close the door and watch his face as he takes in the room. I've put up posters of his game and a big forest-print backdrop. I've stacked large cardboard boxes and painted them green to make pillars.

"Video game night," I announce, spreading my arms wide. "But in real life."

I walk over to the breakfast bar, Drayton watching my every move with utter awe. "These are our weapons." I pick up two Nerf guns. There's also a ton of ammo and a couple of blindfolds. "There's a little twist. We're doing the hush version of Nerf wars. So one of us has to hunt the other while blindfolded. The person being hunted has to keep dead quiet."

Drayton props his hands on his hips, watching me as I walk back toward him with a gun and a blindfold.

"After this, there's a movie set up outside with a projector and a blow-up couch and blankets and food."

I wave the blindfold and the gun, letting him decide which role he wants first. He just stares at me with that soft smile he gets sometimes. The one where it's obvious how much he loves me.

"This is real fucking cute, Cheer." He takes the blindfold out of my hand and then uses his finger to gesture for me to turn around. I smile and turn my back to him. He slips the blindfold over my eyes. "This is hot."

"I bet."

Once the blindfold is secure, he holds my shoulders, turns me back around, and kisses me. It's not quick, but it is gentle and slow; his lips linger on mine, and his hands cup my face. His tongue swipes my mouth as he nips my lower lip, and I have to take a deep breath. Removing one sense really heightens the others, that's for sure.

He takes the gun from me, loads it up, and hands it back.

"Good luck, baby."

It's a good thing I turned the music down low because I have to rely on my sense of hearing very heavily. I use one hand to guide myself around the living room and the cardboard pillars; occasionally, I hear his feet on the carpet and the subtle shuffle of him moving. At one point, I walk straight into a cardboard pillar and knock it over, and Drayton bursts out laughing. He runs when I start shooting in his direction, and he has the audacity to kiss me as he flies past. I know when I get him, though, because he hisses.

We switch places, and I get into the far corner of the room, between the sofa and the TV cabinet, and press myself up against the wall. He walks closer and closer, and I hold my breath to keep from laughing because for some reason it's the funniest thing ever. When he's right in front of me, I wince as he stretches out his arm and runs it along the wall, coming into contact with my face.

I launch off the wall to jump over the couch, but he expertly wraps his arm around my waist, pulls me back into him, and drops me on the couch backward, blindfold still on and Nerf gun in one hand. I'm giggling furiously as he lifts the blindfold and smirks at me.

"You could see, you cheater."

"Baby, I don't need to see you to handle your body. I know it like the back of my hand."

That's hot. "You didn't shoot me, though. I'm not out. Yet."

His gaze roams over my body as he drops the Nerf gun and the blindfold on the floor. "That shit hurts, I'm not doing that." He leans over me, one knee on the couch, one leg on the floor, hands beside my head. "I'll kiss you instead."

He kisses my shoulder. "Got you." He kisses my collarbone. "Got you again." He kisses my ribs. "And again."

CHAPTER 18

DRAYTON

Five weeks to go

Dallas and I are in the kitchen at my house decorating a cake. This was an idea we both had. We found a cool-as-fuck professional cake on Pinterest and decided to recreate it. We got about three minutes in and realized my kitchen has almost nothing in the way of cake decorating equipment, or even baking in general, and we had to go to Target to stock up.

The cake in the photo has three tiers. It's yellow and has bumblebees on it and a little rattle thing on top. We decided to do a practice run and see if we could make the cake for Gabby's baby shower.

I think the fuck not.

"I don't get why the icing is like that." Dallas stands back and looks at how her little piping bag swirls are melting. "The ones in the photo are holding their shape so well."

She's covered in icing: it's on her apron, her face, her arms. I'm thinking about licking her clean.

"Let me find out," I say, pulling up Google on my phone. I search "buttercream fail reasons," and a list pops up with suggestions like not enough icing sugar, too much water, or the wrong food dye. "Well, there's a lot of things we potentially fucked up."

Dallas looks sad, and then she peers over at where I've been painting the wooden rattle to go on top. "That looks really cute. The bees are so good."

"Thank you, baby." I give her a kiss and smack her on the ass. "I think throw some more icing sugar in the bowl and thicken it up."

She shrugs and gets on with it. We've been at this for most of the day, and we're just now getting to decorating. I don't know if that's because I'm easily distracted and end up with my tongue down Dallas's throat every five minutes or if this is just an insanely long process. I've never made a cake before.

Dallas pours icing sugar into the bowl, and I stand behind her, grabbing her butt with both hands. "You know what my favorite cake flavor is?"

"I couldn't possibly begin to guess."

I kiss her head and squeeze. "Yours."

"You don't say."

I wrap my arms around her shoulders and hold her tight, my face pressed against the side of hers while she stirs the icing. "I love you," I murmur.

"I love you too."

Gabs and Josh wander in from the pool area, both holding iced drinks. They slip onto the stools on the other side of the breakfast bar.

"How's this all going?" Josh asks, his expression making it obvious that he's got some negative thoughts about Dallas's icing swirls. I glare at him from behind her, suggesting he fix his face right now. He gets the message.

Gabs doesn't. "I can just . . . buy a cake."

"Hey." Dallas pouts. "This is just a trial, to work out the kinks."

I straighten up and drop my hold on Dallas, pointing a finger at Gabs. "Your best friend is making you a cake. Show some appreciation."

"Aw," Gabby coos. "That's true. That's sweet."

"Look." Dallas starts refilling her piping bag. "I'm aware it looks . . . different right now. But that's why I'm doing this. To find out what I need to do better next time."

She twists the piping bag, holds it to the cake, and a nice swirl comes out, holding its shape. It looks heaps better.

"That's the one, baby." I rub her back, and she smiles at me, all proud of herself and adorable.

"See." She looks pointedly at her best friend. "Trial run."

Gabby smiles at her. "Oh, I wanted to ask, before I forget, do you want to come to the ultrasound tomorrow? We're going to do a gender reveal at the baby shower, but I thought you could be the one the technician tells, so someone knows."

Dallas clutches her chest with a gasp and gets icing all over her cleavage. Looks delicious. "I would be honored. You're sure? You don't want it to be your mom?"

"I love my mom," Gabby says. "But I want my best friend there. You too, Drayton. You guys are both such a big part of our lives."

I'm surprised to get an invite, that's for sure. I look between her and Josh. "You sure?"

They both nod. "Yeah."

Dallas inflates with a deep breath, her gaze shining. "I can't wait."

The girls go over the details, what time and all of that shit. Dallas has work, but she thinks she can start an hour late.

"What kind of gender reveal are you going to do?" Dallas asks, dropping the piping bag and sliding over to the sink to rinse her hands.

"Something simple," Gabs says, Josh nodding in agreement. "Like, blue or pink filling in some cupcakes. Just something basic. I don't want a whole fanfare; I don't want something with confetti that has to get cleaned up, and nothing that'll pollute the environment."

Dallas dries her hands and listens carefully. "Got it. I'm kind of surprised, though. I thought you'd want something a little crazier. You love theatrics."

"I do . . . sometimes. But sometimes I feel like gender reveals are a little excessive for what the occasion actually is. Like, as long as my baby is healthy, I don't mind if she's a boy or a girl."

Dallas blinks at her. "You just said 'if she's a boy or a girl.'"

Gabs gives her a duh look. "Yeah, well, I know she's a girl."

There's a collective laugh at her certainty. It's hard to imagine Josh as a girl dad. I don't know why, but I can't imagine the connection. I would never tell him that, though.

Later, Dallas and I move upstairs; she's watching the music video channel and dancing along to the routines, picking them up with ease. I watch her while I pack a few things into one of my moving boxes. It's something I should spend a little more time on, but there's not that much I want to take with me anyway.

I wrap a framed photo of Abby and me and drop it into the box, along with some of our childhood trinkets. Dallas spins and looks at me with a big smile and her hair in her face before she pushes it back.

"What are you doing?" she asks, a little out of breath as she plonks herself down on the bed. "Packing?"

"Yeah, all my special things. Get in."

She laughs as I point at the box, and then she watches me for a moment, her face becoming more curious. "You're hanging in there? It's not too hard?"

I look at her as I pick the box up and put it on the floor. That familiar sense of heading into a conversation I don't want to be in. She cares, that's all it is. She wants me to tell her if I'm feeling anxious. It's fucking hard to pretend I'm upset when I'm more excited about this move than anything else.

"It has to be done," I tell her with a quick lift of the shoulders.

She frowns, her shoulders dropping. "You keep telling me that."

"It's true."

She purses her lips, looking away, her fingers fidgeting in her lap. For fuck's sake. Now she's upset, and I'm starting to run out of patience with this idea. I'm not telling her right now, though. She'll spend the next month in a mood with me, and I'll have ruined summer. She can be mad at me in California.

"Baby," I say. "We can't keep having this conversation."

She stands up. "I get it. It has to be done. I just don't get how it doesn't even seem to . . . bother you. I cried my eyes out when I started packing. I'm in a constant state of dread at the thought of being apart from you, and you're like, 'Whatever.'"

"No, Dallas, I'm not—"

"You have a specific coping method, and it's to pretend the truth doesn't exist, but it's still weird for me to see. To feel like I'm so easy to leave behind. You didn't even seem excited that I'm seriously considering moving to Texas next fall. It's like you're expecting this to be over by then."

She looks at me with all the vulnerability in the world on her face, and I know she didn't mean to reference Abby when she said I like to pretend the truth doesn't exist, but I still heard it. I swallow hard. I feel like there's no right thing to say here. I've tried telling her she's my entire world, and it's like she doesn't want to hear it.

"What do you want me to do, Dallas?" I ask, walking up close to her, feeling frustrated over this constant circling. "What do you want me to do? Do you want me to break the fuck down, right here? Do you want me to spend the rest of summer acting like I'm on death row? Do you want me to cry and throw a fit at how it feels to spend even a week apart from you? I can't do that. I won't. If you don't comprehend how much I love you and how much I need you in my life, I don't know why you wanna drag this out."

She steps back, and that was definitely the wrong thing to say, but I was running out of ways to twist my damn words.

"Maybe I don't," she snaps, snatching her bag up off the floor and storming out of the room. I watch her go and let out a deep sigh, rubbing my hand down my face.

"That's not a breakup," I shout as loud as I can. "You go cool off. I'll get a kiss good night later."

~

It's after midnight when I pull up at Dallas's, my bike engine loud and disturbing, but I couldn't care less. I park in the driveway, kill the engine, and kick my stand down. The curtain in her bedroom flickers a little as I pull my helmet off. If I woke her up, she's going to be even harder to reason with. Whatever, I'll take it. I'm not spending the rest of the night tossing and turning because I upset my girlfriend and I know she's in bed hurting.

When I get to the front door, I test the handle. It's unlocked. That's a good start. It's dark inside, and I walk quietly through the house, passing Nathan's door. I'm sure I woke him up, but he doesn't come out and tell me to fuck off.

When I get to Dallas's room, I open the door, go inside, and close it. "Thanks for leaving the door unlocked," I whisper. She's curled up in bed with her back to me. She doesn't respond.

"Come on, baby," I say. "I know you want to apologize to me."

She's sitting up and facing me before I can even blink. I knew that would work. "Apologize?"

I grin at her, ignoring the lethal death stare she's giving me. Walking over to the edge of the bed, I kneel down and rest my elbows on her mattress. "I came here to take you on our next date."

Dallas narrows her eyes and glances over at her alarm clock. "It's almost one in the morning."

"Romance doesn't abide by time."

"My sleep does."

Man, she's going to make me work for it tonight. I reach for her hand, and she doesn't pull it back. Clutching it, I bring it to my mouth and kiss her knuckles. "Dallas, I love you. You know, deep down, that I love you more than life itself, and you know that I'm not going to just move on and forget about us at the end of summer. You also know that I'm upholding the deal we made to have the best summer we possibly could. You're making it a little hard, though."

"Oh, am I?"

I reach for her face and cup her cheek, drawing her in closer. "You have to stop picking fights with me. We're supposed to be having a good time. We can worry about the future later; it's not going anywhere."

Her scowl softens, and she drops her gaze as my thumb strokes her cheek, brushing the corner of her mouth.

"Have I ever given you a reason to believe I'm not totally obsessed with you?" I ask.

"No."

"Do you really believe I'm totally at ease at the thought of not seeing each other for months and months?"

"Also no," she mumbles. "I wasn't being fair."

"I didn't come here to get into it again or force an apology out of you," I say, giving her a quick kiss. "I came to pick you up. You up for it?"

She smiles softly and nods, giving me another kiss before she gets out of bed. She quickly gets dressed in a pair of shorts and a cropped hoodie, and then she follows me outside, leaving a note for Nathan on the counter that explains where she's gone. Once I'm on the bike, she climbs on behind me and wraps her arms around my middle. I love it when she's back there, tucked in and holding on tight.

I walk the bike backward out of the drive before I kick the starter and then tear off down the street. There's almost no one out right now, just the odd car here and there, but we're alone for the most part. I flick the throttle and pick up speed, leaning into the bends and going uphill toward my house. The trees get thicker, my headlight illuminating the awning that leaves create across the road. It feels like we're flying, and I know Dallas is back there laughing; I can feel her chest rumbling on my back.

I weave up the drive and pull up in front of the garage doors. Dallas slides off the bike while I remove my helmet, and then I turn to her. She lifts her own helmet off, and I fix her hair for her, smoothing the strands and running my fingers through it. Once she's sorted, I get off the bike and take her hand.

"You said we had a date?"

"This isn't the first time we've had a date in the backyard," I remind her.

"That's true."

I unlatch the garden gate and gesture for her to go ahead. When we walk around the corner, she finds what I spent the last few hours organizing. Over in the furthest corner I've set up a speaker and a camera set up on a tripod. The lights wrapped around the trees are glowing, there are lanterns hanging from the low branches, and the hose is sitting there, if she feels so inclined.

We walk across the grass, and she looks up at me when we get to the spot I've prepared. Her gaze settles on the camera.

"What are we filming?"

I can tell from her tone that she thinks I'm about to suggest something freaky as hell, and I laugh.

"A music video," I tell her and watch her brows lift. "Not a sex tape. Not this time."

She ignores me and looks around, surprised. "A music video?"

"It's just for fun, baby. I know you dance all the time, but I thought this would make a good date idea. I'll even join in if you want. I'll stand there with my shirt off and you can just dance around me. Throw it back a little."

She covers her mouth, eyes shining with amusement.

"It's not a test or an assessment or an audition. It's just us having a good time. You relax, do what you love. Have fun with it."

She turns toward me and stares up with those beautiful eyes of hers. "I feel like this calls for being a bit goofy."

"Keep it goofy, then. Lean into it. It's not going to be on TV."

She props her hands on her hips and looks around again, bottom lip between her teeth like she's contemplating how to proceed.

"I bought this expensive fucking camera." I point to it. "So get to shaking that ass, woman."

She tilts her head, a challenging stare on her face.

"That was my creepy director impression," I say. "Start with picking a song."

She swipes through her playlist, the one she uses for most of her dance routines. The music comes through the speaker loud enough for us to hear, but I don't think it'll disturb the household. Oh well if it does. Dallas decides to look through some early 2000s songs instead, and as she goes through them, she becomes more relaxed, laughing at the possibility of doing something by Sean Kingston or Soulja Boy or Flo Rida or Jason Derulo.

Dallas gasps, looking at her phone screen with excitement, and then she starts giggling hysterically. "Oh, I have the perfect idea." She's practically bouncing as she points at the camera. "Get that thing rolling and then come back."

I do what I'm told, getting the camera lined up so Dallas is centered in the frame, the trees and lights behind her creating a moody background that I somehow feel will not be the right setting for what she has planned. Doesn't matter, though.

Once it's all set, I walk back to her, and she tells me to stand behind her. "Okay, you have to mouth the words to this while I dance. You have to be in character too."

She's still beside herself with laughter.

"Baby, I don't even know what the song is."

She hits Play and slides her phone back into her pocket as "Whatever You Like" by T.I starts playing through the speaker. Now I start laughing because of course she'd pick this and make me sing to it.

"Ready?"

"Yes, ma'am."

I end up laughing more than pretending to sing. Though I'm surprised at how easily the lyrics come back to me. Dallas dances around me, playing right into a 2000s diva getting her bag as she struts her fine legs. She runs her hand down my chest and drops and throws her ass back on me. She's being a total clown, but she still looks damn fine doing it. Whenever we look at each other, we cackle, and I play my part, looking at her shake her ass, grabbing her waist, kissing her neck. Honestly, singing about how much I want to spoil her and how much I need her body and want her body and looking at her like she's a damn snack is easy.

The song comes to an end. Fast. We were having so much fun. Dallas strikes a silly pose, and I snatch her up by the waist and hoist her legs around my hips, giving her a long, hard kiss. The next song starts. "You're Beautiful" by James Blunt.

Dallas pulls back and looks at me with wide eyes, full of delight. "I love this song."

She slides down my body and steps back, her gaze going distant for a moment as she listens to the song, counting the beat. Then she starts to move, and this time, it's an entirely different dance. She moves with this fluid grace, her body totally in tune with the sound, as if she and the song are one and the same, progressing together. She moves like an angel, and I watch, unable to take my eyes off her.

The song chants the title over and over, and it's like it's telling her specifically, because she is. She's so beautiful. The lights and lanterns glitter behind her, the barely-there breeze touches her hair in a way that seems rehearsed. I'm so gone for her, and I wouldn't change a damn thing.

She comes to a stop, a soft, content smile on her mouth, as if she's in a daze. I hope she remembers why she wanted to go to CalArts. I hope moments like this remind her what she's worked so hard for her. I walk over to her and slip an arm around her waist, drawing her in.

"I want you to have everything you've ever wanted in life," I tell her, probably for the hundredth time in our relationship, but sure, I'll tell her again. "You're going to go to your dream school, and whatever challenges that comes with, you'll face, like the badass I know you are."

She tilts her head and throws her arms around my neck, grinning at me. "Did you set this up so I'd remember what I'm aiming for?"

"You know what you're aiming for. I'm just reminding you that I'm your biggest fan."

She stands on tiptoe and kisses me.

CHAPTER 19

DALLAS

Five weeks to go

I'm going to be exhausted later this afternoon. I haven't slept all night. As much as I'd tried to sleep before Drayton showed up to make things right between us and take me on a spontaneous date, I was too upset over our little argument. He was right, of course. I was making it difficult to just enjoy our time together, and it isn't fair to expect him to cope with his feelings in the same way I do. I promised him we'd have a good summer together, and I need to quit acting like he isn't going to miss me. Of course he is. Stupid insecurities.

I walk back into my house at almost seven in the morning. Drayton dropped me off so I could get some rest and shower before Gabby's ultrasound this afternoon. We spent the rest of the night dancing in his backyard, making silly little videos, kissing, and talking; we even made breakfast at five-thirty on the grill in the outdoor kitchen. I feel all mushy, and I can't stop smiling because it was the perfect date, and he always knows how to make that happen.

The music video idea was so cute, and it was the perfect reminder of how I feel when I dance and choreograph movement. It also reminded me how much he loves it when I'm doing what I love. He's been supporting me from the moment we met, and no matter how much he'll miss me, he'd never let me doubt what I'm working toward, and he'd never make it about himself.

Nathan comes into the living room a moment after I close the front door, still in his sleep shorts and T-shirt. "I just saw your note," he says, gesturing at the countertop. "Got up to get a coffee and realized it was sitting there. You good?"

"Yeah." I slip my shoes off at the door and drop down onto the couch. The exhaustion is catching up with me. "Drayton planned one of his surprise dates, so he picked me up."

Nathan's brows pull together in confusion. "Was that at like one in the morning? I remember hearing his bike, but I thought he was just coming over. I went straight back to sleep after I contemplated murdering him for a second."

I laugh, watching my brother get himself a hot drink.

"I hate that loud bike," he mumbles.

"You're such an old man."

"Yeah, no, I am," he says with exasperation. "I'm also tired of Ilona across the road complaining to me about it whenever I leave the house."

"Ah, well." I dismissively wave my hand. "It won't be long until we're both gone and you won't have to hear it again."

Nathan stirs his coffee with a spoon, looking across the room at me with a pursed mouth, a little sadness in his gaze. After he's poured me an orange juice, he comes over to the couch and sits down, handing me the glass, his coffee in his other hand. He lets out a long sigh and suddenly seems distracted.

"Besides," I say after I've had a sip. "Drayton and I had a little . . .

argument last night, and he couldn't let the night pass without coming over and fixing it. You know what he's like. It was nothing major, and it was more my fault, but he came over anyway."

Nathan nods, and then he keeps nodding, a little bob of his head while he looks at me with hard lines of worry on his face. I can tell he wants to say something.

"What?" I ask.

"I just wanna . . . chat about something."

I watch him while I drink the orange juice and wonder what it is because it's making him nervous.

He huffs out a breath. "Did you want me to come to California? Is that something I should've thought of and arranged? Am I an idiot?"

That's not what I was expecting. "Oh, no. I mean, I don't know. I honestly never thought about it. I wanted to go to CalArts long before Mom and Dad died, and after they died, you just kept encouraging me to work at that goal. The reality that we were going to go our separate ways didn't really hit me until recently."

"Me too," he agrees. "We're all we've had for such a long time. You were on your path, and I was just living mine, and it really didn't cross my mind we'd actually be so far apart so soon."

The room falls quiet, and if I think about it too hard, I might start crying. "If you had decided to move too, I would've been excited and welcoming. It would've been great. But you not moving hasn't made me resentful or upset. I would never expect that of you."

"I know." He gives me a sad smile. "I would, though, if you felt like you needed me. I would take Drayton up on his offer to have his dad find me a coaching gig. I'd make arrangements. I'd do that for you."

"I know." I parrot his sentiment back to him. "But I would never want you to do it for me. You remember when you told me you'd have ended up at Notre Dame if it weren't for the injury?"

He nods.

"Is getting out of here and starting over somewhere new something you'd want to do? For yourself? Do you have dreams of furthering your career, getting into coaching at a bigger college? You sacrificed a lot to raise me, but you deserve to do whatever you want now."

He looks thoughtful for a moment. "I didn't spend a lot of time fantasizing about the future because I had a job that allowed me to look after you, and that was all I needed. But ever since Drayton mentioned coaching jobs in California, I've thought about maybe seeing what else is out there. I'm thinking of Emma too, but if the right opportunity came along, I'd go for it. She and I are still new, and we'll see what happens."

"Hell yeah," I say, excited at the thought of him spreading his wings. "Any college would be lucky to have you."

He reaches out his fist, and I bump it. "Might even end up in California."

"Like I said, I wouldn't hate that," I say.

"How are you feeling about it all? You were pretty distraught a few weeks ago. You didn't want to go at all then."

"PMS," I explain and clutch my now empty glass between both hands. "But seriously, I'm embracing how much I'm going to miss everyone. I want that school, I want that adventure, and if I want it, I have to go. So, I'll take the good and the sad and just . . . ride the waves, I suppose. If I decide to transfer at some point, it'll be because it was the right thing to do. I'm not going to worry about it right now."

"Very wise."

I'm not sure if it's wise or just the fact that it's what has to be done; I think when it comes to the difficult moments, the things my mind wants to convince me I can't survive, I've always found a way to rewire the fear into acceptance. Plus, every time I dance, I'm reminded about what it means to have been accepted into my dream school, to do something

I'm so passionate about. I'd be a fool to throw something like that away. I think about last night and how Drayton made an effort to remind me how much dance means not only to me but to him too. The fact that he's been acting so okay with us going to different colleges is because he wants me to feel the support he has for me, to not take away that excitement. Not because he doesn't care. Deep down, I've known that the whole time.

~

At work the next day, I'm relieved to see Ryan is back. He comes out of his office when I arrive and props his hands on his hips with a big smile. "Dallas, how are you?"

"I'm good. You? Did you have a nice break?"

"It was great," he says as I put my apron on. "I spent some time at the lake with my family, who all took time out of their busy schedules to be there."

"That's so nice," I say.

"Yeah. Look, can we head into my office for a minute? I need to chat about a couple of things. Wren is hanging around for an extra five minutes to cover."

"Oh." I feel like I'm in trouble. "Sure."

The little office is basic—a desk, a computer, a printer, a filing cabinet, a photo of a younger Ryan outside the diner when he first opened it, and boxes of orders piled up in the corner. Ryan takes a seat behind his desk, and because there's no spare seat, I stand.

"Wren had some things to say about how Jonothan behaved while I was gone," he says, and I purse my lips, hiding a smile. She didn't waste any time. "I want to give you the option to add to that if you also have any feedback on his management skills."

"He doesn't have management skills," I say. "He's rude and talks to the girls like shit. I can put up with it, but he's not a nice person, and he never asks for anything calmly. Not even the first time. It's immediate escalation."

"Okay, that's noted," he says, tapping something out on his computer. "The other thing I noticed was that your friend Gabriella is pregnant. She was in here this morning, and I saw the bump."

I blank; that was the last thing I expected. "Yeah . . ."

He leans back in his seat. "How is she doing? Does she need anything? Does she have some part-time work, or does she need it? Has she got supplies? Can I do anything to help that she might feel too awkward to ask for?"

I smile. Ryan is a great boss, and I'm going to miss working for him. "She's actually in a pretty good position. Her boyfriend's family is also my boyfriend's family."

"Ah." Ryan nods with understanding. "Of course."

"Yeah, she'll be fine, but thank you for offering."

"Don't mention it." He stands up and walks over to the door. "It's not always easy for girls that age. Some of them have almost no help at all."

He opens the door for me.

"Thanks, Ryan."

Wren is picking up some plates from the kitchen window, and I hold my hands out to take them. "You can go now," I say. "Thanks for waiting."

"That's cool." She hands me the plates. "I totally complained about Jonothan and encouraged some of the other girls to as well. If they want to, it's up to them."

"Ryan asked if I had anything to add, which I did. Sometimes it was so tempting to let Drayton hit him like he wanted to."

"He did?" Wren seems so excited at the thought. She hates that man. "Do you think he really would've or he just said it?"

I laugh lightly. "Drayton doesn't really just say things unless he means them, and it wouldn't have been the first time he's punched someone for disrespecting me."

Her jaw drops with utter joy. "That is so hot. You must feel so safe with him."

My heart gets a little gooey. "I do."

It's true. I've never felt safer than when I'm with him, like I can let down all my guards that women have up all the time and I can relax. It's another thing I'll miss when we're apart.

~

Over the next couple weeks, things fall into a peaceful rhythm. I work, I dance, I spend time with Drayton and plan the baby shower. Nathan and Emma spend more time together, at her house or ours, and I love getting to know her.

Drayton and I have more sweet dates. They're never extravagant, they're just time we get to spend together. Drive-in movies, late-night patio dinners under the stars, picnics. We go to the mall and do a throwback to the nineties photo shoot. It's hilarious. The outfits? There's so much denim. The hair? It's big. The poses? We look like we just stepped out of Zoolander. We find moments to laugh. Forgetting that we're coming to the end of summer is exactly what we needed.

This is my person. He always will be, and as much as I'll miss him, I know that won't change.

It's the morning of the baby shower, and Drayton and I have finished the cake. We made most of it last night, but the finishing touches went on this morning. It doesn't look like it should be on Pinterest, but it's not half bad. Ellie thinks it's the best thing she's ever seen and can't stop gushing over the fact that we made it. I do adore her enthusiasm.

Thankfully, Ellie and Leroy are used to hosting events here, so there are six round tables in storage, which we pull out and arrange in the backyard. We top them with the tablecloths and the centerpiece jars with the flowers from Ellie's friend's garden: gorgeous white tulips and yellow daisies.

Drayton picks up the helium balloons, and we place them around the yard, held down by baby bottles full of jelly beans. We blow up more balloons and hang some streamers. Leroy has volunteered to cook hot food on the grill. There's not supposed to be men here, but we wanted someone to cook. Plus, Josh is going to be here, even if it's not super traditional.

It's all coming together, and I stand on the deck to look out at what I've put together. Well, what we've put together.

I feel a hand slide up my back, and then Drayton is there beside me. "You put together a pretty good event, Cheer."

"Not without help," I say, turning into him. "Thank you."

"Always, baby. I'm going to help Dad with the food," he tells me. "Well, that's what Mom said I have to do because I'm not to hang around and make unwanted remarks or hover around you while you're busy. As if I would ever do that."

I tap his chest and go up on tiptoe to get closer to him. "Helping your dad is a great idea."

He laughs and gives me a kiss. "What time is this thing kicking off? You got time to head upstairs?"

"Drayton," I hear Ellie scold, and I peer past his shoulder to see her placing a wrapped gift on the deck table.

"I knew she was there." He winks with a mischievous grin before kissing my forehead and stepping back. "Yeah, Mom, I'm going to go and . . . do something useful."

She watches him walk back inside with a narrow glare. Her gift is the first one on the table. It's an insanely luxurious diaper bag that cost a small fortune. Ellie peers into the kitchen at the clock and claps her hands together. "Josh let me know the two of them are coming up the road now, and then the guests will start arriving in about ten minutes."

"Thanks for letting me do this," I say. I know Ellie prefers things left to a professional team who keep things running smoothly and put up extensive decor.

"Oh, of course," she says. "You've done such an incredible job, sweetheart. It looks beautiful. I'm a little mad, though, because you've shown me that if I want to, I'm perfectly capable of doing things myself."

Leroy walks past then, holding a plate of skewers. He looks amused at Ellie's statement and somewhat unbelieving. She clocks it and sticks her tongue out at him. It's cute and playful, and it reminds me how beautiful a relationship can look all this time later.

There's a loud gasp from behind us, and we turn to find Gabs walking out from the kitchen, Josh trailing behind her. She looks beautiful, her hair down in long waves, a long pale-green dress falling from her body like water. It's off the shoulder, ruched at her cleavage, and flowing with layers of sheer fabric. She looks like a princess.

"This is so cute," she squeals, looking around, and then her focus lands on me. "You did all of this?"

"It was a team effort." I open my arms for her hug, and she squeezes tight. She steps back again, her hand on her chest as she admires the setting.

"It looks awesome," Josh adds, smiling at me. I smile back.

Drayton wanders out of the kitchen with his hands in his pockets and gives Josh a quick nod of greeting as he stands next to him. "Gabs," he says. "You look very nice."

"Aw, thanks." Gabby gives him a quick hug, thanking him for his efforts.

The guests start arriving soon after that: some girls from school, some of the women from the library, Camilla and a few of her friends, Cass—even Emma shows up. She's met Gabs now, so it's not as weird.

It's not a huge group, but there are plenty of people moving about, chattering, placing gifts on the table, and eating. Drayton and his dad man the grill, whip up dips, and heat up pastries. I find myself watching them laugh together while they flip burger patties, and it warms my heart.

Gabby spends an hour opening her gifts, and I think it's safe to say she's not going to have to buy a lot after this. She's been given everything: pacifiers, bibs, a stroller, diapers, swaddle wraps, bottles. There are things there that I don't even know what they're for, but I suppose I'll find out. Gabs ends up in tears over how generous everyone has been.

Then it comes time for the gender reveal. Going to that ultrasound was such an interesting experience, one I've never had before. The technician took us outside of the room to let us know what our best friends were having, and I've been dying keeping it a secret ever since. We decided to incorporate the color into the top tier of the cake. It wasn't too difficult; it just required coloring the cake batter before it baked. It's a simple idea, but that's what Gabby wanted, and we'd already decided to do a cake anyway.

The guests gather around the table on the deck where the cake is sitting, and Drayton and I get a front-row view. Some of the ladies tell us what a fantastic job we've done, and Drayton makes sure everyone knows he painted the rattle himself. He's quite proud of it, as he should be.

Gabby and Josh hold the knife together, Leroy takes photos, and then they cut a small wedge and slide it out to reveal pink. Gabs almost launches the knife into the air when she throws up her hands with excitement.

"I knew it." She bounces on the spot before launching herself at Josh, who has only just had a chance to put the knife down. The two embrace, holding each other tight.

Everyone claps and cheers and congratulates the couple as they start hugging other people. When the technician told us the baby was a girl, I so badly wanted to tell Gabs her instincts were right—it felt like torture keeping that a secret.

It's my turn to give her a hug, and she says, "I told you."

"Well, actually, you guessed. Technically, I told you."

She grins. "Semantics."

The party is a success, the guests leave in a good mood, and Gabs is so overwhelmed with appreciation and joy that she doesn't know what to do with herself. Josh makes her sit down with a tall, cold glass of water and takes care of her while she lets everyone's kindness sink in. Camilla hangs around for a little while to help Ellie wash up, but it's quiet; the two of them don't engage in a lot of conversation, but I suppose they're going to have to get used to spending time together sooner or later.

I'm walking across the back lawn after taking out the trash when Josh meets me halfway with an awkward smile and a soda in his hand. We stop in front of each other.

"You guys did a really good job," he says for the third or fourth time.

"Thanks."

He takes a deep breath, like he's gearing up to say something he doesn't want to. "Look, you're Gabby's best friend, basically her sister, and what you think matters."

"What I think about what?"

"Me."

This should be awkward, but it's not. Not to me.

"There's been some tension," he says with a sheepish smile. "I know you feel protective toward her, and that's a good thing, but I want you to know I'm doing my best."

I slowly nod, not sure how to respond to that. He probably has been doing his best, and the little things that bug me are because of my own irrational feelings, not necessarily because he deserves it.

"Having a baby is an insane amount of pressure," he continues. "I don't know how else to put that. I want Gabs to be able to stay at home with her for as long as she wants, if that's what she wants, and I want to be able to provide them with everything they need. That's a lot to carry.

That's my responsibility, and I take it seriously. I just don't always say or do the right thing."

My shoulders relax, and I feel the sincerity behind his words. "You're still a teenager too, I suppose. We're kind of meant to be focusing on ourselves at this age."

"Yeah." He chuckles. "I have to admit, it's given me a kick in the butt. I was coasting before, working for Ellie and not giving my future too much thought. So this has encouraged me to pursue better opportunities."

"That's good," I say genuinely. "I just want my best friend to be happy, however that looks."

"I want that too."

"Good."

As soon as we've packed up the last of the tables, Drayton and I disappear upstairs and crawl onto his bed. I feel exhausted, but in a good way. I'm relieved Gabs had a good time. I didn't realize how much pressure I felt to get it right. Drayton slings his arm across my waist and drags me into him, spooning me with a tired huff.

"You did good, Cheer," he murmurs, kissing the back of my head. "So good. Should we skip college? We can go straight into event planning. Start an empire."

"That sounds like a good idea," I say to entertain him, feeling heavy-lidded already. Being in his embrace does that to me when I'm tired. He kisses my head again and tightens his hold a little more, getting comfortable.

AUGUST

CHAPTER 20

DALLAS
0 weeks left to go

On the last day of work, I knock on the office door with my apron and badge in hand and find Ryan sitting behind his desk. It was a relief to have him back for the last few weeks. He lifts his head, smiling under his coarse, dark beard.

"All done?" he says, leaning back in his chair. "You're off into the big, wide world."

"Yep," I say, dropping the items on his desk. "Two days to go."

It would've been nice to say it got easier to leave once I made the choice to stop stressing over the decisions I may or may not make in the future. But my feelings fluctuate all the time. One minute, I've never been more sure about anything in my life, and the next, I'm riddled with nerves about being miles away from the people I love. I've come to terms with those feelings: I embrace them, acknowledge them, and then push them aside again. Like Nathan said, those feelings can all exist at once; it doesn't make my choice wrong.

"You nervous?" Ryan asks.

"As much as is normal," I say. "Excited too, though. The hardest part is going to be missing my people."

"Absolutely. It is hard. I have a daughter in Vancouver. She moved there after college to pursue filmmaking. Her mom and brothers, grandparents, and friends are all here in Colorado. Spread out a few hours apart, but close enough to see often. Anyway, she was an absolute mess before she left. I thought she might not get on the flight."

"Really?"

"Oh yeah." Ryan chuckles to himself, as if remembering it clearly. "She did, though. Best thing she ever did for herself. She's got a great job, great group of friends, she's married now, and when we do get to visit her or when she comes here, she's this whole person that she grew into on her own. Does that make sense? Her mom and I gave her the foundation, and she built on it. She came into her own, she overcame challenges, she built her confidence because she had to. It was the best thing for her. She's a really wonderful woman because of the steps she took to become that woman."

My heart hiccups a little at the pride in his voice and the hope he's just given me. "That's incredible," I say. "That's actually really encouraging to hear."

He smiles at me and then stands up, stretching out his hand. I shake it. "It's been a pleasure to have you working here, Dallas. I've emailed a reference to you for future use."

"Thanks, Ryan. You've been a good boss. Jonothan, not so much."

Ryan sits back down and sighs. "I've seen the emails, and rest assured, I'm dealing with it."

"Wren will be relieved."

I say goodbye and close his door on the way out. Wren is sticking order sheets to the kitchen window as I walk past.

"In case I don't see you before I go," I say, "all the best and thanks for always covering my shifts."

"Thanks for always offering them to me." Wren surprises me with a quick hug. "Keep safe out there. If I end up in California, I'll hit you up."

"Definitely do that."

I head out into the parking lot, where Drayton is waiting for me on his bike. Every time I look at him, my heart squeezes at how much I'll miss him. It doesn't matter that I'm excited to go to college or that I believe we'll make it despite the distance, I'm still going to miss him, plain and simple. As I take the helmet from him, I lean in and kiss him, savoring every single moment that's ours.

He smiles against my mouth. "I love you too, baby."

I slip the helmet on and climb onto the back of the bike, securing my arms around his waist.

~

We sit at the top of the lookout twenty minutes later with an afternoon snack of French fries and face each other with a pad of paper and a pen each. I'm not sure what the pen and paper are for yet.

"You've always wanted to get out of here, right?" Drayton asks.

"I always wanted to go to CalArts and dance," I say. "Wanting to get out of here came later on when I realized how much more there was to see and do outside of our small town."

Drayton nods and taps his pen on his paper. "I reckon we should thank this town a little, recognize that we created some fantastic memories here, appreciate that it brought us together, and reminisce on the good times."

A smile lifts my lips. "I love that idea," I say, shimmying my shoulders. "That's so sweet. I never would've thought about doing something like that."

"You look forward—you're always looking forward—and I love that, baby."

My nose scrunches up as I give him a playful smile. "So what's the idea here?"

"We write down our favorite memories of specific situations, swap notepads, and read out loud," he explains.

"Fun. Okay, what memory are we doing first?"

"Favorite . . ." Drayton thinks for a moment. "Memory of a teacher!"

We both start writing on our paper, and after a few minutes, when we're done, we swap notepads.

"I'll start," I say and read Drayton's memory out loud. "'When we were making out on the quad at lunchtime. Ms. Perry shouted at us to quit it as she walked past and then tripped on someone's bag and started ranting about how love was allergic to her.'"

I laugh, remembering what he's talking about. "I hope she's met someone."

"There's someone for everyone," Drayton says. "Right, my turn. 'When Mr. Finch knew I was struggling with English and asked Gabs to help me with the assignment but she ended up doing most of it, and he knew but he didn't fail me and it was our little secret.'"

Drayton lowers the notepad and looks at me with a cute smile. "That's really wholesome, Cheer."

"He was a good teacher."

"You know you'll have to write your own papers in college, right, baby?"

I sigh with exasperation. "Yes, I'm aware. I'm also capable. Just not as eloquent as my best friend."

We give the notepads back and keep taking turns coming up with new questions. Favorite memory in the shopping center. Favorite memory in the diner. Favorite memory at school. Favorite memory on the football field. Not surprisingly, a lot of our memories include each other. It's sweet and sentimental, and in a way, it's closure I didn't realize I needed.

The afternoon sun streams down on where we sit on the blanket, a soft breeze rustling the shrubs around us. I grab a fry and pop it in my mouth. "Favorite memory of trying something new for the first time," I say and watch Drayton's grin turn devious as he starts writing. "And it can't be something sexual."

"Aw." He pouts, scribbling it out.

When we swap notepads, Drayton starts reading. "'When I first rode a motorcycle with the help of my love, who made me feel like I can do anything in the world.' That's fucking cute, babe."

"You say that about everything I write," I giggle, looking at the notepad. "Okay. 'When I tried baking a cake for the first time and realized that I'll always be rich as long as I can keep doing shit like that together. I want to be involved in all the little moments, no matter how trivial.'"

He's grinning at me when I look at him.

"Are these really your favorite memories, or are you just saying that because they're with me?"

"I'm dead serious," he says. "I've tried a lot of new things for the first time, and baking a cake with you was my favorite."

"That's very sweet." I lean over as I hand his notepad back and give him a kiss. "Okay, favorite memory from an away game?"

We scrawl our answers down and swap again. We both laugh as soon as I start reading. "'Skinny-dipping in my aunt's pool followed by a sleepover in the park where you rested in my arms all night and I felt like the luckiest guy in the world.'"

Drayton holds up my notepad, on which I've said almost the exact same thing. "Great minds, Cheer. I still feel like the luckiest guy in the world when you sleep in my arms."

My breath catches a little. "You know what I'm grateful for?"

"What?"

"That I get to leave this town with a newfound appreciation for it. All I ever wanted was to get out of here, and now I get this entire bank of memories to bring me warmth whenever I think about it or visit. It's my hometown, not just the town I grew up in."

Drayton shifts over toward me and wraps his arm around my shoulder, pulling me in close so we can look out over our town. "Did you have a good summer, baby?"

"The best one so far."

"Me too."

"Hard to beat," I tease, nuzzling my nose on his neck and giving it a soft kiss.

"Challenge accepted," he says, and I can hear the smile in his voice. "Good thing we've got the rest of our lives."

~

Gabby and I catch a movie, followed by dinner, and then we head back to my house for a sleepover with chick flicks, face masks, and a charcuterie board that Emma put together for us. She's made little flowers out of pepperoni and fancy patterns with grapes and cheese and crackers. It all tastes good too.

We sit on mattresses in the living room, just like we did when we were kids, and watch 13 Going on 30.

"Does she, like, always remember this alternate life she would've lived?" Gabs asks, tapping her face mask with her fingertip before she shoves a grape into her mouth. "Because when she gets back to being thirteen, she clearly remembers what just happened, so does she spend the rest of her life going, 'Wow, one time I spent months in an alternate reality, and I know what my boyfriend is going to look like when he's an adult. Hot, by the way, he's going to look hot.'"

"Mark Ruffalo is ridiculously cute in this movie," I agree, topping a cracker with cheese and chutney. "That's a good question, though."

"I wish I could see what my life is going to look like when I'm thirty."

"You'll have a twelve-year-old daughter, so probably a battlefield," I say, referencing the Pat Benatar song in this movie, and Gabby starts to giggle.

"That was good." Her laughter subsides, and then she gives me a worried look. "You're probably right, though. Twelve-year-old girls scare me."

"It's a very hormonal time in their lives," I say. "I feel for them. You remember what it was like?"

"Yes." Gabs shudders. "Borderline maniacs. What am I going to do without you being close to tag in? My daughter is going to need her cool aunt."

"I will tag in whenever you need me. I'll be one phone call away."

Gabs chews on a carrot while she stares at the TV screen. "I'll have to move closer to you," she says. "I never really thought about it before, the fact that we might live apart when we have kids. Kinda makes me sad."

"Me too," I say. "As much as I'd love to have kids that are close in age, I am nowhere near ready to go down that path."

"That's fair. My daughter will end up babysitting your children."

We both laugh. "That's so true." I start peeling my face mask off, and Gabs does the same. "Gabby, I wish I could be in two places at once. I wish I could be right by your side and also at college. I am going to miss you more than I can put into words."

Gabby drops her mask onto an empty plate and sticks her bottom lip out at me. "You're getting emotional on me."

My eyes start to well up, and I nod. "Leaving you is going to be one of the hardest things I ever do, I just want you to know that. Oh, man, it's been a while since I've cried about this."

Gabby leans over, her bump between us, and hugs me. "I'm so proud of you," she says, rubbing my back. "This friendship is forever, I promise. You could move all the way to New Zealand and it wouldn't change a thing except for our time zones."

I lean back and wipe the tears falling down my cheek. Gabby is crying too. I bury my face in my palms and take a big breath, doing my best to regain composure. The sound of someone coming into the room gets my attention, and I look over to find Emma bringing her and Nathan's dishes down.

She winces at me. "It's that time of the night, huh?"

Gabby and I start laughing, and I nod.

Emma sets the dishes on the kitchen counter and comes over to the edge of the mattress. She's wearing her pajamas, hair in a messy topknot. I love that she's so at ease and comfortable here.

She sits down on the carpet. "I remember leaving my sister behind in Nevada," she says, shaking her head. "It was so painful. Literally the entire six weeks up until the move I was up and down with doubt and excitement. I'd been offered this great job, and I wanted to take it and experience a change of scenery, but I also wanted to live two minutes from Bri, like I always had, and I couldn't have both."

"I get that," I say.

"I promised her I'd be home in a year," Emma says with a shrug. "But I really love Fort Collins. It's still hard, I miss her all the time, but it makes the time we spend together really special."

Gabs and I share a smile. "Sleepovers until we're eighty?" I ask.

"Absolutely."

Emma smiles and turns her attention to me. "Nathan's really going to miss you, but he's so proud. He talks about you as if you're his inspiration in life."

I melt a little. "Stop or I'll cry again."

Emma reaches over and gives my hand a little squeeze. "I really like him. Really like him. I'm not going to ever hold him back from looking at other jobs, and I wouldn't break up with him if he decided to move. That probably sounds crazy since we haven't been together that long, but it feels right. I just want you to know that he's in good hands, and I'll support him in whatever he does. I know you were worried about leaving him behind."

It's a comfort to hear that from the woman my brother is so clearly head over heels for. "As long as he's supporting you too," I say, spotting Nathan as he appears at the living room entrance and leans against the doorframe. Gabby and I share a subtle smile. 'Treating you like a queen and being your biggest fan. That's what you deserve."

"Believe me." Emma grins. "He is the most thoughtful man I've ever met. He's a really good guy."

"What else?" Nathan says, and Emma jolts, peering back over her shoulder. The two of them look at each other with hearts in their eyes.

"Who said I was talking about you?" Emma teases.

Nathan rolls his eyes and walks into the room, plonking himself down on the couch. Gabby stares at him and clears her throat. "As you can see, this is a girls' night."

Nathan just stares back. "As you can see, this is my living room, and it sounds like I was the topic of conversation."

"Oh, no, no." Gabs holds a hand up to hush him. "We were talking about Drayton's dad. You know how he offered to take Dallas to the Super Bowl in February. So thoughtful."

Nathan's eyes almost fall out of his head as he leans forward, jaw dropping. "He what?"

"Calm down," I say and shoot Gabs a look; she is amused with the way she's stirred things up. "I said no."

Nathan shoots to his feet now, and I have to lean back to see the outrage on his face. "You said no to going to the Super Bowl. For free. Are you insane?"

"What have you done?" I ask Gabs, who's busy sifting through the bowl of candy for sour worms.

"No," Nathan says. "What have you done? I would kill for that opportunity."

"I wanted Drayton and his dad to go together," I explain. "Look, even though Drayton doesn't say it plainly, his relationship with his dad is really important to him, and this was a good chance for them to do something special together. Kind of how Drayton didn't go camping with us because you wanted that time with me. He respected that even though I begged him to come."

Nathan's little laugh is full of sarcasm as he palms his jaw and sits back down. "You're better than him, Dallas. Believe me. You are very thoughtful."

I shake my head and wave him off. "Drayton and I agreed that one day when we can afford it, we will take you to the Super Bowl, I promise."

"You both said that?" he asks disbelievingly.

"Aw, that's nice," Emma coos, Gabs nodding in agreement.

"Yes," I say.

Nathan folds his arms with a deep breath and a small nod. "I won't let you forget that."

I fold my legs on the mattress and sigh. "Men and their balls, honestly. I won't forget it, I swear. Stop being a drama queen."

He rolls his eyes, and Emma giggles, getting up off the floor and walking over to sit next to him on the couch. The two cuddle into each other, and they end up spending most of the night with us, sometimes watching movies but talking for the most part. It evokes that bittersweet feeling of wanting to hold on to moments like these forever but knowing how special it will be to see each other from now on.

CHAPTER 21

DRAYTON
Zero weeks left to go

Tomorrow, we leave.

It's blowing my mind a little bit. Dallas and I have both packed up our rooms and shipped our belongings. The bedrooms aren't empty, not by a long shot. Most of our things are still there for when we come home during breaks, but it's weird nonetheless. Dallas thinks I fly out in a couple of days. She doesn't know that I've already been to the airport and arranged to get on the plane a tiny bit earlier than standard boarding. Just a tiny bit. It was hard to coax them into agreeing, but I'm charming when I want to be.

Nathan is going to keep Dallas distracted in the airport shops so she doesn't get to the boarding lounge before I'm on the flight. He keeps reminding me that I'm being extra and I could just tell her at home and go to the damn airport with her, but that's not dramatic enough for me. I survived the entire summer without spoiling the news, I have to see it through.

When I head inside after I've done my workout, I'm sweaty and disgusting. Josh is in the kitchen making something to eat, his new suit and tie on, looking like a true professional. He got a job in Denver doing some sort of media marketing gig. It's an office job, and it seems to pay well with plenty of opportunity to move up with experience. It's not a bad opportunity for someone who didn't graduate high school, but his experience working for Mom helped him get a foot in the door. His good character references too.

"How's it going?" I ask, wiping sweat off my brow with the bottom of my shirt. "Off to work?"

"Yeah." He glances at the clock with a worried stare. "I was hoping to beat traffic, but I was up all night looking after Gabs. She's not coping well with the heat as she gets bigger."

"No shit," I scoff, leaning on the breakfast bar across from him. "I'm not either, and I'm not carrying the weight of another human."

Josh shrugs in agreement and packs up some sort of salad thing he's just made into a container. He puts it in a bag and slips it over his shoulder. "I should go. I'll see you at dinner tonight."

My parents are having Dallas, Nathan, and Emma here for dinner. We're disguising it as a farewell to her, but it's for both of us. I made Mom swear she wouldn't start crying, but I'm not sure I trust her ability to keep her emotions in check. She can cry when I'm walking out the door tomorrow. Besides, I'm almost positive I'll see her all the damn time. She can afford to fly out to see me as often as she wants.

I have a nice little surprise for my girl, one she'll be pissed at me for showing at dinner tonight, but I don't care. She's going to love it. I head upstairs to shower and change before I go back downstairs and start arranging the kitchen.

I drag the table so it's more central in the room, and then I get the projector from downstairs and set it up so it's aimed at the left wall, in perfect view of the dinner guests when they're all seated. The video I had made is on a little drive that I plug into the projector, and then I use the remote to flick though and make sure it's working. The image comes on, but there's no sound. Looking at the settings, I realize I haven't connected the projector to the speakers in the dining room ceiling. It's all one big smart system that can be connected room by room, or by the entire house if the occasion calls for it. I only really use it outside by the pool.

I restart the video, and the audio works. I switch it all off again, ready for dinner tonight, and then I decide to head out and see Dallas.

I ride my motorbike over because I have to make the most of the time I have left to drive all her neighbors fucking nuts. Nathan too. When I pull into the driveway, I give it a few revs, just for fun. Not that Nathan is here. Community college started back last week, so he's back full time at work. When I head inside, Dallas is in the living room, wearing her tiny little dance shorts and a cropped T-shirt. She's dancing, and the music is loud.

"Hi." She beams, bounding over to kiss me. She stands on tiptoe, giving me a quick peck, and then she looks at me. "Tomorrow."

I slowly nod. "Tomorrow?"

"I leave tomorrow."

"You doing all right?"

She props her hands on her hips and starts pacing. "As long as I don't think too hard, I'm excited. I'm only leaving room for excitement. My stomach doesn't keep bottoming out or anything like that."

I grip her arm and pull her back into me, hands going to her waist and keeping her close. "This is going to be a good thing, baby. I promise."

She softens, melting into me. "I know."

"You keeping hydrated?" I ask, pushing her hair back from her damp face. "Your cheeks are flushed."

"Your favorite." She taps my chest and steps back, going to the kitchen to get her water from the fridge after she's paused the music. "What do you want to do? I didn't realize you were coming this early."

"That's what she said."

She rolls her eyes at me. "Who said that? It wasn't me."

I chuckle and sit down on the couch. "I can leave so you can keep dancing?" I offer, though my settling in gives the opposite impression.

She swallows a gulp of water and shakes her head. "No, it's fine. I've been at it for a few hours."

I almost ask what time she starts work, but she had her last day the other day. "You wanna go and get ice cream?"

"Oh." Her eyes light up with delight. "That sounds good."

She gets into one of her beautiful little dresses, pale blue this time, and we head to the shopping center on my bike. We get Blizzards from Dairy Queen and decide to go for a walk out toward the rocks where the streets get quieter. Trees start to line the roads and offer a bit of shade from the heat. Dallas spoons her ice cream into my mouth for me to try, and then I do the same. I smear some of it on her nose, though, and she giggles when I loop an arm around her shoulder and lick her nose clean.

We walk for over an hour, talking and laughing. Dallas doesn't just walk, though, not in a straight line anyway. It's like she's always dancing. She skips out ahead, walks backward, circles me, a bounce in her step all the time. It looks tiring, but I assume this is how she has such fantastic legs and so much stamina.

At the next trash can, we dump our ice cream cups and then end up going off the path and down one of the many hiking trails. It's the perfect day for it, covered by the trees so we're not getting overheated. The forest surrounds us, and we stop to kiss all the time. I take videos of Dallas admiring her surroundings and catch her on camera when she admits she's going to miss the wide-open space.

Eventually, we start the long walk back to the shopping center. By the time we get there, we're both hungry enough to eat lunch, so we get kebabs and take them back to Dallas's house.

Later that evening, everyone starts gathering for dinner. The projector and the setup of the room have piqued people's interest, but I tell them not to ask questions. Mom pulls me aside and warns me that if I play something inappropriate or embarrassing, she'll be very unhappy. I think she'd like to use a more menacing threat, but I'm past the point of grounding.

Nathan and Emma are standing on the deck, talking to Dad while they have a beer. I'm sure the conversation revolves around football, which is good; at least it's common ground. Mom is setting out the food on the table. She hired a chef for the night. Apparently, the occasion called for it. Gabs and Josh are outside on the deck chairs, and Dallas is setting out plates and glasses.

When it's time to eat, we all sit down and help ourselves to the food laid out. There are mini beef sliders, grilled herbed chicken thighs, garlic mashed potatoes, roast vegetables, and salads. It's too much food, but it does look good. Dad sits at the head of the table, Mom to his left, Josh and Gabs next to her. Dallas is to Dad's right, then me, then Emma, with Nathan at the foot.

"So, Dallas." Mom holds a slider in one hand. "How are you feeling? Have you ever flown alone before?"

Gabby bursts into tears. It's so abrupt and unexpected that the whole room falls silent and stares at her as she slaps a hand across her mouth and apologizes through sobs. "I'm just going to miss her so much."

Dallas sticks out her bottom lip, looking across the table at her best friend as Josh rubs her back. Dad looks fucking perplexed. Nathan and Emma too.

"Those hormones are doing overtime, huh, sweetheart," Mom says sympathetically before giving Dad a warning look to fix his face. He lowers his head and keeps eating.

"I've never flown alone before." Dallas gets back to the point from beside me. "But I've gone to LA enough now that I feel prepared and not so nervous. I'm glad it's not the first time I'm ever going."

"Yes, a little bit of practice does help, doesn't it."

Dallas nods. "I think getting transport after you arrive is the worst part. Like the shuttle to the Uber stands. I won't have Drayton to help me lift my heavy bag this time."

Mom gives her a tight smile and quickly shovels a mouthful of mashed potato into her mouth. She better not break. Dallas quirks her brow the tiniest bit, confused at my mom's reaction, but she doesn't linger on it. She keeps eating, and I shoot Mom a warning glare.

Gabby has calmed down now; her face is splotchy and her eyes are glassy, but she's back to eating. I can't fucking imagine what my video is going to do to her. Mom asks Emma about herself, never one to leave some-one out of the conversation. I finish my plate pretty fast and lean back, slinging an arm over Dallas's chair, my fingers grazing her bare shoulder.

"Do you two spend most of your time here or in Fort Collins?" Mom asks Emma, clutching her wineglass in her hand.

Emma and Nathan share a look, tilting their heads. "I would say my place. I'm in Castle Rock semi-often, but I think most of the time we're in Fort Collins. I have my own house, so it's quieter."

Mom's brows go up to her damn hairline, and she moves her atten-tion to Dallas and me. Dallas, with a full mouth, chews slowly and looks at Mom like she has no idea how to respond.

I sigh. "Yeah, fair. We can get pretty loud."

Mom puts her glass down and drops her head into her hands.

"Oh, no." Emma straightens up in her seat and waves her hand. "No, no, I didn't mean it like that. Oh, I just meant there's no one else there. Like, it's not loud at Nathan's house. There's not an excess of noise. It's just, there're no other people at my house."

Girl is panicking.

Dad clears his throat with a smile and shakes his head. "We understand. Our son has the ability to make his presence well known."

I recoil. "That doesn't sound like a compliment."

"What made you think I was trying to compliment you?"

Dallas is still chewing, staring straight at Gabs, who has gone from sad tears to amused ones.

"These two are lovely to be around." Emma gestures at us. "I enjoy seeing them when I'm there. There's no . . . loudness. I didn't mean it like that."

"That bike is pretty loud," Nathan mumbles, and I grin.

Dallas gives him an exasperated look. "You have got to give that a rest."

Mom lifts her glass again. "No, I agree. That thing is a total disturbance. Especially when he's sitting there revving it on the driveway for no reason."

Nathan stretches out his arm at Mom. "Thank you!"

Mom looks at me. "You do that there too? Oh, Drayton."

"God forbid a man likes to feel thunder between his thighs."

Dallas almost chokes on her food as she bursts into laughter, and that pleases me. Her laughter always pleases me. Mom looks disgusted, Dad shakes his head at me, and I don't bother finding out what face Nathan is pulling. I'm sure I can guess. Gabby and Josh shake with laughter across the table, and I decide that's a good cue to move on.

"Anyway." I stand up, walk over to the projector, and pick up the remote. "I have a surprise for the guest of honor, the love of my life, the future mother of my children."

I look over at Dallas, who watches me with intrigue and a little bit of fear. Not unreasonable of her, I suppose. I press Play and gesture at the wall behind the table. Gabs and Josh turn in their chairs, as does Mom, and Dad and Nathan twist a little. The rest of us are already facing that direction. I sit back down as the intro music starts. It's the James Blunt song Dallas danced to. "You're Beautiful." She comes onto the screen in the backyard, dancing. She's so stunning, it hurts.

She slaps her hand down on my thigh. "What the fuck," she hisses. "You did not."

"Just wait," I whisper, taking her death-like grip off my leg and holding her hand.

The footage of her dancing is quick, and then it changes to a video of us painting portraits of each other on her living room floor. The song lowers in volume so our voices come into focus, our laughter at revealing the terrible job we'd done, and then I appear, a recording I secretly took when she went to the bathroom. "I love you, Dallas. This will be the best summer ever."

I peer over at Dallas and find her staring at the screen with her lips parted and a glistening gaze.

The video continues in the same sequence. Dance clips followed by a video of us on a date, followed by my secret little recording about how much I love her and how the summer is going to be perfect. There are videos of us at the drive-in, playing board games, swimming in the lake, on our trip to California, having our date in the library, painting each other's white clothes, playing a video game in real life, and baking the cake together. As it nears the end, I come into view, and Dallas is in the background. It's from a few days ago when she stopped at a kid's lemonade stand to show her support.

"So, you leave soon," I say, peering back over my shoulder to make sure she's not listening. "This has been the best summer ever, Dallas. I wish I could describe how much I love you and how much I mean it when I say the rest of our summers are only going to get better."

I blow a kiss at the screen, and it flicks back to Dallas's solo dance in the backyard, which slowly fades out to black with the end of the song. The editor I hired did a good fucking job.

Dallas is beside me in tears. I wrap an arm around her shoulders and drag her into my chest.

"At the dinner table?" she sobs.

"Yeah, baby."

"I love you," she mumbles.

Gabs is wiping her tears, and Josh is looking at me like I just set an impossible standard that he can't meet. Mom is also shedding a few tears, Emma too. Nathan and Dad aren't so emotional, but I feel like I can see the pride in Dad's face, and that's good enough for me.

Dallas wraps her arms around me and brings her mouth close to my ear. "That was so beautiful," she whispers.

"You are beautiful."

"Can I have that video?"

"It's all yours."

~

I spent the morning with Cass and the kids. Dallas and I don't fly out until this afternoon, and she knew I was going to see them. She seemed confused about why I would see them on our last morning together, but I told her Cass needed help with a job. Which wasn't an entire lie. When I got there, she made me help her put together an IKEA bookshelf for her bedroom.

It was a chance to say goodbye, but it's also a reason to pretend I won't make it back in time to see her off at the airport.

She's not going to like that.

But then I'll be there waiting and all will be well. I hope.

Saying goodbye to my little cousins was harder than I thought it would be, but I know I'll still see them often. I savor their small cuddles, but Cass and I agree not to tell them I'm moving. Lucy has been so fragile since her dad left. The word moving could trigger feelings in her that she doesn't know how to process because she associates it with the day her dad decided to fuck off. I don't want to do that to her; I don't want her to think I'm abandoning her. She knows I'm going to school, but we keep the whole thing vague.

When I get home, I'm quick to make sure my bags are packed and my charger is in my carry-on. My suitcase thuds down beside me on the staircase as I find Mom and Dad waiting beside the front door. Beside the portrait of our family. I take a quick look at Abby and wish she was doing this with me. I had a copy of that picture made so I can have one in my dorm with me.

"You don't get to sneak off without saying goodbye," Mom tells me, holding a tissue in her hand, her eyes already red-rimmed and watering.

"Mom, come on, I wasn't going to leave without a word."

Dad tilts his head at me. "A whispered 'goodbye' as you walk out the front door doesn't count."

They know me so well. Yeah, I might've taken off, but that's only because my method of getting through the emotional shit with them is avoidance. We've all sort of done it our entire lives. More so after Abigail died. I'm going to miss them, and part of me feels this weird sense of guilt over leaving. I know it's ridiculous, but I'm their last child, their only child. I know it's time. Dad would never want me to stay and miss out on college, but deep down, this little flicker of emotion exists. I do a good job of ignoring it for the most part.

Dad puts his hand on my shoulder and looks at me. "I'm really proud of you, son. You worked hard all through school, you kept up with your grades, your training, and your commitments, and it's all paid off."

I swallow the lump in my throat and lower my head, feeling an overwhelming flood of emotion that I was entirely unprepared for.

"Not only that," he continues, "but seeing how much you love that girl makes me proud of the man you've become. Outside of those achievements, you are a good person and you have a good heart, and that's priceless, Drayton. I'm just . . . I'm so proud."

I bite the inside of my cheek, feeling a burn in my nose. I quickly throw my arms around him, hiding the lone tear that falls down my cheek, and I hug him. His words make me feel like a kid again; they bring me back to the time when all I wanted was to impress him. It's not that he never told me I had done a good job or that he was proud of me, but whenever he did, it validated me in a way I've never been able to understand.

To me, Dad is the gold standard—in his career, in his marriage, in his strength. I've seen him overcome so much in our lives, and while it changed him, he never completely disappeared. He was always a committed and loyal family man. We had our issues in the past, but I know he's only ever wanted the best for me.

He pats me on the back, and we part. Mom is a blubbering mess and barely gives me a second before she's throwing her arms around me in a tight hug. "Oh, I'm going to miss you, honey."

"Mom, you're welcome to drop in whenever you want. Flights between Denver and LAX aren't going to break your bank account."

"Yeah," she says, stepping back and wiping her face. "But I won't be that mother who clings to her son while he's trying to get through college. I'll see you when I see you."

"I love you, Mom. Thank you . . . for being the only mom in the world who could've dealt with me. For loving me through it all. For understanding me."

Her chin wobbles. "It's been my greatest honor, sweetheart."

~

At the airport, the staff members I talked to about getting on the plane as early as I can assist me before I spot Dallas in the boarding lounge. They walk me on with the passengers in wheelchairs and small children and get me seated. Nathan must've done his part and kept her distracted with farewells and whatever else. I shot her a message earlier to let her know I got caught up and wouldn't be there to say goodbye. I imagine she did not like that.

I sit in the window seat and wait, my leg bouncing as soon as people start boarding. When I finally see her coming down the aisle, I lower my head behind the seat in front of me. She stops beside the seats, her focus on the aisle numbers, and then slings off her backpack, putting it in the overhead compartment. When she finally looks at me, her mouth falls open.

"Wh—Dra—what the fuck?"

She's standing in the middle of the aisle, stopping the flow of people heading to their seats. She's not usually so oblivious, so I take it this is a mind-blowing shock.

"You should sit down, Cheer." I gesture at the seat. "The flight attendant looks kind of irritated."

With her eyes locked on me, she falls into the seat. "What's going on?"

"I thought we should catch the same flight? We can share an Uber. I mean, we'll have to split off once you've settled into your dorm room because I have to settle into mine at UCLA, but it's not that far."

Her eyes widen. "UCLA?"

"Yeah. UCLA. In Califor—"

She cuts me off. "You're going to UCLA?"

I look at her and admire her existence, the fact that she's here beside me and this is really happening because even though I knew, it's still bewildering to me as well. "I am, Cheer."

She's dead still for a moment, and then she punches me in the arm. "What the hell?"

I rub my arm and lean back from her. "Damn, can we save that shit for the bedroom? Or the dorm room?"

She looks distressed. "Why didn't you tell me? I mean, how is this possible? I thought you didn't write a letter of intent?"

"I did," I say, risking more violence. "Months ago. It was risky, but I pulled it off. Dad changed his tune after the whole prom night bullshit. He agreed to let me do a walk-on wherever I wanted, but I'd done the letter of intent."

"You did it months ago?"

"Mm-hmm. Dad gave me the green light to choose which school I went to, but he flipped one last time when I told him that I'd already sorted out UCLA. We're fine now, though."

Better than fine. Things between Dad and me are better than ever.

"How come you didn't tell me?" she asks. "All of that . . . tension over it. You could've said something."

"I didn't want to get your hopes up just in case it didn't happen or I couldn't change my dad's mind."

She softens then, her frustrations melting away. I slide a hand onto her knee; she's wearing a sexy little romper. "You're going to be so close," she says, and it sounds like relief in her voice.

I cup her chin and drag her in. "So close."

We kiss, and I don't care who sees. It's passionate and not all that appropriate for such a crowded place, but I literally couldn't give a fuck. I pour an entire summer's worth of unspoken words into this kiss. The relief I feel over her finally knowing the truth is like a damn aphrodisiac.

She breaks away and leans back. "I know when your kissing is leading toward more. We are on a plane."

I keep hold of her face and truly wish we were somewhere else. I give her another quick kiss.

"I can't believe you didn't tell me the truth all summer." She leans back and folds her arms, pouting again. "You're a liar."

"Technically, I never lied. I skated very expertly around the truth. It was hard. I thought about telling you, more than once."

She glares at me. "Why didn't you?"

"Because you needed to make this move for yourself, and you needed to know you were strong enough to get on this flight and go, no matter how hard it was. You didn't change your mind or change course because of me or anyone else. You did what you've always wanted to do and worked hard for, and I'm proud of you, baby."

Her gaze softens, and I know I'm forgiven.

"Plus, we made the most of our summer, didn't we?"

She smiles and nods. "Yeah, I guess we did."

"I love you, Cheer."

"I love you too, quarterback."

ABOUT THE AUTHOR

Tay Marley is the author of the Wattpad YA hit The QB Bad Boy and Me, the basis for the movie Sidelined, as well as other YA and adult novels. With a passion for romance, happy endings, and strong women, she loves to write stories that set the reader's standards for love oh so high. When she's not writing or reading, she's teaching her three children how to be their own leading characters.